Book Cover Illustration
Karen Alejandra González Ibarra

Developmental Editing
Ema Barnes & Dominic Wakeford

Proof Editing
Kristen M. Quirk

For permission requests, write to the publisher, addressed "Attention: Permissions Coordinator," at the address below.

Publisher Information
Bolt & Company Books
An Imprint of Redwood Press
Redwood Publishing Company
1441 Kapiolani Boulevard, Suite 1114
PMB 272939
Honolulu, HI 86814-4406
ISBN: 979-8-218-99714-4

REDWOOD
PRESS

bolt & company

JUSTICE & LIBERTY
A ROMANTIC COMEDY IN FIVE ACTS

Written by Regan M. Humphrey

For Queer Youth Everywhere
I love you, I see you, and I'm so glad you're here

For Leslie Zampetti
who made me take myself and this book seriously

And for Foluke
the spring fire to my summer sea

ACT I.

SCENE I.

— 8:30 a.m. —

JUSTICE.

> ***Birds Only Fly Where We Can See Them***
> *Birds only fly where we can see.*
> *Not where planes fly.*
> *Not above the clouds.*
> *Below.*
> *Where we can see them.*

No, no, no. No way.
That was shit. Cross all that out.
Okay. Let's try this again.
Justice scribbled down another poem.

> ***Did You Know?***
> *Birds sing at 3 a.m.*

While the rest of us don't.
Because we're asleep.

JESUS CHRIST.

Just forget it. Justice Garrison *was not* a poet. He folded the page up and sighed.

Justice *understood* poets, even though he wasn't one. He understood the feeling that someone else was flowing through him—the mood one got into when they're so nuts about someone that they wanted to break out the free verse.

If it were Justice, he'd just go up and tell them he was nuts about them. He wouldn't waste time pretending like he had any sort of gift for limericks or lyrics.

No, that was Adam's job—Adam Grosch, the shiny, all-American try- hard sitting a few seats up who was practicing his poems to himself.

Guaranteed, *he'd* be the first to volunteer when Ms. Fairchild forced them to read their poems next period.

Wait...

Justice had it.

In English, a little before Ms. Fairchild called *him* up to present, he would just conveniently paper-cut himself. It would work like magic. The sight of blood instantly made Justice clammy and feverish. And just like that, he'd be off to the nurse's office. (On his way there, he could ditch the god- awful poems he just wrote.)

Case closed.

Honestly, he deserved some points for proactivity.

Typically Justice waited until he got *to* English class to do the homework that was due that day, but today he decided not to procrastinate and do it one period beforehand.

He'd tried. That was enough.

Usually the pandemonium of his homeroom comforted him.

He'd listen in on various conversations or take part in a few himself, but he was kind of flustered this morning.

Mom was on an international flight schedule for a few weeks. Her being a flight attendant was cool and all (the souvenirs were *dope*) but while she was gone, Hope, his older sister, was in charge.

Which basically meant Justice was on his own. No rides to school.

Eating out almost every night.

Hope's bony, hungry-looking dance-major college friends doing nail art in the den and making the whole house smell like alcohol and acrylics. And the punk rock Hope listened to, over and over, every fucking night as loud as her stereo would go—it was the worst.

It reminded him of Liberty Fucking Marshall.

Ugh.

Justice flopped back in his desk chair, letting his eyes casually wander across the jungle toward Liberty's seat.

Empty.

Her Rebel Rebel backpack wasn't slung over her chair. No one in the room was actively ignoring her, so all evidence pointed to the conclusion that Liberty wasn't here today.

Maybe she stopped to ruin a perfectly good friendship on her way to school this morning, or, after a little light backstabbing, she got caught in traffic.

Justice didn't waste another brain cell on her absence. Instead, he retrieved his sketchbook from his bag.

Stressful mornings were survived through angry doodles and angry doodles alone. Shading hard and fast, Justice sketched a pyramid with an evil eye at the top.

The eye used its sinister powers to vaporize a small, little

Liberty Marshall, until all that remained was a goo stain, a few David Bowie records, and those ironic military boots she was always wearing.

Beneath the sketch, he scribbled the caption *Teslear Strikes Again!*

And then, completely horrified, he crumpled up the page and shoved it into his bag.

Teslear, the spirit of an evil gaze trapped in a pyramid, who killed with one look, was a comic strip villain Liberty made up. Back when sketches and storylines weren't just a way to pass his shitty days. Back when colors, lines, and characters were a language, one he and Liberty spoke together.

Justice wished he could spit the thought right out of his mouth. What did he have to gargle with to get the taste of betrayal off his tongue?

— 9:20 a.m. —

Homeroom let out like a fire, with students rushing the doors.

Justice sometimes imagined that the kids surging through the hallways of Paul St. Merris Charter School—PSM, to the initiated —was an allegory for too much sugar in a bloodstream. But then, Justice was always imagining. He divided the world around him into colors, shapes, faces, and stories— into *feelings* he could capture with his pen.

He was what one might call an extrovert.

He was a walking school directory. He knew everyone by first and last name. He could map out friendships, feuds, and flirtations. High school for him was just like sketching a portrait.

The details were what made it vivid—details like Jenny Estrada's new haircut or the capes Rachel Florence wore everywhere. Gabe West's laugh. Kwame's mad soccer skills. Or the fountain of dreadlocks that spurted up from Caleb Frost's head. Or—the gravitational pull of Magdalena de la Cruz.

Justice dropped the skateboard under his arm and hopped on.

Who could blame him for wanting to be next to her right this second?

He glided toward the front office, where Magdalena leaned against the glass, either waiting for something or just generally blessing the hallway with her presence.

Justice Garrison would write a poem for Magdalena de la Cruz. And then he would rip it up and burn it and never tell her about it because it would be *awful,* but he would sit down and write the hell out of it first.

Justice hopped off quick before a teacher saw him. And Magdalena noticed him right away.

"Hey, Justice."

Score.

"Mags." He felt that familiar energy buzzing through him—it was like...an urgency to live life. It was the kind of energy that made him get straight to the point.

And *to the point* he got. Sort of.

"Do you...I was thinking we could...Wanna hit Kade Park after school?"

As far as Justice was concerned, there was only one place in Massachusetts where you asked a girl like Magdalena de la Cruz to be your girlfriend: Kade Park, by the pond, beneath the twin poplar trees.

And he'd just drummed up the nerve.

Magdalena's singular dimple dipped into her cheek when she smiled.

Justice had always wanted to rest his thumb there.

If he ever got the chance to kiss her... "Yeah," Magdalena said. "Let's do it."

Excitement thundered through him so loud and strong, he almost didn't hear someone scoff nearby.

Justice glanced, and there she stood. The eyesore herself.

Ladies, gentlemen, and everyone both, not, and in between, Justice Garrison would like to present the queen of messing up good things: Liberty Marshall.

LIBERTY.

Liberty tried not to pop her eyes out of her skull when she rolled them. Five minutes.

She'd only been in school for five minutes. She was already having a bad day. Couldn't she have a few minutes of peace before the sight of friggin' Justice Garrison corrupted her eyes?

At least during freshman year he was still the gangly string bean she knew in middle school. He didn't stand out in any crowd, though she could always pick him out.

But *now,* two years later, he was a fucking billboard. He was broad and athletic. Tall as a tree. And he wore an acid-green skateboard helmet everywhere, so he looked like a giant neon popsicle when you saw him coming down the hall. He was impossible not to notice.

Even Liberty's grade A avoidance skills didn't save her, especially not in moments like these when Justice came to see *Switzerland.* (That was her nickname for Magdalena.)

Basically, Justice and Liberty were warring states and the only time they forced themselves to be civil was around Magdalena de la Cruz, Liberty's best friend and...probably the love of her life. The three of them did Model UN together and, fittingly, Mags represented the famously neutral front.

And most of the time, it was fine.

Mags spent 90 percent of her day with Liberty, and if Justice got some face time in during that other 10 percent, who cared?

But *this*? Right now?

Justice asking Magdalena to *Kade Park* first thing in the morning?

It was a declaration of war.

Liberty could see it in Justice's stupid turd eyes. He was going to ask Magdalena out.

He was trying to *steal Mags* from Liberty.

As if turning everyone they knew against her wasn't enough. As if backdoor defamation didn't do it for him.

Why was he so bloodthirsty? Of the hundreds of girls at this school, he truly had to pick the only one Liberty adored?

"Hi, Ms. Marshall." Magdalena's voice slowed Liberty's doom spiral.

Around Mags, Liberty's thoughts just kind of...dissolved to sparkles and swirls, like a bath bomb in water.

If Mags hadn't spoken up, Liberty might have actually forgotten that her mom was with her. She'd come in this morning to make sure Liberty didn't receive any penalty for being late.

Maybe there wouldn't be any damage to her perfect attendance record, but getting here late had definitely cost her something.

"Hey—" her mom greeted Mags, but then stiffened suddenly. Liberty realized what was happening too late.

Her mother, who really hadn't seen Justice in three years, gasped when she saw him.

No, no, no, no.

"Justice Jackson!" Liberty's mom inflated with excitement, blurting out her old nickname for the jackass in question. "Look at you, you're so tall!"

Meanwhile, mortification tore into Liberty like a rabid animal.

Tell me this isn't happening, she begged.

Liberty forced herself to ascertain Justice's reaction.

He looked like he'd just been caught mid-shit, so basically

they were on the same page. She could almost see him cringing on the inside. What came next was a taco full of awkward.

An awko-taco, if you will. Maybe Justice meant to wave. Liberty wasn't sure.

What happened instead was a weird hand throw. It was far too unenthusiastic and aneurystic to be considered a greeting of any kind.

Liberty was honestly surprised he managed that much. Pretending to wave at her mom was about the only kindness Justice Garrison had shown Liberty in three years—*if* we assumed that's what he intended, and it wasn't a sudden, rare, horror-induced arm spasm.

And then, worse—infinitely, exponentially worse—her mom bit into the awko-taco in the worst way possible.

"Get over here," she sang, arms outstretched. She then proceeded to wrap Justice in a hug.

He was so tall, and her mom was so short, that it looked more like a cheerful koala embracing a dead tree.

Over her mom's shoulder, Justice and Liberty exchanged a look. If this didn't embarrass Liberty so thoroughly, she probably would have reveled in Justice's suffering. But instead they just looked at each other with blank, horrified faces, sharing in their joint hell.

The truth was that they used to share a lot of things.

Unbidden scenes from their childhood raced through Liberty's memory. Eating ice cream when they were seven, ice-cold chocolate dripping down their chins. Camping in Justice's backyard when they were nine. The pair of them in middle school, vigorously playing video games in Justice's sauna of an attic.

They used to be best friends.

Crazy, inseparable, friends for life, best friends, but it's whatever. Eighth grade comes for us all.

The point was that Liberty, even after telling her mom that

she and Justice weren't close anymore, never quite told her why they ended. Probably because Liberty didn't actually know.

But it didn't really matter, did it?

Justice and Liberty weren't just ex-friends.

As things currently stood, Justice and Liberty were arch-enemies.

SCENE II.

— 9:30 a.m. —

JUSTICE.

Justice had never been so happy that he had to get to class. Ever.

He burst into Ms. Fairchild's classroom like it was the first bit of solid land he'd found after swimming for months.

Her room smelled like freshly Lysoled linoleum and sharpened pencils. Usually, portraits of famous writers lined the walls, staring students down like a tribunal of purposefully blurry, impressionistic white people.

Today, however, the posters were down.

In honor of Shakespeare's birthday, Ms. Fairchild had redecorated.

Expensive plastic theatrical masks dangled from the ceiling, turning in slow circles from the air of a groaning HVAC unit. Dolls and Elizabethan puppets slumped in the corners of the room, and fake crowns and swords from Dante's Costumes had been hot-glued to her cork board walls.

She'd strung up pages with famous Shakespeare quotes on them, because *of course she did.* (Ms. Fairchild was way too extra to just buy a pack of streamers.) She'd even taken the time to illustrate "POETRY" on the white board in extra-large, extra-neat cursive.

The room was graveyard quiet as Justice and his classmates prayed that Ms. Fairchild had contracted a random bout of middle-age amnesia and forgotten all about her plan to make them read their poems aloud to each other.

They sort of got their wish.

She let everyone spend half an hour of class reading over their poems and deciding which one they wanted to share. (Justice used that time to cleanse his mind of Liberty's bullshit.)

When it finally did come time to present, like a spell, the hand of Adam Grosch shot up like a rocket. His auburn hair and marsh-green eyes actually twinkled. The room snickered and cheered him on.

Justice lamented that he had no popcorn.

"Adam," Ms. Fairchild waved him up to the front. Justice braced himself.

Once installed ahead of his classmates, Adam held up his sheet of paper and announced, "This poem is called 'Get Down Goblin.'"

Oh, hell.

Justice dug his teeth into his bottom lip to keep from laughing.

Back when he and Adam were in seventh grade, they found this lady on YouTube. She was from 1994, and she'd made this really special song and music video called "Get Down Goblin."

That song and video were super, ultra, mega cringey, but maybe not as cringey as what was about to transpire here today.

"Who's that knocking at my door?" Adam began. "Not a goblin, I hope, but an angel." Justice let his eyes fall closed, gathering all his strength to keep from guffawing. "Who's that knocking on my door? Not a wolf, vampire, or ghost, but Mary Magdalene."

WHAT IS HE SAYING?!?!

"Get down, Goblin. For here is she. I love she."

The room broke into laughter and applause, drowning Justice's unabashed cackling underneath.

Just wait till Justice told Washington.

LIBERTY.

Question 7. Label this anatomical diagram with the proper names for bones and muscles.

Liberty blinked at the homework instructions. Usually, she and her homework had an understanding.

Her homework would ask her to do something she knew how to do and she would, you know...*know* how to do it.

And yet, this morning, the usual arrangement was off.

She rifled through her notes for guidance, when her cell phone suddenly buzzed, right off the table and into her lap.

A text from George. She sent back:

> You know anything about bones and muscles?

George replied with a GIF of Queen Elizabeth II dressed in a periwinkle suit and matching hat, unamused and blinking.

Liberty cracked a smile. That would be a *no*.

Liberty flipped two more pages before her phone buzzed again with a jab from George:

> WHO in their right mind chooses Medical Science as an elective anyway?

Here was a question that begged a sassy reply, but Liberty's brain froze, thinking of the truth.

There were only four elective offerings that semester.

Medical Science, Introduction to Broadcasting, Costume Design, and International Politics. She'd taken International Politics in the fall, but she knew for a fact that Justice was taking Broadcasting and Washington was taking Costume Design, which left her with only one (unfortunately horrible) ex-friend-free option.

Finally, she wrote back:

> People who want to be doctors when they grow up

> You hate doctors

> Ha ha

Obviously she'd wanted to take broadcasting.

It was the only logical choice, and for one simple reason: Liberty had her own online radio show.

No one else at her high school could say the same.

There was certainly no one who would have enjoyed the class more than her or practically applied the curriculum better than she would have.

In terms of impossibly wonderful things—aside from a shot at dating Magdalena—the opportunity to take a class on Broadcasting was at the top of her list.

And that's precisely why she should have expected Justice Garrison to ruin it for her by deciding to take it himself.

Last fall, she, Justice, Washington, and Magdalena had taken International Politics together—as if Model UN and PSM's Rainbow Coalition wasn't enough *together* time—and it was HELL. Liberty winced, just thinking about it.

Finally, she replied to George.

> I don't hate doctors. I hate hospitals.

Liberty wasn't thinking about this morning at all as she typed the words. But then George texted back, and all the anxious, bitter emotions of that morning refluxed through her system anyway.

> How's your grandad, btw?

Liberty hated how some text messages were visceral.

Some messages weren't just little words on a little screen; some of them came alive, like spirits.

She read George's message, but instead she felt it like he was sitting right there next to her.

She heard his rich, British voice ask her, out loud...*How's your grandad, by the way?*

"How's your pain in the ass?" is more like it, Liberty thought. A sharp pang followed, though, like someone pinched her heart. It was guilt—sticky, cloying, bitter guilt.

*What? Just because he's my grandpa and just because he was hospitalized this morning, I can't be mad at him for...*Liberty's thought was interrupted, and at the same time, involuntarily, her pencil stopped writing.

Whatever, she resolved.

Some sentences weren't meant to be finished.

LATER, MAGDALENA LIFTED HER HEAD TO ASK, "HAVE YOU STARTED ON our World History homework yet?"

Sharing silence with Magdalena came so easily to Liberty that she sometimes forgot Magdalena was there at all, until moments like these... moments Liberty dearly wished she could immortalize in some way.

The way Magdalena's curls rested on her shoulders, the freckle on her lower lip, the way the midmorning light hit her face and made her eyes look 4K.

"We had World History homework?" Liberty mumbled.

"Something about the Qing dynasty." Magdalena did a little shrug that Liberty adored more than she should have. "I left my notebook at home."

Again, Liberty rifled through her notes, hoping for a miracle. Nonesuch arrived.

Liberty relayed the bad news and, almost immediately, a thought struck Magdalena. With a buoyant smile, she said, "Oh, I know! I'll just borrow Justice's notes in Trig."

Magdalena happily returned to her work, leaving Liberty alone to recoil at her words.

A vile combination of annoyance and repugnance revved through Liberty's fragile system. *I'll just borrow Justice's notes in trig? Why don't you just marry him, too?*

She immediately regretted thinking angry thoughts about Magdalena, but she couldn't help herself.

Her anger was a faulty engine, one that rattled around inside her until it eventually exploded, spewing her hurt and pain on the nearest target. The nearest target was usually herself.

And as for the explosion, it was usually an anxiety attack the size of Canada—a spiral of fear, shame, self-blame, and heartbreak that left her paralyzed and more broken than she already felt, a little bit every day.

At least, that's how Donna would've summarized it. Donna Coburn, the school psychologist.

Everyone called her Coby, but she let Liberty call her Donna. It shouldn't have, but that small fact made Liberty feel special. It made her feel like she was real and her pain was real.

Donna could see it, which meant that the insistent voice in Liberty's head, telling her she was imagining her life and her problems, overthinking everything, that she was invisible, pretty much to everyone, but especially to the people she loved most... that voice wasn't 100 percent correct, at least not 100 percent of the time.

And that was something, right?

Thinking about Donna made Liberty remember the day they met—which brought her mind back to Justice (barf) and Magdalena borrowing his notes next period (barf squared)—in the fall of Liberty's freshman year.

That fateful day went something like this.

WHERE: Dr. Sorkin's ninth grade English class.

WHEN: September sometime, before 10:00 a.m. most likely.

WHAT: Dr. Sorkin (approximately 546 years old) decides to divide his class into pairs for a group project. "Liberty Marshall," he declared, pronouncing her first name like a rushed sneeze, *Libidee*, "and Jack Weymouth."

To this, **JACK WEYMOUTH** (fifteen, and somehow already a gay icon) scoffed. The room laughed. Liberty did not.

LIBERTY'S ANXIETY LEVEL: two out of ten.

When the time came, **LIBERTY MARSHALL** (fourteen, still recovering from eighth grade exit wounds) approached Jack's desk. Moving down the aisle, she stumbled and almost fell—

Someone tripped her.

Again, the room laughed. Again, Liberty did not. Instead, her cheeks began to heat, the back of her neck felt slick, and her heart thumped, tight and resounding, like a little anxious drum.

LIBERTY'S ANXIETY LEVEL: four out of ten.

Liberty turned to see who'd done it, but there were no feet in the aisle and her classmates' laughing faces unsteadied her resolve. Even if she knew who'd tripped her, what did it matter?

She wasn't going to confront them. No way. The last time she confronted someone...

Well, never mind.

Before Liberty turned back, she noticed the only face in the room (besides hers) without a laugh between its lips. It belonged to JUSTICE GARRISON (fourteen, a dumbass with a skateboard).

No, he wasn't laughing. He looked exasperated, inconvenienced, like some great imposition had been forced upon him. He wasn't even looking at Liberty. But she didn't look away, and finally he lifted his eyes.

"Sorry," he muttered, as though admitting culpability made him physically ill.

It was the most unwilling apology Liberty ever received, but for a moment, it confused her. She heard the word sorry on his lips, and she thought of all the things she wanted him to be sorry for.

She thought about all the times she'd wanted to apologize to him. She didn't know what she'd ever done to make him hate her like this, but maybe apologizing for it was more important than understanding what to be sorry for.

But then, Justice said, "My board slipped." And instantly, Liberty understood.

Just one year ago, if Liberty tripped in a class and found herself humiliated by her classmates' amusement, Justice Garrison would've stood up, like the class clown and good friend he was, and thrown himself to the ground comically and hysterically, just to make Liberty laugh.

Justice, the guy who used to stand up for her, was now the guy who tripped her with his skateboard as she was walking down the aisle.

LIBERTY'S ANXIETY LEVEL: six out of ten. Liberty turned away at once.

Her eyes, hot and stinging, would well up at any second if she didn't hurry out of this moment into the next. She got to Jack's desk, perfectly and symmetrically organized with purple pencils, pens, and notebooks. (Jack had already discovered that purple was his power color.)

Liberty remembered his outfit even now. He wore a purple denim jacket, a lavender paisley ascot, small flakes of glitter in his dirty blond hair, and a withering look on his face that could spoil milk. Before Liberty said a word, Jack held up a hand to stop her.

"Don't even think about it, Ronald Reagan," he said with a flourish.

What could he mean by that? Liberty didn't have time to wonder.

Jack promptly raised a hand and in a clear, resonant voice called the attention of the room to him as he asked for Dr. Sorkin's attention. Jack liked to call all their professors by their first name, just to be contrary, just to keep everyone guessing.

"Um, Philip? Yes, hi, excuse me. I'd like a new partner please. Religious reasons."

LIBERTY'S ANXIETY LEVEL: eight out of ten.

Dr. Sorkin arched an eyebrow. "Mr. Weymouth, what seems to be the problem?"

"Working with bigots—" he paused to serve Liberty with an icy cold glare, "—is against my religion."

The room cackled. Liberty had never felt the full weight of the word *disgraced* before that moment. She was so upset she couldn't speak at all. She was barely breathing.

Bigot. Why in the world would someone call her that?

LIBERTY'S ANXIETY LEVEL: thirteen out of ten.

Her vision went splotchy, like her body was malfunctioning. Her hands were so cold, she almost couldn't feel them. She was beyond tears.

She was in full panic mode—

KNOCK KNOCK.

Enter **DONNA COBURN** (forties, cool psychologist lady) with a question for Dr. Sorkin. She stopped when she saw Liberty's face. "You'd better come with me, dear," she resolved.

"Yes, please," Jack purred. "Take her away."

Liberty left the room to the soundtrack of ridicule. In the hallway, the tears came fast and furious.

"I'm Dr. Coburn," the woman said. "But I think you'd better call me Donna. That's what my friends call me, and I have a feeling you and I are going to be friends."

LONG, TERRIBLE STORY SHORT, MAGDALENA'S FRIENDSHIP WITH JUSTICE turned Liberty's stomach.

It always had.

Liberty knew their friendship was secretly a snake, one that would bite and probably kill her at a later date.

Well, that later date had arrived.

Because this morning, after Justice's sickening and drooly attempt at flirtation, Magdalena agreed to hang out with him at Kade Park.

Liberty wouldn't be there. She wasn't invited.

And she knew Justice would use the opportunity to do what he'd wanted to do since meeting Magdalena freshman year, what *Liberty* had wanted to do since the summer after eighth grade, what Liberty could *never* do for fear of ruining her friendship with Magdalena—ask her out on a date.

Maybe to someone else Liberty's fears looked ridiculous.

Borrowing someone's notes and jumping the broom together weren't the same, but to Liberty, it was inevitable that Magdalena would one day choose Justice over her.

All their other classmates had done it. That was simply the way it was.

Liberty snuck a glance at her best friend, furiously working to finish a Physics worksheet, pure focus on her beautiful face.

Some people are meant to be loved, Liberty thought. Like Magdalena. Like Justice.

And some people... are not. Liberty dropped her eyes.

It hurt like hell, knowing she'd one day lose Magdalena to Justice, but it also made sickeningly horrible sense.

Truth was, Justice brought them together, and it felt like Justice would be the one to tear them apart. The laws of love and friendship could be so... *cruel,* almost draconian, Liberty groused to herself.

Draconian, she remembered.

It was one of the words that would be on their vocabulary quiz on Monday in English.

English. Oh, shit.

Liberty checked the time. 10:00 a.m.

First period was over in twenty minutes, and she'd forgotten all about her English homework. Ms. Fairchild wanted them all to write poems. The poem was supposed to mimic a Shakespearean sonnet or something?

Liberty hadn't quite finished hers. It was missing two lines at the end.

She grabbed her English notebook and started scribbling.

All Liberty could think was, what would Shakespeare write a poem about if he were alive today? What would he write if he were writing a poem from beyond the grave?

One more glance at Magdalena and Liberty suddenly felt inspired to write the poem's final lines. Once finished, she drew back to admire her work. Though she didn't think it possible last class when Ms. Fairchild assigned it, now she thought she might actually get an A.

This was a pretty good poem, if she did say so herself.

Come closer, I shall call thee my friend.
For one last tale, thine ears I do bend.
Long hath I been abroad from the earth.
But one true defense durst beg my return.
My ink hath dried, my quill hath quit,
And still I tarry to tell thee this:
Love's but heady wine, pour'd from a fickle cup.
A phrase I'm told describes love best: "It sucks."

Liberty read her poem to herself ten times fast.

It was a poem she could be proud of, and that was a good thing—Ms. Fairchild planned to print all the poems from her various classes onto colored paper and hang them from the ceiling of her classroom for everyone to enjoy.

Liberty was secretly excited for this, not because she was eager to display her poem, but because she couldn't wait to read Justice's work.

There were a few things in this world that Justice was universally good at—making friends, ditching them for no reason and never telling them why, being the center of attention, playing soccer, skateboarding, and drawing.

And there were a few things in this world that Justice was universally bad at—apologizing, acting like a sane, kind human being, and creative writing. His poem was bound to be a dumpster fire, and Liberty was prepared to bring marshmallows.

SHE CHECKED THE TIME AGAIN. 10:10 A.M. EXCELLENT.

Liberty still had time to finalize the musical lineup for the next episode of her radio show. Ever since she started last year, she'd produced two episodes a month, now thirty-four episodes in all.

Even if no one at her school knew about her show, her ten thousand listeners did. (Them, plus George and Magdalena.)

Either way, colleges were going to eat it up. Liberty was sure of it.

Thinking about college was probably the final push she needed to reclaim her childhood dream. (She'd given up on radio between eighth and tenth grade for reasons she would prefer to redact from history.) But truthfully, Liberty had always been interested in radio.

Ever since she was a kid…

Aside from his genes, there was only one thing of her dad's that Liberty currently had in her possession: an old tape recorder and microphone from times of old.

(During the stone age, her dad had his own radio show, too.)

As a kid, after teaching herself to use it, Liberty used to record herself talking about anything, everything.

Sometimes, she'd tape a news broadcast on TV, play it back until she'd memorized everything the news anchor said, and then she'd grab Dad's recorder and practice her reporting.

In middle school, government and civics classes were her favorite. Other than recess with Justice and Washington, those classes were the highlight of her days.

She loved the idea of order and rules, guidelines and parameters that made her world make sense. She loved math for the same reason.

If mathematics soothed her inner chaos into neat lines of numbers and equations, learning about government gave her hope that she could someday use her chaos to create order.

Her life used to make sense.

Her relationships used to make sense.

She used to be a cheerful brainiac with exquisite, if emerging, musical taste, and two great friends for life.

But everything went to shit.

If her middle school self was twelve going on thirty—a successful attorney/journalist/diplomat in the making—then her high school self was seventeen going on 1979.

Her aesthetic was different now.

She'd ditched cheerful brainiac for punk alien visiting from the past. Why? Punk understood her.

Punk was political, like she was. Punk was in pain, like she was.

Punk was angry and defiant and anxious, like she was.

When asked to identify itself, Punk would check the box labeled "Other." Punk would eat alone in a cafeteria or start a riot. Punk would make some noise to drown out her cries.

Punk would distract someone from seeing her pain. Punk would stand up for her in a room full of critics. Punk would never trip her up or change its mind about her or leave her by herself; punk would never abandon her.

What more could she love about it?

There was a time when Liberty resisted her inner chaos, when she tried to smooth the edges of her wrinkly soul with math and social studies and good friends.

But now, those days were over.

Chaos was all she had left, and she wore it like a cataphract. With pride. With relish.

Life was a battlefield, punk rock was her armor, and her radio show was her greatest display of strength. Her show, *Liberty for All*, was a love letter to the genre of music that shone a light into her deepest darkness.

Her creed was simple: Punk now, and punk forever.

She'd been stumped for days about the title of episode thirty-five. She still didn't have any ideas.

Sometimes, she put the track list for a show together first and then looked for the theme that tied all the songs together. Other times, she had a theme in mind and picked the music to go with it.

All she had today was a craving for escapism. She wanted to escape the impending doom of Magdalena and Justice. She wanted to escape the car ride from this morning with her mom.

Actually, today, she wanted to escape everything having to do with her mom altogether. She wanted to escape the reality of her grandpa in the hospital. She wanted to get away from it all so badly, she'd never even texted George back—

Focus on the task at hand, Liberty, she begged herself.

She found a blank page in her black, heavily tattooed note-book, the one she only used for show-related ideas and took with her everywhere in case inspiration caught her by surprise. On her phone, she scrolled through her extensive iTunes library, on the hunt for her next show's music:

Needles & Pins—The Ramones
Please Take Me Home—Blink-182
Rock the Casbah—The Clash
Helena (So Long & Goodnight)—My Chemical Romance
Re-Ignition—Bad Brains
Cult of Personality—Living Colour
Misery Business—Paramore

Liberty jumped at the bell.

When she lifted her head, she found Magdalena's eyes watching her. A tickle ran up her spine.

"Ready to go?" Liberty dispensed the words mechanically. WHY IS IT LIKE THIS? she wanted to scream.

Why did her crush on Magdalena turn her into the Tin Man, rusted still, unable to move? Wasn't love supposed to make you happy? And at peace? All Liberty felt was little bursts of lust and panic.

She'd been in love only once before, and it was *nothing* like this.

— 10:30 a.m. —

JUSTICE.

Justice Garrison glided (like an angel) into Mr. Bell's classroom, precisely one millisecond before the bell rang.

The room applauded him as he hopped off his board and picked it up in time to evade Mr. Bell's disapproving sneer. He couldn't report Justice for skateboarding indoors if he didn't see it, but he could condescend all he liked. (And Mr. Bell liked.)

"Cutting it close again, are we?" He fixed Justice to the spot with those six little words. There was something about provoking this man that was its own reward.

Justice just felt like smiling whenever he glared.

"Morning, Mr. Bell." Justice tried to keep the smile inside his mouth instead of on his face. He made a beeline for the back of the room, by the windows where he and Washington sat.

Washington's face was frozen. It always got like that when he wanted to SCREAM laugh but was trying to keep it together. Justice smacked Washington's shoulder as he dropped his things and slid onto the stool beside his.

Justice was surprised to find Mr. Bell's eyes still watching him. Clearly, his itch for condescension wasn't satisfied yet.

In a strange way, Justice felt flattered that he'd caused a grown man, a respectable educator of many years and experience, to feel butt-hurt by simply rolling into his classroom.

It made him feel powerful.

Justice sat up tall in his seat and tried to look alive; he wanted to look ready for whatever came next.

"Mr. Garrison, would you be so kind as to give us an example of circular motion and gravitation?"

Cheap shot, Justice thought.

Quizzing students on a lesson you haven't taught yet?

Setting students up to fail was one of Mr. Bell's superpowers, which is why Justice took great pleasure in the opportunity to let the air out of his teacher's horribly inflated ego.

Nice and slow, like a high-pitched balloon fart.

"Hmmmmmmm," Justice mulled. Mr. Bell rolled his eyes. "I think the best example of circular motion and gravitation would have to be..." He paused for dramatic effect.

"Out with it, Garrison."

Justice savored the moment a little longer. "Mr. Bell, I think the best example of circular motion and gravitation would really have to be... making out."

The room collapsed into a cacophony of giggles and guffaws. Mr. Bell looked ready to pop.

This part, Justice *loved*.

Justice loved it when white people got so angry or embarrassed that they started to go red from their neck all the way to their hairline.

He'd only seen it a few times, but this shit was magical to him.

Watching Mr. Bell's skin color go from sugar cookie to king crab leg was something to be awed and amused by.

Even Washington had lost it now.

It was important for Washington to hold his laughter in sometimes because he had the loudest barking laugh you'd ever heard. It was a sound synonymous with mockery, even for their teachers.

Washington tried to leash his cackling until he was outside of class, but thanks to Justice, all bets were off.

"I know what you're probably thinking," Justice surged on.

"That's completely incorrect, Justice, in every way, but! Hear me out."

The whole class would hear him out. Justice was focused on the ruby- red ring inching up from the collar of Mr. Bell's crisp Oxford shirt.

"When you make out with someone, your heads—" Justice mimed with both of his hands, like he was holding two skulls and making them kiss by rotating his hands, "—go in little circles like this."

His classmates continued to snicker and snort as the ring of red rose toward Mr. Bell's chin. His cheeks were rapidly reddening.

Justice was so excited he almost forgot his demonstration and laughed at himself. "And your tongues go—"

Before he could stick his tongue out, Mr. Bell stalked to the board and resumed writing out the equation he was in the middle of preparing before Justice arrived.

He slammed the tip of his Expo marker loud enough to silence any further giggling, reducing the room to the noise of angry marker squeaks and muffled snickers.

"Turn in your books to page—" He growled the words, but Justice wasn't quite done with him yet. When Mr. Bell turned back to face the class, he found Justice's arm in the air.

"Wait, Mr. Bell, I'm serious. Are you honestly saying that a person's lips can't have a gravitational pull?"

Magdalena's did.

Justice thought about kissing her all the time.

Mr. Bell ignored Justice and his question and forced class to start.

Killjoy.

ABOVE THE WHITEBOARD, THE WORDS AP PHYSICS WERE WRITTEN IN an elaborate mural made from more fuzzy rainbow pipe cleaners than should be purchasable by law.

Or at least, that's what Justice was thinking when Washington leaned over to him and said, "You're bad."

"Thank you, I try," he murmured back.

"So, what happened?" Justice glanced right into Washington's hazel brown lie-detector eyes. "You only turn into a Provoke-a-saurus Rex when something's got you in a mood."

The pro and con of having a best friend is that they know you well, sometimes too well.

Justice had been so excited to tell Washington about the comedic gold that was Adam's dumb poetry, and here he was instead about to tell him about running into Liberty.

Way to kill his bad poetry buzz...

He'd been trying very hard for the past hour not to notice it, but Justice could still smell the honeyed perfume of Jeanine Marshall on his clothes. Ugh.

The whole affair made him want to break something expensive and pin it on Liberty. *I mean, can't she control her own mom?* Like, what kind of psychopath lets their mom hug a teenager that's not related to them in broad daylight, in the middle of a high school hallway?

If Justice didn't have an invincible reputation, he would've had to carry the shame of being mom-hug-boy until graduation. That is exactly the kind of torture Liberty Marshall would attempt to bring down on him.

She was so—so—why couldn't he think of the words to best describe her cunning? He'd been on a roll today, but now he had nothing.

"Um, hello?"

Justice blinked back to reality. "Fine. Yes. Something did

happen to me today. Something disgusting. And inappropriate. I think I can safely say I'll be scarred until the end of junior year."

"Really?" Washington arched a perfectly plucked eyebrow. "Did you run into a white supremacist snacking on literal feces?"

"Worse." The taste in Justice's mouth got suddenly stale. "Liberty."

It was hard enough to say her name, harder still to continue with his story. Especially when Washington got all tense.

Whenever Justice mentioned Liberty, or when Washington was forced to interact with Liberty directly (like in Rainbow Coalition meetings or that time in English they were paired together for a project sophomore year), he locked up like a prison door and got all strange.

Justice didn't really get it.

At first, Justice thought Washington's weirdness was about the ex- friend factor. But there are plenty of people Washington used to be friends with in elementary and middle school who go to PSM with them that he's completely cordial and normal around now.

Then Justice thought, maybe it was because Liberty was a bitch and a half to deal with. But half the people in this school were like that, and Washington didn't hold that against anyone else.

Justice always got the feeling there was something more to it.

Maybe something went down between Washington and Liberty that he didn't know about. And his curiosity always begged him to ask Washington about it when he got like this, but the other 98% of him would rather die than resemble (even vaguely) someone who was interested in Liberty Marshall.

(Been there, done that, barely escaped with his soul.)

Justice wanted to break-dance right out of this conversation before he even finished his sentence.

Talking about Liberty sucked for him and sucked for Washington. Let's just get this over with.

"I was talking to Mags, and then Liberty showed up with her mom.

And her mom...talked to me," he hedged.

Talking wasn't as bad as hugging, but it was close enough that Washington would understand how nauseated Justice felt, without Justice going into the gorier details.

Those details, which he desperately wanted to repress.

Justice shook his head. "I bet she planned it."

"How is Jeanine?" Washington replied with a faux fondness. His question made Justice think, which was unusual.

Usually, Justice didn't think unless he wanted to.

But for some reason, Washington's question made Justice visualize Jeanine Marshall's face in his mind.

He'd seen her a million times. It was actually possible he'd seen Jeanine Marshall more than he'd seen his own mom.

That thought hurt in a way he was unwilling to face— *Be good*, his mother's voice echoed through his memory. Her high heels clicking down the driveway.

That little black ugly standard-issue suitcase airlines gave stewardesses, rolling behind her, mocking him.

He remembered being little, suddenly, and thinking, *I wish I was a suitcase, so I could go with her.*

Pathetic.

Justice never wanted to be that pathetic ever again.

He would've saved himself a lot of time, energy, and friendship if he'd just learned his lesson then and there, before he even met Liberty— Women will break your heart with a smile on their face.

THERE WERE STILL FORTY MINUTES OF CLASS LEFT, BUT JUSTICE RAN OUT of fucks about five minutes ago.

He'd been sketching the world outside the windows of Mr. Bell's classroom with much success. His landscape work was definitely getting better. But Justice still preferred to draw people, *faces*.

He loved to draw complex facial expressions. He loved it when he could read the mind of a person rendered in a portrait. The metaphysical pleasure of that...it was trippy in the best way.

He'd been drawing since he could hold a crayon.

Even as a toddler, while his other friends were drawing spaceships and dinosaurs and firetrucks, he was more interested in faces. He used to stare at people all the time as a kid.

His parents admonished him for it a million times.

It's not polite to stare, they'd say.

It's not polite to get divorced either, Justice dreamed of telling them.

It's not polite to divide all the stuff in our house and take half of it with you when you move out, Dad.

It's not polite to be halfway around the world all the time, not giving a shit, Mom.

Justice had just begun to shade the road when a box truck broke his focus. (The cab was bright green, just like his helmet. Hard to miss.) It looked like a baby semi truck who hadn't yet grown into the full length of its trailer. It was cute.

It huffed to a stop, idling by the curb in front of PSM long enough for Justice to take in the colorful illustration on the truck's side. A pair of lutes were positioned like crossbones beneath a skull. But where the skull should be was an illustration of some old, unamused guy.

Written in a circle around the image were the words *What You Will Shakespeare Company*.

What does a Shakespeare company do exactly? Justice wondered.

It's not like they made Shakespeares and distributed them across the land. Although, they could.

Everybody liked bobble-heads...

Before he could finish that thought, the truck pulled up to the PSM driveway and turned in.

Spare thoughts disappeared as his mind drifted back to the instant replay of his psychological altercation with Mr. Bell at the start of class.

Justice thought back over every word he said with pride.

He might not be a creative writer, but he was most definitely a creative talker and that was better, honestly.

If he was a good creative writer, he'd write better poems. His being a good creative talker got him a date with Magdalena this morning (sort of), and if he was lucky, his talents might get him kissed too.

You know how when boys are little they sometimes think girls are gross? Justice was never like that, which is surprising, considering that his older sister Hope is and has always been a total troll.

Justice had always thought boys and girls were great. And perhaps because of this he'd discovered the joy of kisses early on in life.

When he was seven years old, to be exact. His first kiss—

Justice stopped himself.

He didn't want to think about his first kiss.

It was a memory too good to be forgotten, but too tainted to be remembered with any kind of fondness.

Justice called that the Liberty Marshall effect.

She was just like radiation. She didn't destroy good memories. She just made them so toxic to the touch that you couldn't go near them anymore, not without getting sick to your bones.

Her face appeared suspiciously in his mind, the same way it

suspiciously rains when you're already having a bad day. He hated how when he thought about Liberty, the creative center in his mind still activated. He'd sketched her face so many times that when he thought about her face, he also thought about how he'd draw it.

He saw her actual face and a charcoal sketch of her face.

There were certain parts of her face he could always get right, like her forehead, eyebrows, and hair. And there were parts of her face he could never sketch a true likeness of.

Like her eyes. And—*why am I even thinking about this?!*

Justice was so desperate for a distraction that he decided to pay attention in class. When he tuned back in, Mr. Bell was mid-sentence.

"—company who'll be performing for us this afternoon needs help setting up. Any students who are willing to volunteer will be excused from class between now and the start of Club period—"

A few hands went up around the room, and Justice was shocked to find that his hand was one of them.

He looked up at his arm, which had risen on its own, and found Washington's fingers around his wrist.

Justice didn't know what it was like to volunteer, but he did know what it was like to be volunteered.

"Dude," he hissed to Washington, but his voice was drowned under the scuffle of every other person in the room also raising their hands.

Everyone wanted to be excused from Mr. Bell's class.

"Please, please, please," Washington whispered under his breath, as Mr. Bell supplied a condescending laugh.

"Unfortunately, not all of you may volunteer. I was asked to provide four students only. The first four hands I saw were... Quentin Bluth, Andrew Lang, Washington Ardmore, and—" It clearly pained him to say it. "—Justice Garrison. The four of you may be excused. Take your things and report to the theater."

Justice still had virtually no idea what was going on or what Washington had just volunteered them for, but the look on Washington's face was undeniable.

His lips were slightly pursed, like he had his cheek between his teeth. And his eyes were all forlorn and sparkly.

Justice glanced around the room at the other students preparing to leave.

Andrew Lang crossed his field of vision.

Ah, yes, Justice thought to himself. Crushes make people do crazy things.

"What time is it?" Washington asked, hurriedly standing from his stool and straightening his pastel jeans and adjusting his hideous floral-print button-down shirt.

Justice checked. "Eleven o' five. Why?"

"That gives me fifteen minutes to try and get Andy to notice me," Washington blurted out, clearly on accident.

His head snapped up after the words left his mouth, shock and disbelief plain on his face.

Justice snorted as he hiked his book bag onto his shoulder. "Come on, lover boy."

In the hallway, Justice tried to pump Washington for information, but he seemed to be hypnotized by Andy's back as they walked together-ish—the four of them, Q, Andy, Washington, and Justice—toward the new wing of PSM.

Finally, Justice gave up and asked Q. (They were workout buddies in P.E.) "So what are we doing?"

Quentin was a nice guy, who always looked like a defecting army soldier because he kept his dark hair buzzed and the look on his face serious.

It was impossible to tell he was nice unless you saw him with a dog. In fact, Justice and Liberty might be the only people in this whole school who knew Q was nice.

They'd discovered this a long time ago...the time Justice accidentally lost Judge, Liberty's fat American bulldog.

Q still asked Liberty about Judge from time to time, or so Justice heard. Not that he gave one single fuck.

Quentin gave him a blank frown. "Helping a theater company." "We're helping a theater company do what?"

"Set up."

"Set up what?"

"For Much Ado," Andy chimed in, turning back to smile at them.

You didn't have to be into guys to understand why Andrew Lang was an attractive young man. (It helped, but was not a prerequisite.) The guy smiled with his whole face.

Even his perfectly coiffed hair smiled when he smiled. He was the all-around nicest guy they knew.

And he had a really kissable face, Justice thought. Is that a weird thing to think about someone?

Lips were Justice's favorite facial feature.

They were the most fun for him to draw. The way he drew someone's lips spoke volumes about what they were feeling or thinking.

Lips were also his favorite body part because of their involvement in the act of kissing, and he'd come to the conclusion, through observation and experience, that the best kisses involved good lips.

And Andrew Lang most definitely had them.

"Gesundheit," Justice said to that sneeze of a word that just came out of Andy's mouth. "Now, what are we setting up for?"

Andy laughed. Justice saw Washington melt a little in his periphery. "You know, Much Ado About Nothing. The Shakespeare play? The one we're reading for English."

Error Code 404. File not found.

"These acting people are putting on the play today," Q eloquently added.

It was then that a faraway bell rang in Justice's mind.

Something about today being a half day with a performance in the afternoon. This must be that.

As the boys navigated to the theater, they passed the front office, and Justice was painfully reminded of Jeanine Marshall.

Again.

In the three seconds he allowed himself to relive that morning's events, he realized that when he saw Jeanine Marshall that morning, she wasn't her usual sunshine-y self.

I mean, she was, but something was off.

She'd looked like a woman dealing with something hard, and the way she'd hugged him…it was like she never wanted to lose anything precious ever again.

SCENE III.

— 11:20 a.m. —

LIBERTY.

Second period ended, like death by lethal injection. Quick, but still not quick enough.

An anticlimactic end to the hefty prison sentence that is P.E. Liberty knew it was completely and totally cliche, but P.E. was her idea of hell.

(The only thing that could have made it worse was Justice Garrison being in the same section as her. Thank God she didn't have to fail publicly in front of *him* three days a week.)

Their teacher, Coach Hennessy, was a *total* hardass clearly out to prove that America made a mistake by not letting her advance to the Olympics or something.

Liberty didn't hate her *too* much.

After all, Liberty would be pissed, too, if she were a high school P.E. teacher.

Obviously, there was some sort of industrial-strength pole up

Coach Hennessy's ass, and that was okay. Probably wasn't her fault. But did she have to take it out on *them*?

Today was intervals day, which was a small, unassuming term that meant absolute child abuse.

Coach Hennessy made them run the track behind the school, and every time she blew her whistle, they had to speed up.

The only people who got to sit out Cruella De Vil's bid for cruel and unusual punishment were Katy Sanchez (sprained ankle), Oricai Desmond (allergy attack, lucky bastard), and Jack Weymouth (ugh).

Jack kept a beach blanket and a pair of swim trunks in his locker so that whenever he got the opportunity to sit out P.E., he could work on his *tan*.

At the beginning of class, after Coach explained today's activity, Jack said, "Excuse me, Deborah? I need to be excused from class today."

"Reason." Coach Hennessy was as laconic as they came.

If she could communicate without putting herself through the trouble of being monosyllabic, she invariably would.

"I'm on my period," he'd enunciated.

Then, the entire class watched in amusement as Coach Hennessy tried to process his words and come up with a one-word response that meant *No way in hell, but also, you could be trans, what do I know, I'm just a horrible P.E. teacher.*

Finally, she settled on, "Fine," much to Jack's irritatingly smug excitement.

And then, for the next *hour,* wearing cat-eye sunglasses, lip gloss so glossy it could refract light, and lavender swim trunks, Jack proceeded to provide mocking color commentary as everyone else jogged past him on his towel.

While waiting for the class to complete another lap, he flipped through the pages of Allure Magazine.

Somehow, without looking up, he'd deliver lines like, "Lift

those knees, Tessa!" And "Roll your shorts down, Jessica. If Victoria can keep her secret, so can you!"

As Liberty crawled by him, moribund and out of breath from all the cardiac activity, he'd said, "Run any faster and you'd make a good horse for the Pony Express."

"Bite me, you overgrown eggplant," she'd wheezed, out of earshot.

Liberty had so hoped at the start of last semester that this would be the year she had zero classes with Jack Weymouth.

They'd shared *six* classes freshman year, and three sophomore year, and this year her wish *almost* came true. She only had one class with him, but *P.E.?*

Really?

Was that meant to be some kind of joke?

Why couldn't they share a study hall—a.k.a. a period where they would never, ever interact under any circumstances?

Liberty would sit with Magdalena in their favorite corner of the library, and Jack would sit in his favorite corner of the library, where they kept the books on how to be mean and stylish at the same time.

It was bad enough seeing Jack during club period.

It didn't help that right beforehand he got to see her sweat, trip, stumble, and otherwise endanger the lives of her peers by attempting to play sports.

Whoever decided club period should come after second period was obviously a sadist who had it out for Liberty.

Having to do club period right after P.E. was low, just down-right *mean.*

It would be like forcing death row inmates to perform a slapstick comedy routine before you strapped them into the chair.

All Liberty could see in her mind, as she dragged her feet from the gym all the way to Room 408, was herself, dressed like a rodeo clown, strapped into an electric chair, waiting for someone merciful to pull the lever.

Clowns.

That gave her an idea for episode thirty-five's track list. She could play Clowns by t.A.T.u.! But...could she?

Would that be too experimental? Her listeners had come to expect pure punk from her, and t.A.T.u.'s desperate, anxious, angelic, gay, pop-punk—while a delicious cocktail of so many things Liberty loved—wasn't exactly punk rock in the... Judeo-Christian sense of the world.

She was texting George about it before she'd even finished thinking it through. She glanced at his message from earlier, the one she'd purposefully ignored and was still ignoring. *How's your grandad, btw?*

> Doing a poll. Playing t.A.T.u on LFA. Yes or no?

After Liberty typed and sent that message, she dared check for any others from her mom.

Nothing.

Liberty tried to force herself to relax.

If something was more wrong with her grandpa than there had been this morning, her mom would've texted her, right?

Thinking of her mom only led to thoughts that depressed Liberty. The hallway, Mom hugging Justice, the thirty seconds before that when Liberty watched Justice falling all over himself with Magdalena.

That was another thing she hated about him.

People loved him even when he was messy.

Even when he was tripping all over his words, half-drooling, looking and sounding like a complete idiot, he was still lovable.

Must be nice, Liberty thought bitterly.

She looked up and, much to her own dismay, discovered that

despite manifold efforts to walk in slow motion, she'd already made it to her next destination.

The halls were becoming increasingly empty as students funneled into their respective club rooms. Liberty was the only one paralyzed outside of hers.

All at once, her anxiety attacked, burying her alive beneath piles of panic.

Her brain raced back through the conversation she had with Mom that morning in the car. There was nothing quite like fighting tears on a car ride from point A to B.

How exposed and trapped and little you feel…

All those feelings returned now, as her mind careened through unknown nightmare scenario after nightmare scenario.

She extrapolated from the events of this morning until she could almost feel her heart breaking.

Justice talking to Magdalena, him asking her out, him asking her to be his girlfriend, her saying yes, her distancing herself from Liberty, just like Justice and Washington did.

Just like Liberty's dad did.

Just like Liberty's mom had that morning.

And Liberty would end up so alone and so afraid to talk to Magdalena, but wanting to so desperately, that one day she'd see Mags in the hall, and it would be just like that day with Justice a few years back—

"Liberty Marshall, when they said good things come to those who wait, they were *not* talking about you," Jack threw the words over his shoulder as he strode past her, straight into Room 408.

Liberty barely had time to register the insult, she felt so out of control, standing there on her own.

Maybe Jack was right in his own twisted, hateful way. What was she standing there for?

What was she waiting on?

She should just leave. Right now. Today had already been a killer, and it wasn't even half over.

She was already dealing with a double dose of family drama. That was enough to warrant a self-care day all by itself, without the added incentives of being publicly humiliated by her mother and ditched by her best friend for her arch nemesis.

(No, that hadn't happened yet, but after this morning, she felt best- friendless again already.)

She never wanted to think about today in P.E. again.

The question was, after all the grade A horseshit she'd been forced to deal with all day, could she really handle the bloodbath that was a Rainbow Coalition meeting?

Rainbow Coalition was PSM's LGBTQ+ awareness/alliance club. Magdalena founded it, because she's brilliant, and because if Liberty had founded it—as she'd always intended to do when she got to high school—no one would have come.

Thanks to guys like Jack, Justice, and Washington, people at this school thought Liberty was a...

Liberty could hardly think the word, it was so dumb.

Homophobe.

They thought she was a homophobe.

Even her faithful attendance at Rainbow Coalition meetings didn't seem to convince anyone otherwise. Liberty was willing to bet people thought she attended the meetings as, like, a strange form of remedial learning.

Like homophobe exposure therapy.

In the beginning, she'd made more of an effort to dismantle the shitty reputation that had been foisted upon her by previously discussed assholes.

When it was time for the RC to elect their governing body, Liberty threw her name in the hat for everything she could. But despite her clear executive leadership skills and *excellent* ideas, she was snubbed.

Snubbed, snubbed, and snubbed some more.

She didn't make president (went to Magdalena), she didn't make vice president (went to *Justice*), and she didn't make secretary (went to Adam Grosch, who probably can't even spell secretary).

Liberty didn't even make *treasurer*, whose job is literally to count money and write numbers down on a sheet of paper!

They wouldn't even let her lead any of the boring subcommittees, like the Signage Committee or the Programming Committee (they elected Jack, Liberty could say less).

Even though Liberty was herself a member of the LGBTQ+ community, even though she'd never done or said anything homophobic *in her life*, much less to any of these people, they'd systematically sidelined her from taking part in club activities.

The only reason they didn't outright kick her out was because she and Magdalena were best friends.

And one would think Magdalena's spotless social reputation would buoy Liberty's trash panda of a reputation, but *no*. This was an unfortunate example of coexistence.

Liberty had discovered that the universal admiration people felt for Magdalena could happily coexist with the wrongful disdain they felt for Liberty.

All of her great ideas went unconsidered. All of her opinions were unappreciated.

If the words came from her mouth, they were wrong. But if the same words came from Justice, they were the most inspired words anyone had ever spoken.

Add in some forced cardio and body-shaming and it would be worse than P.E.

And there was nothing she could do about it. Except, for once, maybe ditch an RC meeting.

She could go home, binge *Once Upon A Time* with Judge, take a nap, work on her show.

The possibilities were endless.

If only she could get her feet to move...

Her phone suddenly buzzed and she almost dropped it. George.

> BIG YES to tATu!

In the few minutes it took him to text back, Liberty'd forgotten what they were even talking about.

She typed and sent a new message.

> Doing another poll. Should I ditch RC?
> Yes or no.

> And deprive me of my favorite pastime? I
> vote no.

Liberty sighed. George had spoken.

MAYBE LIBERTY SHOULD'VE MENTIONED THAT GEORGE IS HER ONLY friend (not including her dog) who doesn't go to Paul St. Merris Charter School.

George doesn't actually go to any of the high schools nearby, and that's because he lives in London now.

With his mom.

Here's the 411 on George Monsouri-Amand.

George is a seventeen-year-old American-born British-Moroccan bisexual intellectual.

But he didn't used to be.

He used to be a burly, macho fourteen-year-old problem child having a bad eighth grade year.

That's right.

George, along with Liberty, Justice, and Washington, all went to the same middle school. But it was in eighth grade that his world-traveling, dream-team, archeologist parents decided to divorce.

(Justice wasn't alone in the Shitty Parental Situation department.)

And as if starting high school wasn't perilous enough, it was decided that George would leave their sunny, adorable, perfect town of Green River, Massachusetts and start high school in the UK.

George, at the time, was partially in support of this decision. There's nothing like a fresh start somewhere new once you've burned all your bridges to ash.

Though the last thing he wanted was to leave the US, the grief of his parents' pending divorce (and the breakup of his family) destabilized him to the point of acting out in school.

His parents saw his fighting fellow students, bullying others, and neglecting his schoolwork as a cry for help, one they believed a change of scenery might answer.

Liberty saw his behavior patterns a little differently.

The look in his eyes when he flirted with girls was the same look he got when he antagonized boys in their class.

The adults in their lives looked at George and saw a discipline problem. Liberty looked and saw a budding bisexual, poorly handling the discovery of his sexuality.

That's what made her reach out to him.

After discovering her own sexuality in sixth grade, she proceeded to watch her friends and classmates come to their own realizations.

Liberty was special though.

She thought about it like having a third eye.

The same way some people just *know* when it's about to rain. She had a similar instinct about baby gays.

It was like she could hear their sexuality in its infancy, crying out from deep inside their souls.

Liberty was never wrong.

Every person she'd ever identified as a baby gay in her mind, no matter how heterosexual they presented on the outside, came out eventually.

And George was no exception.

Liberty imagined that, at the time, George was drawn to her self- awareness. He wasn't ready yet to admit what Liberty could already begin to see—that he was bi.

Somehow, in all the chaos of his life, and hers, George and Liberty began to develop a friendship as eighth grade wore on. But they didn't really get close until Liberty, Justice, and Washington had their catastrophic, world- ending falling out.

Their friend group broke up, and George soon became Liberty's only source of refuge.

The safe harbor they shared together would be short-lived, however, because after summer, George would be moving and likely never coming back.

To be honest, Liberty hadn't expected their friendship to last this long. Why should she have?

Friends she'd known longer had ditched her for dumb reasons. It seemed logical to expect that she and George would drift apart for reasonable ones.

Long distance is hard on any relationship, but somehow it had only seemed to bring her and George closer, in the two and half years they'd been apart.

George would text her whenever he got homesick.

Or whenever he thought of a funny joke that his British friends wouldn't get.

Or that time when he got his first post-coming-out crush on a guy in third year, while he was still in second.

Liberty was virtually there for all his high school milestones, really, when she thought about it.

Their late night FaceTimes. Their epic Snapchat streaks. The memes? *All* the memes.

They hung out almost every day of his last summer in the US. Aside from the few weeks when Liberty was at camp and all she could do was write George letters, they were together a lot.

And now that he was in London and had been there for more than two years, Liberty was pleasantly surprised by the way it didn't feel like he'd left her life at all.

In fact, she and George had rituals, and one of them was helping Liberty survive the bloodbath that was RC meetings.

Since Liberty was officially/unofficially forbidden from doing anything in the club, she relegated herself to the back of the room and live- streamed her reactions to all the stupid shit they did in these meetings to George via text.

It was so entertaining to him and so necessary to Liberty's survival that they did it consistently, week after week. Honestly, Liberty didn't know how she would get through these meetings without him.

Today, the only reason she was in the room at all was because of George. If he hadn't texted when he did, she would've been home by now.

But *no*.

No truancy for Liberty Marshall.

Not today, on the worst of all bad days.

No, instead, she was in her usual corner, by the window (for an easy escape, if at any point the tedium turned lethal), taking glorified meeting minutes.

Liberty was essentially an unpaid, under-appreciated, and unauthorized stenographer in the honorable court of pain and suffering, Judge Magdalena de la Cruz presiding.

"I bring this club meeting to order," Magdalena said, right on cue. An eager message from George came next.

What's on the agenda for today?

Liberty rolled her eyes just thinking about it, as her thumbs flew into a summary of today's drama.

Everybody knows Gay Pride Month is in June. But PSM lets out for summer vacation in May. So the club decided to celebrate GPM in May, so as not to miss out on "prime awareness and programming opportunities." The issue is that May starts at the end of next week, and the only thing we've decided on is that Magdalena's going to give a speech.

"Well, *I* think we should organize a gay pride parade," Jack chimed in the second Magdalena opened the floor for discussion.

"We don't have time to organize a town-wide gay pride parade. And even if we did, it would be a hard sell, since there's going to be another one in like five minutes," Adam piped up.

It wasn't quite the resounding shutdown Liberty wanted whenever Jack put an idea forward, but it would do for now.

"Yes, thank you, Goblin Boy, for making that clear."

Goblin Boy? Liberty's eyebrows raised.

A few people snickered around the room, Justice looked like he was choking on the laugh he was trying to keep in, and Adam turned a bit pink and seemed to be looking everywhere but at Magdalena. (Liberty texted George about it.)

Jack re-crossed his legs and continued.

"I wasn't talking about inviting the whole of Green River. I think we should host a *PSM* pride parade. We'll parade through the halls, all the way to the track and field—"

Then, another idea hit Jack. (Liberty wanted to hit Jack too.)

"Ooooh, I know! We can use the leftover powder we used for our Holi celebration last month to do like, a rainbow color-war thing at the end."

A murmur of excitement suffused through the room.

And Liberty, without thinking about it at all, piped up suddenly, loud enough that everyone could hear her.

"That's cultural appropriation, isn't it?" Silence settled.

A few people looked Liberty's way. Not everyone.

It looked like it *pained* Jack to do it. "Was someone talking to you?"

"Repurposing materials from a sacred religious festival because you think it's cute..." She didn't finish her sentence because the end of it was obvious.

Liberty looked around at the faces of her classmates.

Seriously? *No one* was going to agree with her completely valid objection just because it came from *her*?

"What if we did a color-war with water balloons, but the water inside the balloons was bath-bomb water, so it's sparkly and colorful?" Magdalena suggested, ever the diplomat.

"I love that idea," Justice and Adam said at once.

"You're brilliant. I love you." Jack proceeded to air-kiss Magdalena on both cheeks.

Liberty, for a moment, was so consumed with rage that she wanted to rip the fire extinguisher from the wall, hose down her classmates in fire retardant, set the place on fire, and then watch to see who lived and who didn't.

There was nothing for her to do except text George every single last detail, and she did.

Once she'd finished eviscerating her enemies via text, she put her phone down and looked up, right into the staring eyes of Justice Garrison.

Her heart skipped, like a kid with some jump rope. His copper-eyed gaze petrified her.

She couldn't remember the last time she'd made eye contact with Justice Garrison.

The full, real, uninterrupted, see-into-a-soul kind of eye contact where you can't look away before the other person does, and you feel like you'll fall down the rabbit hole at any second.

The rabbit hole of who this person is.

The rabbit hole of all their secret thoughts and fears and pleasures.

How could Liberty have forgotten that Justice had a staring problem?

Not because he looks at people too much. But because when he really looks at you, really *sees* you, you never want him to look away.

JUSTICE.

"Earth to Justice," Washington hissed, except he was all tense, so he just sounded like a human imitating vending machine sounds. "You're staring at *Liberty Marshall.*"

Christ. Justice snapped out of it, dropping his gaze to the club forms on the table in front of him. *What the hell is wrong with me today?*

He saw her over there texting *George.*

(That's right. Justice knows about their little arrangement. Liberty spent every RC meeting spitting acid and texting George about it. Cute, if you think two murderous crocodiles on a virtual date is cute.)

Next thing he knew, he and Liberty were engaged in a non-hostile stare down. It was weird seeing her whole face head-on like that, looking at her, *really* looking at her.

He'd done such a good job teaching himself to avoid her that sometimes he forgot how easy it was to look at her.

Even if you got him under oath, he would never admit out loud that Liberty Marshall was easy on the eyes.

She was a chainsaw to the heart, a knife to the back, a menace to society, a danger to normal people everywhere, but she was still...you know.

Gorgeous or whatever.

The only consolation prize for Justice in Liberty's looks was that they didn't earn her any friends. She was walking proof that a person's character far outweighs how attractive they are.

And thank God.

If Liberty were more popular, he'd probably have to talk to her. How repulsive.

Justice didn't know how George Monsouri-Amand could *stand* to be friends with her.

Oh wait, yes he could.

There's three thousand miles of distance between them.

Even Justice could probably stand to be friends with Liberty if he had a three thousand mile buffer.

Oh, wait, wait, here's another reason they're still *such* great friends: They're both terrible people.

That's why they're friends on social media and they leave comments on each other's posts and they've got inside jokes and they text every single day.

Justice actually wasn't sure about that last charge, but he was willing to bet money on it.

Back when the RC meetings first started, after Liberty went through her painful try-hard phase where she attempted to jive with everyone and everyone said no, Justice forever used to see Liberty endlessly texting someone at the back of the room.

And Justice always thought to himself, *Who the fuck is she texting?*

Liberty only has one friend, and Magdalena's here.

And then one day, she dropped her phone as he was walking down the aisle, and in the split second before she picked it up, he saw her open Messages app and saw that she was texting someone named GMA.

Now, a normal person would've assumed this meant *Grandma.* But Justice knew (and knew Liberty Marshall) better than that.

Those were George's initials.

It was a running joke of theirs that she referred to him as GMA. George thought it was funny.

Well, you know what? *Fuck George Monsouri-Amand,* okay? HE'S THE WORST.

When Justice really thought about it, George was the real reason that he, Liberty, and Washington stopped being friends. He's the reason. He—

"What do you think, Justice?" It was Magdalena's voice. Justice lifted his head.

He'd zoned out again. Awkward.

He didn't want to look like an idiot in front of Mags, so he read the cues visible on her beautiful face—to try and quickly suss out whether she wanted him to agree or disagree, whether the idea in question was good or not—and said, "I think it's a wonderful idea."

Magdalena closed her mouth at once.

It was so slight Justice thought he'd imagined it, but an ounce of doubt flickered through her nutty brown eyes.

What? Justice thought. *What did I do? What did I just agree to? Why does she look uneasy?*

He glanced at Washington, who was looking at him, flat-out panicked, tense to the nth degree.

The only one in the room genuinely smiling was Jack, which

could only mean that Justice had just agreed to something that would bring chaos down upon them all.

Finally, he looked back to Magdalena who'd taped a smile on her face. "Great," she said. "Okay. Well, then." She was clearly trying to regroup. "In that case, Justice, you and Liberty will be in charge of DJ-ing the parade."

WHAT?! HE AND LIBERTY WERE WHAT?!

"Um," he began to backpedal, but how?

He'd missed the whole conversation and admitting that now would make him look like King of the Assholes.

Jack's smile widened. "Violence anticipated."

No, no, no, no, no, no, no, no, no, no, no, no, no, no, no, no, no, no, no, no, no, no, no, no, no, no, no, no, no, no, no, no, no, no, no, no, no, no, no, no, no, no, no, no, no, no, no, NO.

This *cannot* be happening.

WHAT ARE THE ODDS that of ALL the things he could have blindly agreed to in order to impress Magdalena, he'd agreed to do the one thing he'd *never* do to impress Magdalena?

He wouldn't work with Liberty Marshall if you paid him in skateboards signed by legends. There was nothing, *nothing,* Justice wouldn't do or say to get out of this, and—suddenly, Justice realized that his only ally in this catastrophe of an idea was Liberty herself.

Other than her, surely no one hated the idea of working with him as much as he loathed the idea of working with *her.* Which meant that both of them probably wanted out.

He glanced at her, a déjà vu feeling tickling his spine.

The déjà vu was definitely about this morning, he guessed. When her mom hugged him, and the two of them shared in their mutual mortification.

He expected to share another one of those with Liberty, but when he looked her way, she was furiously texting, staring at nothing but her phone's screen.

Her messages with *George*.

Same old, same old, his brain thought. *George was more important to her then, he's more important to her now.*

The thought made his blood boil.

The thing is that Justice and Liberty used to be a team. And not just any team. They used to be *the dream team.*

Anything they did together, they did amazingly. They did it better than anyone else. Anything at all.

If they baked something together—something neither of them had ever made, like the cake for Hope's eighteenth birthday party—it turned out delicious.

If they wrote a comic together, it came out compelling and beautiful, like they ripped it out of a book at Barnes & Noble.

If they swam together, they discovered new levels of difficulty for underwater tricks.

If they walked together, they discovered secret trails and paths that led to gorgeous meads in the woods by the river.

If they danced together, people filmed.

Once upon a time, they were the best team in the whole world. They were the best *friends* in the whole world. And until George showed up, Justice didn't think anyone could ever come between them.

But boy, was he wrong.

And that was the sickest part of this whole situation.

As much as Justice didn't want to work with Liberty and he knew she didn't want to work with him, if they did work together, they would kick ass.

Someone would probably ask them to DJ the town's pride parade, and from there, the capital's, and from there, pride parades around the world.

Justice used to be sure that there was *nothing* they couldn't face if they did it together. And for that and a million other tiny stupid reasons, there was a time when Justice wanted to be so much more than just friends with Liberty Marshall.

But just like back then, she was blowing him off.

She didn't even have the decency to look at him after they'd both been sentenced to Rainbow Coalition jail.

Chatting with some homophobic bully three thousand miles away was more important to her.

Why did all the women in his life think something halfway around the world was more interesting, pressing, and important than him?

What was it about him that was so...*impossible* to pay attention to? Justice was getting angrier by the second.

It was like there was a closet in his brain full of all the stuff that made him angry, and once something fell off the anger shelf, everything started falling one by one until Justice was so mad he could hulk-smash a table with his bare hands.

His parents forced him and Hope to see a therapist once, while they were in the middle of the divorce.

They'd only attended one session.

After that, his parents were fighting so much that they couldn't decide on who should foot the therapy bill, and splitting it was, for some baffling reason, too complicated.

Justice only remembered one thing from his one therapy session, and that was a technique the shrink taught him to help him diffuse his rage.

Write everything angering you down on a sheet of paper, she told him. *Make a list.*

At the time, it was the dumbest advice he'd ever heard in his life, but he'd tried a few times since then and it actually did seem to help.

He was already pulling a sheet of paper from his notebook when Magdalena announced, "Let's use the rest of the period to get to work."

The room devolved into people separating into cliques and side conversations while working on their assignments for the parade. Washington got up as soon as Magdalena released the room and strode right out the door.

Justice glanced at Liberty one final time, who was *still* texting, before finding a private-ish part of the room to start working on his list.

He couldn't have anyone looking over his shoulder...

HATE LIST

1. I hate how she's always texting him.
2. I hate *him.* I hate GMA.
3. I hate his fucking hair and his fake British accent and his perfect, fancy parents who take him with them on their international adventures, unlike some parents I know.
4. I hate how expressive his eyes are. I hate that his lips are perfect.
5. I hate how girls used to fall all over him. I hope he ages really badly like all the other British people. I hope he looks like Prince Phillip—just full walking corpse— when he's like 60.
6. I hate how he posts these pictures of himself kissing guys on Facebook. He's just flaunting his sexuality all over the place, like *Everyone pay attention to me, I'm a reformed recidivist who understands myself and who I am so perfectly now that I have no qualms about sharing my love with the world via Facebook.* Like he's the only guy who's ever kissed another guy before.

Justice had kissed guys before. Okay, guy singular.
One guy.

It was Washington. And it was a long time ago, and it shouldn't have happened, but it did and it was actually fine, because Washington, also, has great lips and at the time, Justice had a lot of pent-up kissing energy—NOT THE POINT.

You wouldn't find Justice flaunting his kiss-capades on fucking FACEBOOK. Because it's impolite. And no one asked to see pictures of his tongue down someone's throat.

7. I hate his body. Everything about it. No one who's not trying to get swole for an action movie should have muscles like that, just walking around. That's ridiculous. What does he need them for? Carrying books to class? I feel like guys who go out of their way to make themselves look like Arnold Schwarzenegger when they're seventeen are just like, toxic masculine try-hards with body-image issues who think muscles are a substitute for brains or talent. George isn't even an athlete. Literally, why does he go to the gym, other than to impress people? What a sheep.

8. I hate, hate, hate, hate, hate Liberty's dumb radio show, and her dumb followers. Oh yeah, she probably thinks no one knows about her show. Well, joke's on her. Washington found it, and when he showed me, I almost broke his phone. How dare she. What kind of backstabbing, heartless—

What no one knows is that Justice and Liberty wanted to start a podcast.

They started talking about it in seventh grade, when Liberty was getting really into civics and Model UN. The podcast was going to be called...*ugh.*

Justice couldn't even think about this without getting riled up. The podcast was going to be called *Justice and Liberty for All.* It was going to be a show where he and Liberty gave a teenage perspective on current events and political issues.

That was *their* thing.

They were going to do it together.

They'd even convinced their parents to send them to the same broadcasting camp the summer after eighth grade so they could learn the tricks of the trade.

With his parents divorcing and him and Liberty falling out, he'd forgotten about camp that summer until he casually overheard Liberty talking to George about this *new* camp she was going to go to.

The saddest part about that is if Liberty had gone to broadcasting camp with Justice after eighth grade, the two of them probably would've made up.

They probably would have fixed things.

And the reason Justice believes that is because he spent every day of broadcasting camp on his own, thinking about her, and thinking about how, if she'd been there, they would have dominated that camp together.

They would have...what did it matter now?

This semester, Justice had even chosen Broadcasting as his elective course, just to see if she'd be there.

How pathetic was *that*?

There was this weird, slimy part of him that wanted to know if any of the dreams he and Liberty had together still meant anything to her.

Justice could barely admit that to himself in his *mind*, much less commit the horrible truth to paper.

He rushed on with his list.

9. I HATE that she let George be a guest on her dumb
   radio show. George. The guy who's three thousand

miles away. She let him participate virtually for an episode of her show.

10. I hate that she named her show *Liberty for All.* We came up with *Justice and Liberty for All together,* and then she stole the name and cut me out of it. Surgically removed any trace of me like I'm a damn tumor.

Something must be seriously wrong with him today.

He was making his list, but it wasn't making him feel better. Not at all. Not even a little bit.

LIBERTY.

By some stroke of divine sadism, Liberty and Justice had been paired to do the music for the pride parade. And by "stroke of divine sadism," she was referring to Adam Grosch saying, after she volunteered to DJ, *What if Liberty and Justice DJed together?*

Which was a great suggestion on Adam's part.

After the RC meeting, he should go to the White House and suggest we give the U.S. nuclear launch codes to Vladimir Putin.

The same second she told George about it, he responded.

What? Are you the last human beings on EARTH? You and Justice working *together*?

As in together, together?

You do know that the definition of the word "together" does not include murdering him?

And then came the question that Liberty knew, just *knew,* would come next.

How'd Dewey take it?

Perhaps Liberty should have explained about Dewey.

Dewey is Washington's real name.

Washington's real, complete God-given name was Dewey Campbell Ardmore.

Now, for obvious reasons having to do with Dewey hoping to get a date sometime this century, he made the decision at the start of freshman year to rebrand, a word which here means *get Justice to come up with a completely dumb and somewhat plausible nickname for him to use in high school.*

Liberty was not there, of course, for the nickname brainstorm, but if she had to guess—knowing everything she knew about Justice and Washington—it probably went something like this:

JUSTICE: Hmmmmm. Dewey Campbell Ardmore. What about if we called you Dew? Like Scooby-Doo?!

DEWEY: Veto.

JUSTICE: I got it. Your new nickname will be Mountain Dew. Get it?

DEWEY: I'm not nicknaming myself after a soda that looks and tastes like piss. Try again.

JUSTICE: How about Camp the Man? Or D. Bell! Or Ardmore, just Ardmore, like a cool mononym. Like Beyoncé. Or DMX.

DEWEY: ...

JUSTICE: I got it. Washington. DEWEY: ???

JUSTICE: Your initials are DC. What do you think of when someone says DC? Washington.

[DEWEY has left the chat.]

[WASHINGTON has entered the chat.]

WASHINGTON: Approved.

JUSTICE: I'm so good at nicknames.

WASHINGTON: No, you're not. Now, can we please make out?

Okay, it probably went 90 percent like that.

The point is that *everyone*—everyone at PSM, probably everyone in the state of Massachusetts, even George thousands of miles away—could see that Washington Ardmore was madly and miserably and so disgustingly in love with Justice Garrison.

Liberty should know.

She was the first person on the planet to figure that out. She was there at ground zero. George was probably the second person to connect the heart-shaped dots.

Actually, Liberty wouldn't be surprised if George found out about Washington's crush, *long* before she did. And the reason is because George has always been interested in Washington.

Well, not Washington.

Dewey. The guy he was before he got to high school.

Before he decided that pastels and fugly floral prints were his thing.

Liberty always thought, in the beginning, that Washington was trying to keep up with Jack, whose style and flamboyance were clearly intimidating.

Jack established his iconic purple monochrome look on day one of freshman year. Jack was gay and out and proud and fortified by an impenetrable force field of hyperfeminine performance value and his scathing, epigrammatic wit.

He was then, as he is now, more or less impervious to the devastating power high school held over the teenage psyche.

Worse, he was *privy* to high school's destructive power. He used it like a whip, the fact that high school was hard for most people.

How in the world was Dewey supposed to compete with him? He was a shy, creative gay wallflower, hopelessly in love with his best friend, too scarred from middle school to branch out, with a backwards-ass historical name that sounded like some author they'd be forced to read in twelfth grade lit.

He and Jack were two very different types of gay guy, which Liberty assumed left him with two options.

Option A: Try to compete with Jack in his lane (attempting to out-jack Jack, in a sense), which is utterly impossible, something Liberty suspected Washington discovered early on.

Or...

Option B: Become someone completely new, who's different from Jack, but won't be fully and completely eclipsed by Jack's long, unamused shadow.

Dewey went with Option B, a decision George probably would've hated, if he'd been there with them freshman year.

Luckily, George was spared some of the horror of his middle school crush going through an unflattering transformation.

But still, Liberty was convinced that no amount of ugly could stop George from asking her about Washington. Because when you like someone, you can't help yourself.

He left the room as soon as he could without drawing attention to himself.

Liberty reported faithfully.

Seriously? After all these years of uninterrupted Justice time, he still gets jealous over you?

Liberty's heart did a little alley-oop, reading that last message. Washington.

Jealous over *her?*

Liberty didn't want to think about that.

It would only lead to her thinking about the day everything blew up, and then she'd invariably start crying and that was *the last* thing she could stand to go through on a day like today.

She put the thought out of her mind and turned the tables on George.

> Why? You care?

Whenever she teased George, he didn't respond right away, which made Liberty giggle to herself.

Busted.

If George went to PSM, Liberty bet he and Washington would be dating right now. Washington was so desperate to be noticed, and George had so much spare attention to lavish on whoever he chose.

George and Washington, she thought happily. Hey, wait.

George Washington.

Their names went together. She'd never noticed that before. Unfortunately for Liberty, her name only went with one other and it was the name of the person she loathed most in this world.

Justice and Liberty.

Momentarily she allowed herself to remember how much she used to love it when people said their names like that, side by side.

Like ice cream in a cone. Or pen and paper.

Or blue and sky. They used to fit.

Not that Justice ever cared. How could he have?

He was too busy ripping their friendship to shreds. He was too busy taking Washington's side.

Justice *always* took Washington's side.

He'd always cared *way more* about Washington than he'd ever cared about her. Liberty knew that from the beginning, when she showed up in second grade.

Justice and Washington had an in-progress friendship.

They'd been tight for many years. They were a package deal, and Liberty was clearly the outsider.

Why she'd ever imagined for one single second that if both she and Washington had feelings for Justice, he would pick her over Washington was laughable to her now.

What a stupid thought.

She'd never thought anything so stupid in her life.

Maybe if she'd realized a little sooner how utterly laughable her feelings were, she'd still have Justice and Washington for friends.

(Not that she wanted to hang out with those two idiots.)

One thing Liberty had never figured out, though, was why Washington had always acted so strangely around her after the deterioration of their friendship.

She would've understood if he treated her with the apathy deserving of a severed acquaintance, or even if he'd acted supremely smug or pitying or vainglorious around her.

Because he'd won, after all.

Their friendship fell apart and he got Justice and Liberty got nothing. Winner takes all.

Washington got his best friend and his true love. It hurt to even *think* those words.

Liberty lost *two best friends* and the only guy she'd ever... in one fell swoop, you know?

In one fell swoop, she was friendless. She was isolated.

Someone started a weird rumor about her being homophobic, and whatever reputation she had before was bulldozed to make room for the proverbial face tattoo she seemed to have now—the one that read BIGOT, the one that made everyone discredit and avoid her.

The way things went down seemed to, in every way, advantage Washington over Liberty, and yet when the two of them were in the same room together, he acted like he suddenly had to take an enormous shit and acting normal around her might unleash his bowels involuntarily.

Her other question about his behavior was one she was... frankly too afraid to ever voice out loud for fear of jinxing it into existence.

Why weren't he and Justice dating?

The two of them had been single since the eighth grade. They were constantly together.

Justice now despised Liberty, which meant that whatever fear Washington may have had about Liberty interposing in the past —however improbable the scenario of Justice choosing her over him evidently was— should be gone now.

In Liberty's worst, wildest dreams, and every day of high school, she'd secretly feared one morning she'd wake up and discover Justice and Washington dating.

That was the scariest thing she could think of.

Because if Justice and Washington dated, they'd get married and move someplace iconic for a pair of dudes in love to move— San Francisco, she'd always imagined—and adopt a bunch of kids and go on to live this beautiful life she would have no hope of ever being a part of.

Not that she would even want to live in the same *country* as them, if they got together.

But the point is that *if* they ever got together, the heartbreak Liberty carried around with her every day would be complete.

Total. Final. Irreparable.

Something inside her ached, just thinking about it.

Some wounds don't heal.

The only reason Liberty could conceive of, as to why they weren't together this very minute, was the matter of Justice being an idiot, especially when it came to himself.

And she had to concede that it was...technically *possible* that Justice had yet to realize that he was probably bisexual or pan.

Liberty didn't know how that could possibly be, nor did she know why it even mattered.

Whether Justice understood his sexuality or not, how could that possibly stop Washington from making *his* feelings known?

As far as Liberty was concerned, Justice Garrison would fall for the first person who tripped him.

If someone he loved and cherished, like Washington, asked to date him, Liberty would put her money on Justice saying yes. Hands down.

There was no way Washington didn't know that.

Liberty knew it, and she'd only been his friend for five years. The two of them were going on fourteen or something. (Barf.)

Justice had been Washington's first kiss for Christ's sake, speaking of barf! And not like a cousin kiss, either. Justice was Washington's first *make out.*

Liberty had very unfortunately seen the video footage of said kiss. She'd been at the party where said kiss took place, but thankfully in another room.

Gay guys who were secretly in love with their best friends would *kill* to have that kind of romantic momentum on their side.

But if even that wasn't enough to convince Washington to act, what about the way Justice used to blatantly check George out, that conflicted mix of hate and admiration in his eyes? Come on.

Obviously, Justice's sexuality was more complex than just... girls only.

If only for the fact that he loved Magdalena—a wonderful, amazing girl, who was also trans—Liberty was convinced that Justice was the type of person who loved people, not parts.

Not genders. Not assignments.

Washington was one of the great loves of his life, right up there with skateboarding and comics.

Surely that meant something.

In the eighth grade at least, it meant Liberty was shit out of luck. In the friends department, she ended 0-2.

George changed that.

It was at that moment, she was overcome by how much she missed having George around. Magdalena was a top-notch best friend most of the time. But Rainbow Coalition meetings were one place where Liberty had to fend for herself.

It was harder on her than she realized, and without George on the phone texting her for moral support, she wasn't sure she'd be able to stand these meetings at all.

Liberty meant every word, when she finally texted him back.

> I wish you were here.

Slowly, he responded...

> Are you sitting down?

> Yeah. What is it?

> I've got some news you're going to love. I hope.

> I was going to FaceTime you later, but...

Liberty watched the three little dots hop as George typed. She felt the phone buzz in her hands when the text arrived, and when she read it, she quickly discovered it was the *best news* she'd gotten all day.

> My mom was chosen to lead this big fancy archeological expedition thing. And if I go with her, she'd have to home school me for my last year of high school. And we all agree that would be pretty shit the year before I go to university, so instead... we decided that I'll move back to the states for my last year of high school! I'll be with my dad.

Liberty was so shocked and surprised and unbelievably excited that she couldn't stop her thumbs from FLYING into a reply, but she didn't hit send because suddenly there was Jack, standing over her, rapping on her desk.

"Yoo-hoo," he said. She glanced up at his puckish face. "DJ girl, don't forget to include Queen in the parade playlist." He wagged his finger at her. "Freddy Mercury did not die of AIDS to be snubbed by a persona non grata like yourself."

Liberty didn't know which was more offensive.

The fact that Jack actually thought she wouldn't know to play Queen at a gay pride parade or the fact that he'd used Freddie Mercury's death to insult her.

Liberty sucked in a breath to brace herself. "Sure, Jack."

"Oh!" He remembered something. "Now, I know his music is a bit slow, but you've also got to play some Andy Bey. Anything out of that man's mouth and I'm in *heaven*." A sharp little grin came to Jack's face. "Anything out of yours, on the other hand…*hell*."

Usually, Liberty didn't bother participating. What was the point?

No one took her ideas seriously, and on the rare occasion they did, Justice or Jack Weymouth would find some way to torpedo the notion before it caught any real traction.

Today, for some reason, she refused to keep her peace.

"Jack, you do know that valuing black people when they make music you like and not valuing them when they say things you don't like is a form of racism."

Jack's perfectly mascaraed eyelashes began to flit up and down. He blinked, rapid-fire and drew his head back, chin dipping against his neck.

Affronted. Gobsmacked.

His punching bag had punched back.

The volume of chatter in the room dimmed—probably because the rumble before the fight was palpable, just like thunder before a storm.

Liberty could feel eyes on them from every direction.

"*Excuse me?*" Jack spat.

"I just wanted to remind you that being part of an oppressed demographic doesn't mean you can't oppress others."

"Are you insinuating that I—" The *impossibility* of what he was about to say next was clear on his disbelieving face. "—am *racist?*"

Liberty shrugged. "You know what they say...*if the hood fits.*" The room devolved into a harmony of *Ooooooooos.* "Food for thought."

Liberty's heart galloped in her chest.

Jack, ironically, was turning more purple than his outfit.

And Liberty, in some small way, felt redeemed. Did she actually believe Jack was racist? No, not really.

Certainly no more than anyone else.

(To call him a jerk would be an understatement, though.)

Ultimately, Liberty considered it a good thing that maybe now Jack might have a semblance of compassion when it came to blindly accusing someone of a prejudice they didn't have.

His accusing Liberty of being homophobic was so utterly *ridiculous* that she'd continuously refused to dignify the insult by contradicting it.

The idea that *Liberty* could be a homophobe? Her?

The first person to talk to Jack Weymouth in middle school? Way before he'd emerged from his cocoon into the colorful gay butterfly he was now, Liberty understood him.

She knew why he kept to himself and couldn't seem to settle anywhere in their giant sixth grade class. She'd been the one to reach out to him and buoy him until he found his crowd. And even after all that, he could call her a bigot?

He could defame her near and far as a homophobe?

Fuck Jack Weymouth. Let him stew in the same disgrace he'd forced upon her. There was a wise old saying Liberty'd heard somewhere recently that applied to this situation perfectly: *Karma's a bitch.*

The only thing that stopped her from laughing to herself about it was the look on Magdalena's face—there was nothing but concern and disappointment in her coffee brown eyes.

Liberty always feared Magdalena might look at her that way. She had no idea that day would be *today*.

— 12:00 p.m. —

The PSM cafeteria looked like a food court at a high-end shopping mall. It was an open corral of tables and benches surrounded on all sides by various glowing, inviting cuisine stations. Eight stations to be exact.

Sal's Salad Corner, Pizza, Pasta & Calzones, Vegans Anonymous, Pescatarian Junction, Deserts by Desiree, Soups and Stuff, Whole Grain Train, and, last but not least, the... Backyard Barbecue Buffet.

Sometimes it felt like charter schools trolled themselves.

Liberty and Magdalena split up as they normally did, grabbed food from their favorite stations, and reconvened at their usual table—the one in the center of the room, equidistant from all the food stations *and* all the exits.

It was a little too out-in-the-open for Liberty's taste; she preferred corner tables, just like cops, so that her back was to the wall and she could see everything going on in the place without actually having to be a part of it.

But Liberty had never felt like a different seating arrangement was something she could ask Magdalena for.

Their friendship was a gift to Liberty, but she was smart

enough to know that to Magdalena—who would never in a million years admit it—their friendship was probably an encumbrance.

Why do you hang out with that weird mean girl? Liberty imagined people asking Mags the moment she stepped out of earshot. *Don't you know she, like, hates gay people?*

Magdalena had never once mentioned it, Liberty's unfounded and repulsive reputation. She didn't complain at all about any of it. And honestly, the fact that she didn't made Liberty uneasy.

Because it meant rare moments like these—when Liberty ran out of fucks—were suddenly very high stakes.

What if Magdalena, out of kindness and empathy (or most likely pity), was keeping all of her grievances about their friendship to herself?

Bottling pent-up annoyance and resentment toward Liberty, like soda in a can. What if Liberty snapping on Jack was tantamount to Liberty shaking all the carbonated cans of Magdalena's disappointment?

What would happen if Magdalena exploded on her? Would their friendship survive?

Survival. Yeah. That's how it all started.

The summer after eighth grade, Liberty was desperate.

It was the first summer in six years where she and Justice weren't going to see each other every day.

They weren't going to see each other at all. Or at least, that's what Liberty wanted.

Several weeks prior, they'd *begged* and pleaded with their parents to let them go to Broadcasting camp together. Long story short, Liberty couldn't face him.

She couldn't show up at that camp and act like she really

wanted to be there if she also had to pretend like Justice didn't exist, or that they didn't know each other, or that just a few weeks ago, she wasn't spending her every waking hour thinking about him.

Liberty couldn't bear the idea that she might show up at broadcasting camp and he wouldn't be there. Somehow, the thought of *him* skipping camp to avoid *her* was way more emotionally devastating than *her* skipping camp to avoid *him*.

All she wanted was to go somewhere that summer where she wouldn't think of Justice at all. The answer to her prayer came in the form of (brace yourself) Camp Sunflower, an all-girls sleep-away camp on a hundred-acre sunflower farm.

No boys, no bullshit.

It was the perfect place.

And it was there that she met and befriended Magdalena. Mags was shorter then.

Her hair fell only a little past her ears, and it was growing in uneven.

She hadn't switched to contacts yet.

That was the first summer after her transition, and she was so insecure that she wore pants and long-sleeved shirts almost the entire time.

Looking at her now with her big barrel curls, wearing jean skirts and colorful tops—unafraid of her own beauty—it was hard to believe the days and nights they spent together at Camp Sunflower were real at all.

Magdalena used to be a girl who was afraid of not being seen like one, and now she was a girl who stood up for every girl, boy, and nonbinary person who felt that way.

Liberty wished she could say that her own transition from thirteen- year-old Liberty to seventeen-year-old Liberty had been as graceful, but alas, the truth was not her friend.

She remembered the way the sun filtered through the canopy

above them, making the shadows of leaves and branches flicker across Magdalena's skin.

She was alone, reading. She looked miserable, and Liberty'd said,

Did your parents make you come here?

No, she'd replied too quickly. *I'm here because I want to be. I... always wanted to go somewhere where I could be around other girls.*

Then how come you spend all of your time here by yourself? Liberty remembered saying.

The short answer to her question was imposter syndrome.

Magdalena had spent her whole life wanting to be counted among the girls, but once she'd transitioned and finally gone to a place where she might get her wish, her courage faltered. Anxiety took over.

Liberty knew *allllllllllll* about that.

It's why they became friends.

Both of them were just trying to survive summer. Back then, they needed each other. Magdalena and Liberty were necessary to each other's survival.

But now?

Magdalena had options.

She could be friends with anyone she wanted. She didn't need Liberty.

The way they'd been sitting at their usual table, eating in silence, it felt like Magdalena didn't want Liberty, either.

It felt like an iron fist was closing around Liberty's heart, like it would keep clenching until her heart turned to dust and there was nothing left.

Her anxiety rose steadily with every silent minute. She felt like she was sliding downhill toward an anxiety attack.

Just leave, that voice in the back of her mind started saying again. *Go home. What's the use in staying? No one needs you here.*

Justice's stupid face kept appearing in her mind.

Probably because Washington was laughing (*always* at the top of his lungs) nearby. And Washington laughing meant Justice was entertaining him, as usual.

Justice entertained everyone. Justice entertained Magdalena. Why else would she agree to hang out with him after school, if she didn't enjoy spending time with him?

The fraying seams of Liberty's mind began to unravel a bit further as thought after thought raced through her head. The only available weapon to help her end her agony was honesty.

Brutal honesty.

She knew hearing the honest-to-God truth might crush her flat, but at least the suspense would be over, and if she found out now that Magdalena was planning on going out with Justice, that would give her the entire weekend to change schools.

Besides, if Liberty glared any harder at the table between them, she'd put a hole in it.

She sucked in a breath and held it before finally lifting her head. Magdalena was on her phone, but Liberty didn't lose her nerve.

"Do you—" she sputtered.

Magdalena met her gaze.

That electricity appeared again, zipping down her spine, like a rollercoaster down a drop.

Liberty had to look away. "Are you..."

In the end, the words came out meek and rushed and ridiculous. "Are you planning to go out with Justice Garrison?"

Magdalena stopped chewing and gulped the food down instead, which sounded like it hurt.

Liberty dared to meet Magdalena's eyes again. There, she searched for the look of someone in love with Justice.

That same look that came to Washington's eyes...she tried to find it in Magdalena's and...

"You mean, about Kade Park?" Mags put her phone down.

Liberty nodded. "Are you going to date him? If he asks you out later today or...*ever,* would you say yes?"

There was suddenly something very interesting about Magdalena's fingers. When Mags looked down at them, it didn't seem that she could look away.

Mags looked like she was wrestling with something of her own. Was she searching for a way to tell Liberty that she was in love with him?

Liberty's heart was beating hard and slow, like her chest was full of honey or molasses or thick, slimy mud.

How do you prepare to have your heart demolished?

What Liberty didn't expect was what (*and how*) Magdalena said, with a coy little expression on her face (COYNESS, ACTUAL COYNESS): "What do you care?"

Liberty felt like someone had just used her head as a gong mallet.

What do you care?

What did that even mean?

Magdalena must have registered the sheer emptiness of Liberty's brain in regard to finding an answer to her question, and quickly amended: "What does it matter if I date Justice or not?"

Liberty was already spiraling, just hearing the words *I date Justice* fall from Magdalena's lips.

It's stupid, she kept telling herself. *I know it's stupid.*

Liberty didn't care that other people wanted to date Magdalena. Of course they wanted to. Mags was everything.

She just didn't, at all, ever, under any circumstances, want Justice to be the one Magdalena said yes to.

And Liberty quickly realized there was no way to voice that without sounding certifiably insane, and her only other option would be to say, *It matters because I love you,* which there was no way she could say.

How in hell would she recover from a confession like that?

"If that's..." The words felt like acid on her tongue. "If dating him is what you want, then I..."

No. Liberty could (and would) lie to a lot of people, but Magdalena was not on the list. She would not do herself the indignity of pretending to be okay with Magdalena dating Justice when she absolutely wasn't (and never would be) down with that.

What a mess.

When Liberty found the courage again to look at her friend, Magdalena looked the way Liberty felt on the inside.

The emotions on Mags' face were scattered, unsteady, changing moment to moment.

She looked hurt and sad.

Magdalena bit into her lower lip, which meant she might actually cry.

What had Liberty done?

"You don't have to worry," Magdalena smiled a smile that scared Liberty. That smile was hollow and empty and false. "I'm not that type of friend."

"Magdalena?"

"Really, Liberty." Her tone changed. Liberty got the sticky feeling that what Magdalena truly felt on the inside and the words that were coming out of her mouth were on completely divergent tracks. "What kind of friend would I be if I knowingly and purposely decided to go out with him?"

Raise your hand if you're lost, Liberty thought to herself. "I literally have no idea what you're talking about."

Magdalena exhaled a short, staccato breath. "It's obvious that you still love him."

A tumbleweed tossed through Liberty's mind. "*Who?*"

"Justice."

It took a whole sixty seconds for Liberty to connect all the puzzle pieces together in her head, and once she'd done that, all she could do was laugh, because the picture the pieces made was PREPOSTEROUS.

It was comical in every imaginable way.

Liberty almost fell out of her seat she was laughing so hard. And it was just like going into a coughing fit where one cough triggered another and another.

Every time she tried to stop laughing, more laughter came.

Magdalena was staring at her, face blank, like she was the one who was lost.

"Sorry," Liberty wheezed, when her sides were sore. "Just...let me get this straight. For some unimaginable reason, you think that *I* am in love with..."

Liberty turned for emphasis to point toward Justice's table, but when she looked over to where he usually sat, she found him staring at her.

Again.

Their eyes locked together.

Everything funny about that moment died instantaneously. It was the same look he gave her third period.

That unfettered gaze...it made her heart trip and fall and trip while trying to get up and then fall on its face again.

It made her neck feel hot. She forced herself to look back at Magdalena.

All of her blasé and amusement about this subject was gone. Liberty was completely sober and serious this time.

"You're wrong."

"I know that me and Justice hanging out has always bothered you," she admits.

Because I love you, not because I could ever again love that boorish, BRAINLESS—

"It's because he sucks, not because I care whether he lives or dies." Liberty clarified. "I do not...*love*..." She couldn't even put *love* and *Justice* in the same sentence. "I don't feel that way about him."

Never in a million years would Liberty have guessed that *this* was the conversation they'd be having at lunch today.

"You're not into him," Mags confirmed. "Not even a little?"

"Absolutely not." Instead of feeling like the truth though, those words felt strange. Fuzzy. Like a stray hair she had to get off her tongue.

"You don't...want to be with him?" Was that *hope* twinkling in Magdalena's eyes?

"I'd rather fall down the stairs."

But now Liberty was confused again.

Why was it important to Magdalena whether Liberty liked Justice or not? It was power reversal time. "What do *you* care?"

Suspicion inflated inside Liberty.

What if Magdalena was in love with Justice, and the only reason she'd been holding back from going after him was her thinking that *Liberty* still liked him?

Wait. *No.*

An anvil dropped through Liberty's chest.

Was it possible that Liberty had just...enthusiastically given Magdalena permission...to smash her heart into a million pieces?

Was Liberty telling Mags she felt nothing for Justice the springboard that would launch Magdalena right into his arms?

No. No, there was no way that Liberty was this unintentionally stupid and self-destructive.

This was a self-own of epic proportions. This was worse than swinging the racket at the tennis ball and missing. This was *missing the ball* and managing to hit herself in the same swing.

The worst part of this entire moment was when Liberty realized that pretending she still liked Justice had been the answer all along.

Magdalena was right.

She's an excellent friend. She wasn't the type of person who would date someone her best friend loved.

If Liberty had had the forethought, the gall, the *stomach* to answer yes, when Magdalena asked if she still loved him, Justice would've been off- limits forever.

Even if Magdalena loved him with every fiber of her being, she would have abstained from dating him for Liberty's sake. *That's* how good a friend she was.

Liberty had a shady, but foolproof, opportunity to permanently remove the pain from her ass that was Justice and his stupid little crush.

And she'd just passed it up. For no reason. At all.

She wanted to actually hit herself for being such an idiot, but the flogging would have to wait because Magdalena hadn't responded to Liberty's question.

In fact, her cheeks were turning pink near her nose, and her eyes were on her fingers again.

"What happened with you two anyway?" She finally asked, very noticeably sidestepping Liberty's question.

This question caught Liberty off guard.

Her knees knocked together under the table.

How was it that *this* question felt more vulnerable and intimate than Magdalena point-blank accusing Liberty of being in love with Justice?

"Um, I don't really know? He had a psychotic breakdown and decided to hate me forever." She loathed the pain inside that lifted its sorry head whenever she let herself think about this. Why did it still hurt so much? "He never told me why."

Magdalena tilted her head. "Did you ever talk to him about it?"

"Nope. We haven't had a real conversation since...since before..." Liberty tried to actually remember the last time they'd spoken.

Really spoken to each other.

Oh yeah, she thought somberly. *I remember now.*

❧

EIGHTH GRADE HAD SLOGGED FORTH, LIKE A FUNERAL PROCESSION, approaching the summer after it—or as Liberty had taken to thinking of it: *her grave.*

The despair of being publicly rejected and privately isolated by her two oldest and dearest friends had boiled down to cold, hard panic.

For the whole of Liberty's life, summers had been a time of wonder and adventure, shared with Justice and Dewey at a summer camp of their choosing.

Together, they'd braved *vacation bible school,* theater workshops, and sports camps.

Before the fallout, they'd been looking forward to the Young Broadcasters Summer Program. Justice and Liberty had insisted upon it.

They'd need the training, if they were really going to attempt *Justice and Liberty for All...*but now? There was no Justice and Liberty *at all.*

Their friendship was over and that meant the first summer that Liberty could think of where she would be completely and utterly alone. Not only in her choice of activities, but for three months on *end.*

(She and George weren't officially friends yet.)

No one to walk with on her daily pilgrimage to Dino's Ice Cream Parlor. No one to stargaze with on her trampoline on the warm, clear nights. No one to revel with her in the freedom of late-night phone calls with no early-morning obligations to make them regret it.

No one who'd tap at her window at the stroke of midnight on her birthday.

No one to bemoan high school with.

The immensity of what she'd lost was inescapable. Liberty could hardly bear it.

On the last day of school, she broke.

Impossibly, improbably, she caught Justice alone, before the three o' clock bell. Wearing a grass-stained P.E. uniform and an unwilling look, he faced Liberty and she faced him, desperately hoping the agony of the past several weeks would convert to courage in her blood.

"Hi," was all she could force herself to say for a moment.

Justice, seeming to struggle with his own words, reproduced the same syllable: "Hi."

Liberty suddenly felt that her mouth was full, as though speaking with so many sentences lodged between her teeth would be impolite.

Are you and Dewey together now?

Did Dewey tell you about my feelings?

Did my feelings make you angry?

Were you disgusted?

Is that why you stopped talking to me?

Why did you stop talking to me?

Strangely, Liberty thought of her father. *Don Marshall.*

She often thought of her father's name because knowing his name made her feel closer to him than the word *Dad* ever did. His disinterest in her spanned a decade at least.

Nonsensically, she thought, *Maybe I should ask Dad why Justice doesn't like me anymore.*

Maybe whatever it was inside of Liberty—the bad thing, the thing that repulsed even her parent, preventing someone who was *hardwired* to love her from doing so—was the same thing that now made Justice wrinkle his nose at her if she stepped too close.

That was it, wasn't it?

Liberty must be ugly on the inside and that day on the hill with Dewey, arguing with him, that ugliness shone through and Justice saw it.

She could feel her throat restrict, hot moisture lining the rim of her eyes.

"What are you doing this summer?" She managed to choke out.

"Staying away from *you*," was all he said.

Then, Justice walked away. Liberty let him.

It was the longest conversation they'd had in weeks, and it would be the last time they spoke to one another for two years.

GREAT, WELL, NOW LIBERTY FELT WORSE THAN SHE'D FELT ALL DAY, which was significant because today had been an abnormally rough day.

That memory of the last time she and Justice spoke had pushed her over an edge. And she didn't want to fall, so the best thing she could do was change the subject.

"It's fine. Forget I mentioned it. Let's talk about something else," she finally said.

"Okay." Magdalena seemed to relax only a tiny, tiny bit. Liberty understood why when the next thing out of Magdalena's mouth was, "I don't think you should've said that to Jack."

Liberty exhaled in a huff. "No, of course not. Everyone in the whole world is good and agreeable in your eyes," she retorted, referencing Magdalena's eighteenth century alter ego from *Pride and Prejudice*. "No one deserves scorn, no matter how their provocations beg for it."

Magdalena fixed her with a look. "Don't get all Jane Austen on me, okay? You really hurt Jack's feelings."

"And mine are *fine?*" Her eyebrows rose as she stared into Magdalena's face. "In case you missed it, Jack Weymouth has been calling me a bigot for *three years.* He's been *telling people* that I'm a bigot. Does anyone stand up for me? No."

Magdalena swallowed another bite of mac 'n' cheese before pointing out, "You don't exactly stand up for you, either."

That hurt.

The pain was so acute, the words on Liberty's tongue evaporated into nothing. She closed her mouth, holding a breath in longer than she should have.

That was what clued Magdalena in. She immediately started to apologize, but it was too late.

Liberty pushed back. Again.

She'd been doing that a lot today...

"So... what, Mags? You're saying that since I don't stand up for myself, I deserve it? By making the decision to *not* confront someone about their bad behavior, I'm *asking for it?*"

"That is not what I meant. At all."

Liberty waited for her to go on, except it was clear Magdalena was struggling for the eloquent way to put it.

"I merely meant to point out the hypocrisy." If Magdalena tread any lighter, she'd be flying. "You're upset with people who don't do the same thing you...also don't do."

"Great. Well, next time someone misgenders you or deadnames you, I'll make sure to do absolutely nothing about it. I'll make sure to *not* say anything. I'll just shut my mouth, sit still, and let you handle it on your own. Sound good?"

"Liberty," Magdalena breathed. "We're not talking about me."

"Of course not. The rules are different when it's *you.*"

"What is *that* supposed to mean?"

"You're meant to be loved, Magdalena!" Liberty thoughtlessly blurted out. With her raised voice and God knows what look upon her face, every ounce of blood in Liberty's body turned to self-consciousness and shame.

Magdalena, slowly, equally self-conscious, raised her gaze to Liberty's and the electric charge of their four brown eyes was so potent, so destabilizing, that Liberty again had to look away.

"I don't expect you to understand," Liberty finally said, when the moment around them had lost its intensity.

Liberty had to suck in a deep breath before she could say what else she was thinking.

"No one besides a total transphobic troll would ever say anything mean about you. If you were in trouble, everyone within a ten-mile radius would show up to help. That's just the way it is. You're...meant to be... *cared about*. And I'm... not."

The words sat there on the table between them.

Liberty couldn't take them back, even if she'd wanted to.

"Today, I was fed up with that and I snapped on Jack, who absolutely deserved it, and I won't apologize."

Grace Billings materialized beside their table before Magdalena could utter one word in response. Grace, of course, had come over to ask Magdalena something, and Magdalena, incapable of disappointing anyone, obliged her happily, if not with an edge of surprise and reluctance.

Liberty could only watch them chat for about three seconds before she felt like her brain was going to pop.

She abruptly stood and went to dispose of her lunch tray. If only getting rid of emotional turmoil was as simple as dropping something in a waste bin.

JUSTICE.

First of all, Justice had only been looking at Liberty because of her Washington impression.

Aliens in space probably heard Liberty laughing a few minutes ago. It was a sound Justice hadn't heard in years. It was unsettling to hear that laughter—Liberty's head-thrown-back, from-the-gut laugh—primarily because Liberty hardly smiled at school.

If she laughed at all during the eight hours they were trapped here, she either did it on the inside or made sure it was *never* when Justice was around, because he hadn't seen or heard her laugh one time since they started high school.

The other reason her laughter activated him is because he, well...it's whatever, it's just that *he* used to be the only one who could make her laugh like that.

It used to be that nothing and no one could make Liberty laugh like he could.

Before she'd revealed the horrible creature hidden underneath her then-inviting exterior, the ability to make Liberty laugh was a badge of honor Justice took with him wherever he went.

Whenever he saw something or heard something he knew would crack her up, he'd remember it and tell her about it later. If she did something embarrassing, he'd do the same thing intentionally and make it funny so that she'd stop being self-conscious and laugh at him and his nonsense.

Justice found out early on that laughter was a kind of EpiPen for Liberty. When the world was closing in around her, squeezing her tight, laughter siphoned all the intensity out of life's grip.

Laughter allowed her to breathe. It counteracted her anxiety attacks, soothed her fears. It seemed so small and insignificant, but making her laugh was one way Justice could help Liberty if she was in trouble.

And that annoyed the shit out of him now.

He felt like a retired firefighter who still got nervous every time he heard a siren.

Whenever Liberty seemed down, that impulse to make her

laugh still arrived. That impulse had popped up consistently since Justice met her.

And even now, three years after they'd stopped being friends, he still felt that impulse to be there for her.

It was awful.

Especially because Liberty was a total downer.

She looked and acted like she needed to hear something funny all the time; it was like she was constantly pressing Justice's call button. And he was constantly working not to answer. It was *exhausting*.

"What's exhausting?" Washington asked in his ear.

Justice jumped a little. "What?"

"You were muttering under your breath again," he informed Justice, stabbing a bit of carrot with his fork.

"Was not." Justice glanced toward Liberty and Magdalena's table, just one more time.

The pair of them were almost cartoonish.

Liberty was dressed in black head to toe, with a devastating look on her face. Justice could almost see the invisible storm clouds above her head that refused to let up.

And Magdalena was the complete opposite, effervescent bright, dressed in pinks and pastels, looking literally like a rainbow might extend from the top of her head.

Honestly, Magdalena looked kind of like she'd raided Liberty's middle school wardrobe.

There was a time when Liberty wore more colors and smiled and laughed and talked to people.

The funny thing about disguises? They always wear off eventually.

"And that's *three* times in the past two hours," Washington said in that tight, strained voice.

The one he reserved for any mention of LM.

His words immediately made Justice look at him. "You, staring at Liberty, I mean."

"Not staring at her. I'm staring at Magdalena," Justice defended himself. "And I'm *not* staring!"

He dunked a French fry into the pond of ketchup on his plate and chewed thoughtfully.

Until Washington mentioned her, Justice had temporarily repressed the reality that he and Liberty had been paired to work on music for the premature-gay-pride-parade.

Dread pummeled around in his chest.

"So what is it?" Washington interrupted the comfortable quiet *again,* annoying Justice with that strained tone. "You're starting to like her again?"

"Who?"

Washington set his jaw. "Justice, I'm being serious."

"Who am I starting to like?"

"Thursday Addams," he replied, nodding toward the girls' table. It took all of three seconds for Justice to come to the *INSANE* meaning of Washington words.

And if he wasn't annoyed before, Justice definitely was now. "Very funny."

"I'm not kidding."

"You must be kidding," Justice resolved. "You must be joking because no friend of mine would ever accuse me of starting to like the girl who I would be perfectly happy to never again see in my life."

The words came out like a water spill, soaking the moment between them.

But this conversation was strange. Sacrilegious.

It put Justice on edge.

"What am I supposed to think?" Washington said, mouth full. "Someone suggested you work with Satan's minion and you said, *I think it's a wonderful idea.*"

Justice hated it when Washington imitated his voice.

He always made Justice sound like a jerk.

"It was an accid—" Justice froze mid-sentence. He heard tires screeching to a halt in his head.

Wait, wait, wait, wait, wait.

If Washington Ardmore—Justice's oldest and truest friend, the person who knew him best in the *world*—was under the impression, after that RC meeting, that Justice liked Liberty, who else might be confused?

Justice's eyes went wide as dinner plates, remembering the look on Magdalena's face after he happily agreed to the assignment.

Hadn't she looked surprised? Disappointed? Why wouldn't she be?

He asked to hang out with her *that morning*, and just a few hours later he was eagerly signing up to work with...

A thought dawned on Justice, a scary, terrible, horrible, damnable thought.

What if Liberty...

At some point in the past two and half years... There's no way she hadn't, was there?

Oh, fuck.

Justice plunged both his hands into his hair, raking through his curls for some kind of solution.

Why had it never occurred to him before?

Liberty had probably told Magdalena by now about the pathetic crush Justice used to have on Liberty.

She must've told her. Girls almost exclusively talked about things they thought were cool and weird. Justice having a crush on her once—and only a little bit—years ago obviously and squarely fell in both categories. There's no way that Magdalena didn't know, right?

She must know.

And if she knew that unfortunate awful bit of Justice's history, today in RC when he cheerfully agreed to work with Liberty, maybe she thought his feelings were back.

Justice wanted to jump on top of their table and shout to the entire room that, not including nausea and disdain, he had *ZERO* feelings about Liberty Marshall.

But he couldn't do that.

Not without looking and sounding like (and very much *being*) a jackass.

But it's not like he could go up to Magdalena either and say, *Hey, just want you to know that the only reason I enthusiastically agreed to work with Liberty is because I had no idea that's what I was agreeing to.*

That would paint him as the chump who wasn't listening to her during the RC meeting.

Being the vice president to her president was one of his favorite things about high school. He didn't want her to think, even for a second, that he was mediocre at his job (which he basically was).

What Justice lacked in executive acumen he made up for with humor, people pleasing, great creative ideas, and all around charisma.

He didn't want to mess up the well-manicured reputation he'd worked tirelessly to build these past few years with one bad apology.

No. No, no, no. There had to be a way to fix this— He could clear things up that afternoon at Kade Park!

Wait, but that was a few hours from now and a few hours was a few *years* in Girl Time.

Kade Park wouldn't get here quick enough.

Magdalena could friend-zone him for good in a few hours. He needed a quicker solution.

Something efficient, definitive, decisive. A game-saving goal.

"I knew it," Washington was in the middle of saying. "You only get nuts like this when it's about Liberty. So just say it, okay?"

"WOULD YOU SHUT UP!" Justice barked. "*Dude*, I promise you on Peebles' grave that I do not have feelings for she-who-shall-not-be-named, okay?"

This seemed to appease Washington.

Washington's late pet turtle was genuinely the best reptile you'd ever meet. One did not invoke the holy name of Peebles lightly. Justice knew this.

Washington knew this.

With this one simple statement, it felt as though the natural order of the universe was returning.

Justice blew out his cheeks.

"I believe you..." Washington got back to his salad.

"Good, because I've got a problem the size of fucking Jupiter and I need your help."

"Qué pasa?"

"There's a chance that Magdalena also thinks I...you know, and I need to find a way to debunk the myth without legitimizing it in the first place."

"Well put." Washington dabbed a bit of salad dressing off his lip. "But why?"

"Why what?"

"What does it matter if Magdalena thinks you like punk Barbie?"

"Well, for starters, she's definitely not going to go out with me if she thinks I'm into her best friend."

"Yeah, but you don't even like Mags like that," Washington added, much to Justice's shock and confusion.

"Yeah, I do."

"No, you don't."

"Washington, I like Magdalena de la Cruz."

"I know."

"*Romantically*," Justice stressed.

Washington about choked on his Juicy Juice. "WHAT?"

Justice wasn't sure how they were actually even having this conversation right now.

How was it possible that this came as a surprise to Washington? Why was he acting like Justice liking Magdalena was impossible, when his crush had been in progress for more than a year?

"Justice, *what are you talking about?*" Washington replied, after composing himself. "This is such a weird joke."

"I'm not joking. Why do you think I would joke about something like this?"

"Because there's absolutely no way in the world you can be serious." Washington shrugged.

Justice was speechless.

He'd never been told whether he could be serious or not.

Washington continued. "For starters, this is the first time you've ever mentioned it. And second, what do you even know about Magdalena? Like what do you *really know* about her? Besides the fact that she's smarter than you, trans, and basically all the fun of Liberty without Liberty?"

That shut Justice up.

His mouth fell shut like a drawbridge, and he felt wounded somehow, like Washington had jabbed him someplace he already had a bruise.

Maybe Washington had.

This moment felt strikingly like one from Justice's childhood...

Once, his uncle accused him of eating more cookies than he'd authorized, and even after Justice had stood his ground and told the truth, he was still overruled and sentenced to no more dessert for the rest of his stay, even when it turned out his cousin had been the cookie thief all along.

Justice felt like he was telling his best friend the truth. Why wasn't that good enough?

Whatever.

Washington wanted proof that Justice liked Mags? *Fine.*

Justice sat there and thought about all the things he knew about Magdalena, all the things he liked about her, and in no particular order, made his case.

"She's beautiful, smart, and *so nice.* She's been the same awesome person every minute of every day since we met. Whenever I want to talk to her, she's there and she listens. She never blows me off. She's never once let me down. There. See? Match made in heaven. Will you help me now—"

"Justice, I asked you what you *know* about her."

Justice stopped in his tracks again.

Washington went on. "You know, what do you know about who she actually is? Or what matters to *her?*"

"What are you, the crush police?" Justice was starting to get mad now.

"I'm just saying that thinking someone's cute and nice and being *into them* are different things." He sucked the last of his juice out of the box, like an eight-year-old child dispensing wisdom.

"You think I don't know that?"

"I think...you're impulsive. And I think you have a tendency to see the world in black and white. You can be really all or nothing sometimes—"

"—You've really got a lot to say for someone who's in the same boat."

Washington's eyebrows jumped up into his hair. "W-what?"

"For someone who's in love with a guy and never does anything about it, this little speech of yours is really funny."

Washington rolled his lips together when he got flustered. His cheeks were too brown to blush, but the color in his face definitely became more concentrated.

Almost like an embarrassed glow.

"I...don't know what you're talking about."

"You love Andy, don't you?" Justice whispered. "If Andy somehow got the idea that you were into someone else, you'd want to clear things up, wouldn't you?"

"Justice."

"And if you asked me for my help, I would help you. I wouldn't critique your crush and tell you it wasn't *real* enough."

"Okay, okay. Point taken. Yes. I like him."

"Yeah, and you could waste brain cells fantasizing about Andy in a Spock costume, or—" Justice made sure to pause for dramatic effect, "—you could just ask him out."

"*Absolutely not.*"

"Dude." Justice gave him a look.

"You're as bad as Liberty," Washington harrumphed. Another kick to the gut.

Jesus Christ, today sucked.

He tried to keep his voice calm, even though there could be no disguising the offense he took to his friend comparing him to his enemy.

Washington was immediately apologetic, but what did that matter? The comparison had been made.

The cut had been carved into Justice's skin. The mood between them tanked.

"What is that supposed to mean?" Justice made a fist so hard that his knuckles ached.

He unfurled his fingers, but the upset remained.

"Nothing," Washington said. He paused, measuring his words. "Both of you are just bold. Neither of you has ever been afraid to...jump in."

"What are you talking about?"

Washington pushed out a breath, reluctance clear in his

posture. "Swim camp. Fourth grade. That picture your mom took."

Justice remembered that photo. It captured the exact moment Liberty and Justice leapt over the water, and Washington didn't.

"*Washington*," Justice groaned.

His agitation increased with every millisecond they spent talking about this.

Justice wanted to be done with this conversation.

He wanted to be done with the possibility of Magdalena thinking he liked Liberty.

He wanted to be done with everything, so Justice went into his game-time mindset. The one he used to kill his opponents on the soccer field. He thought hard for a few moments.

Look for the opening, he chanted in his mind. *Just find it, Justice. There's always an—*

"How about this?" he suggested. "I'll just ask Mags out ASAP."

Why not? It was perfect. It would clear up any misunderstanding about who he cared for.

He did have a crush on Mags, and he'd been thinking of asking her out later at Kade Park anyway, right?

Washington chortled. "Uh, yeah. The day you jeopardize everything by asking Magdalena out is the day I do the same with Andy Lang."

"Then saddle up, buddy. I'm going to ask Magdalena out right now." Justice stood immediately, and it took Washington's full strength to drag him back down again.

Washington's expression was grave. "You only result to cowboy metaphors when you're serious."

Justice tried to stand again, his eyes zeroing in Magdalena's smiling face, but Washington again held him back. "Look, I get that fear of rejection isn't a big deal to you, but the rest of us..."

"Why do you automatically assume you'll be rejected?"

"Why do you automatically assume you'll be *accepted?*" Washington countered. "How do you know Magdalena doesn't already have someone *she* likes?"

Justice had never given the idea one single thought. And before he could change that, the bell rang.

Lunch was over.

And if he didn't do something and fast, his chance with Magdalena would be, too.

SCENE IV.

— 12:50 p.m. —

LIBERTY.

Later, when Liberty and Magdalena melted into the cafeteria exodus, the mood between them was still dire.

So Liberty decided to jump off a metaphorical cliff.

"If you dated Justice and he asked you to choose between us, what would you do?"

"I'd dump him," Magdalena answered without a second's hesitation. Liberty felt like *singing*. "I'd never date anyone who thought it was okay to ask me to choose between him and my friends."

Magdalena circled her arms around Liberty's shoulders as they walked, squeezing the two of them together. Magdalena then rubbed her face against Liberty's, like a cat, which as far as Liberty's concerned, just might be a cure for cancer.

The two laughed, the sound of it scrubbing away the muck from Liberty's mind. Liberty hadn't done anything she felt needed to apologize for, but in that moment she still felt forgiven, and it put her at peace.

In the hall, they passed a giant renaissance poster.

An Elizabethan couple stood back to back in the frame, upholding swords. A banner at the bottom read *Much Ado About Nothing*.

The sight of it made Magdalena freeze.

"What?" Liberty said.

"*No way*, I did the history homework," Magdalena lamented.

Liberty gasped theatrically. "Call the police!"

"I did the homework because I thought it was due today," she explained. "I forgot we were celebrating Shakespeare's birthday."

"We're what?"

It was the third time that day that Liberty found herself wishing to leave school and go home.

That morning, she woke up disoriented and confused—her mother had turned off her usual alarm and left her a note about her grandfather—and that was probably why Liberty forgot that she'd planned in advance to ask her mom if she could stay home that day.

Because it was a half-day.

The first half of the day was class-filled as usual, and the second half of the day would consist of someone repeatedly dipping Liberty into a vat of hot grease.

That afternoon, the entire school was to sit through...a *play*. In honor of Shakespeare's birthday.

How barbaric, Liberty thought to herself.

Because her school thought it important to commemorate some dead playwright guy, Liberty would have to sit through two hours of *torture*.

Honestly, compared to theater, Liberty might genuinely prefer a more traditional method.

Like a good old-fashioned stoning.

Or being burned at the stake.

She found herself again dragging her feet as she and Magdalena returned to their lockers to put their stuff away.

The whole school had ten minutes to prepare for what was about to happen, and Liberty planned to use every last minute if she could help it.

Dread and anxiety building inside her, like water rising through an aquifer, she got her locker open. An influx of love overtook her as she looked at the *Labyrinth* poster taped to the inside of her locker's door.

Nothing like David Bowie dressed as a goblin king to help her prepare for the end. She stuffed her black heavily buttoned canvas backpack inside the small metallic closet, wishing she, too, could fit herself inside.

In the process, her phone slipped out of her bag and into her hand. It reminded her—she never replied to George's message!

Maybe she'd get through this play after all.

Obviously, she was going to text him nonstop about his return to Green River for the next two hours, and realistically, *for the next four months*, every single day until she saw his beautiful face again in the flesh.

Liberty was planning to take her phone with her to the show. But when the home screen of her phone came to life, there was a text from her mom staring up at her.

> Sweetheart, they found a tumor.

Several messages were nested beneath it, but Liberty couldn't handle this right now.

At all.

"Ready?" Magdalena chirped, appearing at her side.

Without another thought, Liberty tossed her phone in her locker and slammed it shut.

Now, if she could just get her heart to slow down…

"Ready," she managed.

And that was maybe the first time she'd ever lied to Magdalena.

❧

BELMONT WAS PSM'S NEWLY BUILT THEATER.

It was part of the new wing on campus, and the thing was like a coffin that could fit four thousand people.

Red velvet seats and carpet everywhere. Heavy, weighted doors that swung so slowly they looked like they had their own version of gravity. Cool lighting structures hung from the ceiling and retracted, like this was the fucking Metropolitan Opera House or some shit.

The place was a *zoo* when Liberty and Magdalena slipped in with the last of the stragglers a few minutes after one o'clock.

They took their seats and settled in.

Magdalena took the seat on the aisle, and so as classmates passed, they stopped to say things to her and she said things right back, which was fine.

Liberty was working on her deep breathing.

Stay calm, she told herself. *One breath at a time, in and out.*

Everything's okay. No one's going to die.

Except maybe in the play.

Liberty had no idea what play they were even going to watch. She always tuned out when people talked about stuff like this. And that would've been okay, if she'd just remembered to ask her mom if she could stay home today, but *no.*

Not today.

Almost nothing had gone her way today.

Think happy thoughts, she tried to coach herself. *Dogs. Think about how much you love dogs. Dogs are the best.*

Don't think about Mom at the hospital.

She's always at the hospital.

Don't think about Dad. He sure as hell isn't thinking about you.

And definitely don't think about Grandpa or the tumor or what any of it means, because then you'll just cry.

No fucking crying.

At least not until the lights go down.

Don't think about Lion King. Don't think about Lion King. Don't think. Just don't think.

LIBERTY WAS TEN WHEN IT HAPPENED.

Mom had agreed to work some extra shifts at a hospital two towns over from theirs, and the long hours meant she and Liberty barely spent any time together.

When she was home, she was dead tired.

When she wasn't home...well, she wasn't home, was she? And Liberty was starting to feel it again.

She'd felt it more than once in her young life, the feeling that her mother's work was more important than her.

Liberty hated that feeling.

She did her very best at everything. She got good grades, she never got into trouble, she always followed her mother's instructions to the best of her ability. She was a perfect, model child.

She had to be.

If Liberty didn't try her best to be perfect, her mom wouldn't smile at her or praise her or spend time with her.

Maybe, if she'd been able to show her dad what a good kid she could be, he'd want to visit her more than twice a year...

Moving on.

The good thing about being good was that Liberty felt free to ask for things she wanted, and her mom usually said yes.

And so she asked, "Mom, can we go see a show together?"

Just the two of them. They'd spend the whole day together, and they'd cap it by seeing a show.

And her mom agreed! How wonderful.

It was soon decided that they'd go see *The Lion King* in Boston at the Citizens Bank Opera House.

They road-tripped the two hours from Green River to Boston cheerfully, singing loudly to their favorite songs and playing word games all the while.

They went out to a nice lunch. They'd worn dresses and sparkly jewelry. Mom had even put a bit of makeup on Liberty and done her hair. It was a girls' day for the history books.

They had mezzanine seats at the opera house. They could see the whole stage.

It felt like being inside a palace.

No tall people sat in front of them, so they could see the entire show perfectly. The air inside the theater smelled like old spice and pine.

Liberty was wearing gloves, actual gloves.

Her joy was real and potent. She'd hardly stopped smiling since she woke up that morning.

As for the show, it was excellent.

The songs, the dancing, the *costumes*—everything about it was wonderful and perfect and great in more ways than she could have ever imagined.

And then, Liberty saw a kid.

Maybe only a few years older than her.

She couldn't even remember now what they looked like, what their gender was. All she remembered was the way their head drooped, unnaturally, followed by the rest of their limbs. Knocked out, the kid slumped to the left, fell out of their seat, and collapsed into the aisle.

Liberty almost laughed when she saw it.

Some kid fell asleep watching *Lion King* and then tumbled into the aisle, but when she tapped her mom's arm and pointed the kid out, her mom didn't laugh.

Her mom wasn't amused at all.

Her mom said, "Liberty, stay here," and stood, ducking into the aisle. She zipped over to the young person, just laying there, unmoving. The kid's family started to stand and gather around. Soon ushers came hurrying down the aisle.

Liberty's heart had pounded so loud, she didn't even hear it when the show stopped.

She jumped when the lights came back up.

And then the whole theater started to look and chatter. *What's wrong? What's happened?* They must have all thought. Liberty didn't know, either.

Soon paramedics arrived.

They ran down the aisle with a stretcher.

This was after what felt to Liberty like an eternity of watching that kid laying there, still as any inanimate object in the room. Watching her mom listen for his pulse and talk in firm, short sentences to the kid's family.

Does he have any allergies? Pre-existing medical conditions?

In her ten-year-old ears, the words were big and heavy.

The paramedics strapped the kid onto the stretcher and jogged toward the nearest exit. Applause shook the room, as patrons lauded their efforts, but to Liberty, it was perverse.

Were they cheering because the paramedics were going to help? Or were they cheering so that now they could get back to the show?

The family rushed after the stretcher. And so did Liberty's mom. She threw one look in her daughter's direction. "Stay here," she instructed, echoing her earlier directive.

But her mom might as well have asked Liberty to fly.

Tears sprang, as Liberty watched her mom follow the party out, under the re-dimming lights, as the show resumed.

Liberty was plunged into darkness, all alone, anxiety clawing at every inch of her skin. She thought she might bleed. What if she passed out, falling from her seat right into the aisle, just like that kid?

That thought was enough to make her explode from her seat. Liberty burst into the aisle.

Somehow, she found the will, even though her limbs were like lead and her head was swimming, and she couldn't see in the dark, through her own tears.

Liberty ran, feeling like she might be sick.

She navigated through the dimness to one of the exits and pushed through the doors out into carpeted corridors that led to the lobby.

The place was eerie, mostly deserted, with everyone inside watching the show. But she kept moving.

She kept running.

Liberty ran until she got to the doors that led outside. That's where her mom would be, right?

She ran out to the curb, the fresh air revitalizing her. Liberty turned in circles, looking for the family, for the ambulance, but they were nowhere to be found.

It wasn't long before Liberty felt like she couldn't breathe.

She turned back, intent to go back into the opera house, but the doors were locked.

They were locked.

A splitting pain cracked her forehead in half—that's what it felt like when her panic and anxiety peaked.

She blacked out after that.

Later, her mom would tell her that she fainted.

A good Samaritan found her unconscious on the sidewalk and called an ambulance. In the time it took Liberty's mom to turn the

Citizens Bank Opera House upside down looking for her, Liberty was transported to the nearest children's hospital.

Somehow, the hospital eventually got ahold of her mom.

Liberty woke up in white hospital pajamas with little cars on them. She and her mom cried and spent the night in the hospital, before returning home the next day.

By complete coincidence, that children's hospital was the same one they took the other kid to.

Liberty's mom ran into the family when she arrived.

On the drive home to Green River, Liberty asked her, *What happened to that kid at the show?*

Her mom kept her eyes straight ahead. It took her several minutes before she told Liberty the truth.

They died.

Liberty still remembered the kid's hand, limply hanging over the edge of the stretcher, as the paramedics hurried out.

Just like in the movies.

Died.

Liberty decided then that she would never step foot in a theater again.

AND YET, THERE SHE WAS.

In Belmont with Magdalena and everybody else in this whole fucking school.

Thinking about *The Lion King*, even though she knew thinking about that horrible weekend could only lead to more anxiety, more panic. More thoughts of Mom and hospitals and Grandpa and people dying and—

"—sed to present William Shakespeare's *Much Ado About Nothing!*" The room erupted in applause, as sweeping sixteenth century fanfare wandered into their ears.

Liberty hadn't even noticed the lights go down.

Her anxiety was a 6.348 out of ten, and she desperately needed a way to get her shit together.

And then she realized how doomed she really was because right at that moment, Magdalena snuggled into her.

Magdalena's *bare knee* came together with Liberty's.

She looped her left arm underneath Liberty's right. She extended her head into the bend between Liberty's neck and shoulder.

Liberty turned to stone. She wasn't breathing at all. How could she breathe?

She and Magdalena only got this close on movie nights, and even then, there was a laptop between them on Mags' bed. They'd never done anything like *this* before, where so much of both their bodies were touching.

Literally, if Liberty looked down and Magdalena looked up, they'd be kissing.

What is happening, what is happening, what is happening, what is happening, she thought over and over again, still not breathing. *BREATHE, LIBERTY.*

She allowed herself to take the smallest, tiniest breath and was immediately overwhelmed by the scent of Magdalena's shampoo. Honey lavender sunrise princess magic, whatever the fuck this fragrance was, it was so potent in Liberty's nose it felt psychedelic.

Liberty let her eyes fall closed.

Today went from the third worst day of her life to cuddling with Magdalena during *Hell, The Musical.*

How was Liberty to account for *this?*

Liberty felt a little like she was flying, but she couldn't tell if it was because she liked Magdalena so much or if she was just so surprised and already panicked that she was beginning to disassociate.

Not knowing the difference didn't do her any favors as she worked to calm down.

She tried to focus on the play for a change.

Much Ado About Nothing.

What was this show even about? The audience kept laughing, but Liberty never heard the joke.

Strangely, if you'd asked Liberty earlier in the day, *Hey there, how would you like to snuggle up with your dream girl in a dimly lit room?* Her answer would have been a resounding *Yes please.*

But now that she was here (impossibly) and this was actually happening?

Liberty...well, frankly, she hated it.

Not Magdalena, of course. She could never hate Magdalena.

Just hated the cuddling part.

Liberty already felt restricted, like her lungs might quit at any moment, and having someone—even an angel like Magdalena— in her personal space right now only made her feel like she was sinking faster beneath the waves of anxiety.

But why? She wondered.

She'd had plenty of anxiety attacks around Justice, back in the day. Except that when *he* got in her personal space, it didn't feel like this.

It felt like she was drowning, but Justice was just above her, with a boat and a life jacket and probably some sandwiches.

A tear suddenly rolled from her eye down her cheek and disappeared into Magdalena's hair.

The last time Liberty had an anxiety attack so bad she almost blacked out was her thirteenth birthday party.

For some reason, she decided to sing a song she wrote.

She was nervous to sing. She'd never sung in front of people before. And more than anything, her dad was going to be there.

Her dad.

He'd never heard her sing. But Liberty had hoped with all her heart he'd like her song. After all, he loved music.

It was something Liberty got from him. Surely they could bond over it, if only just a little.

And when she got up to sing, everything started off well.

But her dad was in the middle of a conversation with a group of her older cousins when her mom gathered everyone to hear the song.

Dad and the cousins didn't whisper as they kept talking, even while Liberty sang. And at one point, her dad made a joke that made the whole table erupt in laughter so loudly, her song was drowned out altogether.

Liberty just ran.

Liberty would always rather leave than stay some place she wasn't wanted.

If her dad couldn't give her his undivided attention for a few minutes on her birthday, then...then nothing.

The panic came for her, hard and strong. But so did Justice.

In full form, to cheer her up, he decided to sing for her. One of his favorite songs—Thinkin' Bout You by Frank Ocean.

Only, in the first verse, instead of *A tornado flew around my room before you came,* he sung, *A potato flew around my room before you came,* after an iconic Vine they loved, which made Liberty cry she laughed so hard.

The hilariously incorrect lyrics, plus a few atmospheric high notes and some truly horrific interpretive dancing, and Liberty had forgotten all about her bad birthday.

Justice gave her a piggyback ride back to her house, and despite returning anxiety about seeing her parents and her party guests all over again, being completely wrapped around Justice's body didn't give her even a fraction of the discomfort she felt right now...

Another tear rolled down her cheek.

Thank GOD for the darkness of the theater.

Her throat felt thick and syrupy; her chest was tight.

She thought about Justice, carrying her home, and for thirty seconds, she allowed bitterness and regret to devour her alive.

Magdalena's words returned to her mind, sour and pungent and sharp. *It's obvious you still love him...Justice. What happened with you two anyway?*

I DON'T KNOW, Liberty wanted to scream.

She didn't know what in the world she could've done so wrong that the person she'd cared most about in the world would turn his back on her.

She didn't know and she wanted to.

For one horrible, contrary, excruciating moment, she allowed herself to admit in the darkest, quietest, most private part of her mind that she missed him.

And she hated him for being someone she missed, instead of someone by her side.

Everything about him that she used to love tormented her now, endlessly.

She wished none of it had ever happened.

Eventually, the sadness once again gave way to the truth.

Justice and Liberty were nothing more than a tragedy of the past. Like the Titanic, cold and broken at the bottom of the ocean, never to sail again.

— 1:40 p.m. —

JUSTICE.

The only thing Justice had against theater was that it very much reminded him of his Aunt Shan.

She was gone and had been most of Justice's life now.

But he still remembered how she smelled, like peppermint and thrift store fabrics. When he and Hope were small, she used to take them to see movies once a week at the ninety-nine cent theater in the historic part of Green River.

In short, Aunt Shan would go down in history for two reasons: primarily because she'd taught Justice everything he knew about love, and secondarily, because…if not for Aunt Shan, Justice and Liberty might not have met.

There was a time when Justice thought that Liberty was a gift to him from his Aunt Shan, up in heaven.

But when everything fell apart between them, he felt cheated and foolish. And it wasn't long after that Justice found himself wishing he could trade.

He'd rather have his Aunt Shan back than the scars of his friendship with Liberty.

The year Justice started second grade, his parents told him for weeks that Aunt Shan was preparing for a trip to visit Grandpa.

Justice wouldn't figure out until later that was code for *The breast cancer is winning* and *Soon, there won't be anyone to bring you chocolates on Christmas.*

One weekend, they took Justice to New Arlington Memorial Hospital because they thought it might be his last chance to see Aunt Shan. (They were right.)

BRIEF TRANSCRIPT OF THE LAST TIME JUSTICE EVER TALKED TO AUNT SHAN

Him: When are you coming back from your trip?

Her: I don't know, caterpillar. What will you do while I'm gone?

Him: [Insert something about a second grade school project he doesn't remember]

Her: Will you do something for me?

Him: [Imagine six-year-old Justice nodding]

Her: Will you find more friends? Good friends. Like Dewey.

Him: How do I find them?

Her: It's easy. Find someone wearing...the same thing as you. That's how you'll know that you belong together.

A few weeks later, after Justice started school, in walked Liberty Marshall one morning, wearing a white shirt and a blue jean jacket.

Justice's mom had also dressed *him* in a white shirt and blue jean jacket. Aunt Shan's parting words came back to him, blah, blah, fast forward through one of the best friendships in history, until Liberty broke it.

Justice exhaled, trying for the millionth time in the same fifteen minutes to *focus.* But his brain was in chaos, and he couldn't seem to rein it in.

He'd planned (and by *planned,* he meant completely spur-of-the- moment decided) to ask Magdalena out before lunch was over. Just pull her aside and make his feelings known. But lunch ended, like, three seconds after he made up his mind.

When Magdalena and Liberty did finally arrive at the theater, it was too close to showtime for Justice to get up without a teacher shooing him back to his seat.

Not that it mattered.

They were sitting in the central section of the theater, *way* in the back.

They might as well have been across campus.

Justice's leg bounced up and down, rapidly, restlessly. He couldn't help feeling like he'd lost.

Like he'd blown a game.

Every second that slid past without him clarifying his feelings to Magdalena felt like a new reason why she wouldn't go out with him.

The idea that she could think that he liked Liberty hung over him like a shroud. He felt like the storm clouds that followed

Liberty around had somehow found and attached themselves to him.

There had to be a way for him to fix this, wasn't there?

Wasn't there?

He turned in his seat, yet again making his neck ache, and looked to where they were sitting. He was proud of himself. They were almost to the end of the show's first act, and he hadn't glanced back at them since the show started.

It'd been almost an hour…

But when his eyes found Magdalena and Liberty at the back of the room, his chest suddenly constricted.

His mouth got dry.

Magdalena was bent into the shape of Liberty's body, almost like a spoon. She was as close to Liberty as she could possibly be without being in Liberty's lap.

Magdalena was using Liberty like a body pillow.

The sight of them made something hurt inside Justice. The feeling was hard to explain. It felt like…maybe like, a distant (and really uncomfortable) cousin of jealousy.

But Justice didn't know why he felt anything at all. Liberty and Magdalena were just friends.

Washington's words returned to him, like a curse.

Like a drop of ink in crystal clear water.

How do you know Magdalena doesn't already have someone she likes?

With the lights from the stage illuminating their faces, even from afar, Justice could see their expressions.

Liberty looked like a marble statue. She wasn't even blinking. And Magdalena…Magdalena wasn't watching the show at all.

The look on her face…

It made Justice's stomach twist up.

There was no way that…Magdalena liked Liberty, right?

As gross a thought as that was, Justice knew that it was far from impossible. As someone who had once fallen for...you-know-who himself, he knew that Liberty wasn't without charm. She was without a soul, but Magdalena wouldn't find that out until later.

Until the most inopportune moment possible.

If Magdalena did like Liberty, she wouldn't find out just how much of a backstabber Liberty was until it was too late.

Thinking about that made a different kind of urgency bloom inside of him.

Before he'd only been worried about clarifying his own feelings to Magdalena, but now he was worried that if someone didn't snap her up fast, she'd end up dating Liberty.

And friends don't let friends date toxic people.

Or at least, Justice didn't want to be a friend who did. Now Justice was feeling braver than before.

Asking Magdalena out wasn't simply an important next step in Justice's crush journey. It was now an act of altruism that might shield Magdalena de la Cruz from enduring the mind fuck that was getting over Liberty Marshall after she sucked you in and then brutally broke your heart.

It was more than an act of affection. It was his duty.

As a caring friend.

As a dedicated Rainbow Coalition colleague.

...As an American.

The room broke into applause, cuing the intermission.

But all Justice heard was a theater full of people cheering him on. He had to ask Magdalena out for the greater good, and now was his only chance before the three o' clock bell.

"Hey, you okay?" Washington asked, as soon as Justice was resolved. "You've got a dumb look on your face."

"Bathroom," Justice mumbled, rising from his seat. He knew what he had to do.

Stepping out into the aisle, Justice was immediately met with the DROVES of other students doing the exact same thing. It was intermission, and every person with a small bladder (which seemed to be about 60 percent of the theater) was also getting up to take full advantage of the break.

Justice could barely even see Liberty and Magdalena anymore through all the talking heads and moving bodies all headed the same way he was going.

Seriously? COME ON.

Justice wanted to yell.

He wanted to climb over chairs and cut across the seating sections to get to them, to Magdalena, before it was too late, but he was stuck.

Like a small grain of sand stuck at the top of an hourglass, slowly, slowly, slowly funneling into the bottom.

And just like that hourglass, he was running out of time.

— *1:50 p.m.* —

LIBERTY.

Magdalena didn't extract herself from Liberty until the lights came up at intermission.

Liberty had almost passed out from the lack of the oxygen.

She didn't know what to do or say, as half her body suddenly felt cold and alone. She didn't *dare* look at Magdalena.

Only God knew what kind of look must be on her face... What now?

They'd gone from arguing at lunch to snuggling during the show??? Liberty had whiplash from the way the vibe between them had so rapidly evolved.

It was really strange, honestly.

Liberty had identified the crush she had on Magdalena the summer they met.

She'd acknowledged its presence the entire two and a half

years they'd been friends, but she'd also accepted a long time ago that there was nothing she could do about the way she felt and that there was nothing that might persuade her to broach said feelings to Magdalena.

Not after the *last time* Liberty had an all-consuming crush and that blew up in her face.

No way.

There was no way she would ever hazard her friendship with Magdalena over a little infatuation.

It was too risky.

But at the time that Liberty came to all of these conclusions... she had zero inclinations that Magdalena might share her feelings.

And now, after the cuddle, Liberty didn't know how Mags felt. She didn't know what to believe.

She absolutely didn't want to open herself up to hoping that Magdalena might feel the same way, but wasn't it worth *wondering* about?

Even just a little?

Liberty, holding her breath again, looked over at Magdalena, only to find herself staring into the dark tresses of her hair. She was talking to someone in the aisle—Adam stood over them, smiling his dopey, earnest Adam smile.

Adam was hard not to like.

He was the golden retriever of boys.

Just smiley, happy and pure, with zero ulterior motives other than to make friends.

"Mr. Tanaka has a question about the budget for the indoor-outdoor parade," he told Magdalena, clearly unhappy to bring her anything other than exciting news. "I told him I'd check with you—"

"No worries," Magdalena said, and then without any warning at all, she turned back to Liberty.

If the power and potency of Magdalena's focused gaze trained directly and unflinchingly on her wasn't enough to make Liberty lose it, Magdalena placing her hand on Liberty's bare knee ought to do it.

Just her little dainty fingers on Liberty's leg electrified her enough to jump a car.

"I'll be right back, okay?" Magdalena was up and gone before Liberty could force a heart-stuttering, throat-dry *Okay* out of her mouth.

Smooth, Liberty.

Maybe it was cliché, but Liberty desperately wished she were immune to the rollercoaster of falling in love.

The fact that a few fingers brushing her knee zapped her with a 50,000-watt volt of affection—or that a quick disappearance after an unexpected cuddle session drowned her in loneliness—was beyond absurd.

Liberty covered her face with her hands to try and ward off the deluge of conflicting emotions imminently arriving in her already crowded mind.

Whose idea was today anyway?

When Liberty let her hands fall away, she noticed a shadow looming over her. She looked up and nearly jumped out of her seat in surprise to find fucking Justice Garrison standing there, haunting her.

He had a really stupid look on his face, which could only mean he was in the middle of some big idea of his.

Liberty was already bored.

She wanted to appear and sound—and actually *be*—completely aloof and apathetic in this moment, but she couldn't ignore the way her heart thundered in her chest.

With the chatter surrounding them, and yet no one in their immediate vicinity, this was the most alone they'd been since before they imploded in eighth grade.

Or, actually, since the last time they'd "talked" on the final day of eighth grade.

Focus, Liberty! She commanded herself. *Be disinterested. Be devastating.*

"Shouldn't you be in the balcony?" She asked.

"What?" He replied.

"I heard they opened a VIP section for idiots." Her burn bounced right off him. Recognition didn't even reach his eyes.

"Where's Mags?" He blurted out.

"Doing a club thing with Adam."

"*Where?*" His voice was a few notches above pleading.

It put Liberty on edge. She felt the impulse to ask him if everything was okay, but she would rather die than give him the impression she cared at all about his well-being.

"Mr. Tanaka's office—" Justice disappeared before she could tack on, "—I think?"

Yeesh. What was *his* problem?

Later, the lights began to blink, which meant the second half of this afternoon of torture was about to commence.

Liberty squeezed her eyes shut.

She didn't want to think about the messages that awaited her when she was reunited with her cellular device. She didn't want to think about illness or death or dying or her mom or any of her family members.

Liberty didn't want to think about Magdalena and how she smelled, how she *felt* pressed against her. She didn't want to think about Justice or Washington or Jack or anyone.

She just wanted to turn her brain off in the interim between now and her getting her shit together. Liberty expected that might happen by the time she was thirty.

Why couldn't everything and everyone just leave her alone? Why did everything have to come at her today?

The theater lights stopped blinking and finally began to officially dim. Most seats around the room were full or soon to be, meaning that the flood of people who'd journeyed to the bathroom had all trickled back in by now.

Everyone was back.

Why wasn't Magdalena?

Liberty sat up in her seat as tall as she could, and as the theater turned black, she searched for Washington's curly mop head.

She didn't find him, until the lights on the stage brightened back to warm colors and the actors resumed their onslaught of tedium.

There. On the right side of the house, near the front. Beside him there was an empty seat.

Justice wasn't back either.

A small bud of concern bloomed in Liberty's gut.

Something's not right.

She sat with that feeling, that gnawing, nagging whisper at the back of her mind, as long as she could.

It was about halfway through the second act of the show when she couldn't take it anymore.

Her head hurt—actually, physically hurt—from everything going on inside it. The frequent eruptions of audience laughter only made her head pound more, and every second she didn't spend wondering if Magdalena was okay was spent trying to keep the flashbacks at bay.

Finally, Liberty ducked out into the aisle and hastened through Belmont's mahogany doors back into reality.

Leaving Belmont felt like climbing back through the wardrobe, after being forced into Narnia.

She took deep breaths, the first she'd had in a few hours.

Maybe, now that she was by herself and not being actively triggered by her surroundings, Liberty could finally have a moment to herself.

It was the first she'd had all day.

— 2:30 p.m. —

JUSTICE.

What the actual fuck.

Justice had turned this school upside down looking for Magdalena, Adam, and Mr. Tanaka.

He'd checked Mr. Tanaka's office. That was his first stop.

Nothing.

He'd checked the front office. He checked the Rainbow Coalition club room. He checked the *club office.*

The cafeteria. The gym. The track. Where the hell were they?

Had they decided to hold a mini-RC club meeting in outer space? Without him? Why couldn't he find them anywhere? Justice kicked a rock into the grass at his feet.

He picked his head up and took in the breadth of the PSM campus.

Think. Where would they be?

Justice couldn't think of any other places to look.

In fact, his mind gave up and didn't think about any other places he might look at all. His mind went straight to Liberty.

Was it more likely that Magdalena, Adam, and Mr. Tanaka were meeting on club business in an unfindable location, or was it more likely that Liberty sent Justice on a wild goose chase just to amuse her cold, dead heart?

Anger flared inside him.

Of course.

Justice was at fault here, obviously. His first mistake was trusting that Liberty might tell him one simple truth to begin with, instead of lying.

Why should he have expected anything from her other than dishonesty?

He knew better.

"FUCK!" Justice roared at the empty soccer field in frustration. He was almost out of time, and he'd wasted a good forty-five minutes of it hunting fruitlessly for Magdalena. Liberty Marshall had all but singlehandedly derailed his plans.

She was good, he had to admit.

Ruining things for other people was definitely a well-honed talent of hers. Obviously.

But Justice Garrison never quit.

He never gave up when things went sideways.

There's always an opening. That was his motto. *There's always a way to get what you want from this world.*

And after a few seconds more of puzzling, he realized that his best course of action was to text Magdalena.

He'd text her and ask if they could talk, before heading to Kade Park. Or maybe he'd...

I guess I could, he mused. *Could I? Can I?*

Could he ask her out over text? Was that still a thing people did?

Justice was an in-your-face kind of guy. He preferred to say what he felt and see the reaction on someone else's face. Texting her the big question was not his preference by any means, but time was ticking.

It was now or the friend zone forever.

He needed to go for it and stick the landing like a goddamn champion. Justice dug a hand into his pocket for his phone.

Nothing.

He tried the other pocket—his cell phone, it was gone.

Justice dropped into the three-second panic everyone drops into when they realize they don't know where their phone is.

But then he saw it in his mind and remembered exactly where he'd left it. With his and Washington's stuff, backstage near the loading dock, from earlier that day, when they'd helped the

Shakespeare company people unload their props and set pieces and stuff.

Damn it, he thought, as he broke into a run back toward the school building.

Intermission was definitely long over.

There was probably less than a half hour left of the show.

If he didn't get his phone and text her fast, she might get caught up in the after-school rush and leave before he got a chance to talk to her.

They were still on for Kade Park later, as far as he knew, but Kade Park later was too late. She could be resolved against him by then.

She could be resolved against him even now. Was he doing all of this for no reason?

How do you know Magdalena doesn't have someone she likes?

Washington's question glared at Justice inside his mind.

He didn't want to so much as *think* an answer to that question.

Thoughts had too much power.

Justice didn't have to think about any of it now. He'd made up his mind. He was going to ask her before she left school today. He had to. It was his only shot, if he even had one.

It simply couldn't wait.

After cutting across the soccer field, the new wing of the building came into view. Justice could see the back of the theater, the parking lot, and the promised land—the loading dock, with the What You Will Shakespeare Company box truck stuck inside it.

He sprinted for it, like the winning goal depended on it. His backpack, his skateboard, and the cell phone from which the best relationship in teenage history would begin awaited him there.

SCENE V.

— 2:45 p.m. —

LIBERTY.

Liberty scrunched her eyes shut so tight, she felt it in her already- throbbing forehead.

Migraines were *the worst.*

Her imagination swirled to nothing as she pressed her forehead to a nearby concrete wall.

Magdalena floated to mind for the hundredth time.

Liberty would've texted her long before now, but texting required her phone and she was avoiding that thing at least until three o' clock, maybe even until she got home.

She simply didn't feel up to it.

Maybe that was selfish and awful of her—Grandpa was in the hospital with a tumor, maybe dying, and Liberty couldn't even be bothered to read a text message about it—but Liberty had to take care of herself. Sometimes it felt like absolutely no one else would, if she didn't.

The sound of something rattling broke Liberty out of her

reverie. Eager for any distraction at all, she glanced toward the sound, coming from a classroom a few paces ahead.

She peered inside.

Her eyes scanned the chairs parked around the room, stopping on the one in the far corner, where Adam Grosch sat, Magdalena straddling his lap, their faces sewn together by their tongues.

Magdalena.

Kissing Adam's face off.

In her head, Liberty heard that forever, too-high, hospital *beeeeep* that meant someone was gone, and no amount of resuscitation would bring them back.

It's my heart, she thought, as her chest caved in. Broken was too sweet a word for the total annihilation she felt.

She'd only met this pain once before.

And Liberty did now, what she'd done then.

She back-stepped.

And then she ran away from it with all her strength.

— 2:50 p.m. —

JUSTICE.

Once he got back to the loading dock, Justice was momentarily distracted by the square opening in one wall, where the butt of the What You Will Shakespeare Company's box truck sat open.

Inside it was a small maze of furniture and costume racks. It was neat looking.

If it were three years ago, Justice would have sketched it for Liberty, and she would have said something infuriatingly creative and smart like, *This would make an amazing secret portal! Or a great jump-out spot for a horror movie creature!*

Even when they'd been friends, Liberty infuriated him. He could never get used to her.

Just when he'd memorized her elementary school persona, her middle school persona arrived. She was suddenly a girl who was taller than him and wearing skirts that showed her dimpled knees.

Her hair was down more; she started to smell like things people put in cookies and cakes.

Like vanilla and dried cranberries.

HEY. Justice's mind cut in. *Important mission, remember?*

He grabbed his backpack and his board. His and Washington's things were right where he left them in one corner of the loading dock, the one nearest the doors which led to the black box theater.

Justice stuffed a hand into his bag and rifled.

To free his other hand, he set his skateboard down.

He could feel the line of his phone, squished between two books—

Without warning, the doors across the dock exploded open.

In action movies, it was the sound you heard before the SWAT team burst onto the scene.

Justice looked for some sort of emergency and didn't know what to make of Liberty Marshall sprinting across the concrete, expression abstracted and serial-killer blank.

When Justice told Washington about this later, he'd make up a story about why she was running.

Maybe she was trying to escape another failed friendship, or maybe there was a Doc Martens sale at DSW and—

— *2:53 p.m.* —

Abruptly, three things happened so fast that Justice had to immediately rewind to figure them out.

It was like three frames of a movie.

One second, Liberty's running. The next second she's gone,

and the third second, Justice sees a flying shadow and hears a crash.

As far as Justice could tell, this is what happened:

1. Liberty, bolting like a psychopath out of hell, didn't notice his skateboard on the ground. In her haste, she stepped on it.
2. Somehow she tripped *and* slipped on it at the same time—Justice has no idea how she accomplished this; she must be naturally talented—so that she went down and...
3. Justice's lucky skateboard went flying...straight into the depths of the *What You Will* prop truck.

Ladies, gentlemen, and everyone both, not, and in between, Justice Garrison would like to present Liberty Marshall: the reason he can't have nice things.

ACT II.

SCENE I.

— 2:59 p.m. —

LIBERTY.

From the ground, all Liberty heard was raucous applause. The show was over.

And the noise of it, drifting into the loading dock from the backstage hallway, was *mocking her.*

As though today hadn't destroyed her spirit enough. If you're wondering, Justice didn't help her up.

He didn't even ask if she was okay.

In fact, when Liberty—prostrate, sore-faced, and embarrassed — finally rose to her feet, Justice was nowhere to be found. Aside from the clapping and nearby cheers of excitement, there was silence in the loading dock, nothing and no one around.

Liberty allowed herself to consider whether she'd imagined Justice was there to begin with, but stopped when she heard a slight shuffling coming from the open box truck, half-parked inside.

The inside of that prop truck might make a cool place for a

magical portal, but she thought it would make an even nicer grave. And she'd certainly feel better if she put Justice in *his*.

Liberty punted Justice's book bag out of the way and marched toward the truck.

There was probably a bruise the size and shape of Africa gathering on her cheeks and nose.

The girl of her dreams was secretly running around kissing someone, someone she'd *never* even mentioned to Liberty as a person of interest, AFTER CUDDLING UP WITH *LIBERTY* AT THE PLAY. And in the middle of her escape, Justice managed to fell her with his skateboard.

Today, of all horrible days.

Another person was genuinely hurt because of him and he didn't have the human decency to even *acknowledge that* before he was looking for his *stupid,* Scooby-Doo-decked, not-more-important-than-a-human-being skateboard!

Liberty charged onto the truck, swiveling around a stack of chairs and tables. She ducked through a clothes rack, shoving stale-smelling costumes out of her way, and found Justice between two wardrobes trying to reach above them.

She announced herself by shoving him hard.

He went sideways into a musty chaise lounge, making its wooden legs creak and its prehistoric cushions spit dust into the air.

"WHAT THE HELL IS WRONG WITH YOU?" she erupted.

Justice ripped back up to his feet, facing her head on. "ME?"

This would be so much easier if she were still bigger than him. Liberty used to swing Justice around like those foam noodles people used at pools.

"You're an ASSHOLE." She felt combustible, she was so mad. If someone lit a match in here, the whole truck would go up in flames. "I WISH I'D NEVER MET YOU!"

"THE FEELING IS *MUTUAL!*" He clapped back.

Liberty could scarcely think straight, but she could feel the hurt, drawing up inside like a tidal wave.

This was the first time Liberty and Justice had actually *verbally* acknowledged the animosity between them, and while the insults were flying, she might as well go all in.

She opened her mouth to let him have it, but the anger sizzling in Justice's eyes abruptly cooled.

The tension in his taught, soccer-boy muscles softened. His expression went blunt, like an egg shell after the yolk spills out, something unfocused and queasy coming to his face.

It was then that Liberty noticed her top lip was wet, one moment before the copper tang of blood slipped into her mouth.

She touched the skin above her mouth and discovered that her nose had turned into a blood faucet.

That's what happens when you fall on your face.

The real trouble was Justice, who had always been severely squeamish about blood.

A paper cut gave him the sweats.

It was the kind of thing you were supposed to grow out of, but even in the dimness of the truck, Liberty could tell Justice looked as green as a brown guy could look, watching the blood trickle down her face.

His eyelids drooped. Justice began to sway.

You've got to be fucking kidding me, Liberty groused to herself. *He's going to faint.*

It was too late, Liberty realized, as Justice collapsed into her, completely unconscious.

Together, they slammed to the truck's cold metal floor, four legs and four arms sprawled and smushed in the narrow space.

From above, they must've looked like a drunk, two-headed spider, Liberty thought groggily.

Phosphenes splotched her vision.

Her head swam with pain from the fall.

She didn't hit it too hard, but between her face full of soreness and the blood waterfall (now flowing upstream and down the back of her throat) she was already dizzy—thoughts separating like tufts of cotton balls, rolling across an empty blue sky.

Yikes. *Her head.*

Disoriented by her bloody nose and pounding head, not to mention *trapped* under Justice's giant body draped over hers, Liberty tried to get her bearings.

She blinked rapidly, trying to get her vision to clear. But her sight was distorted by the tears pooling in her eyes. She could feel her body shaking, parts of her were sore from the fall already.

Liberty felt weak and small, like tissue paper. She felt...

The tears welled up faster.

Her vision of the room got farther and farther away.

All the rage of minutes past dissipated into cold, heavy sorrow. Liberty didn't just feel trapped beneath Justice, she felt crushed beneath the weight of everything bad about today. All at once.

Mags was still kissing Adam in her mind, over and over.

She couldn't stop seeing it. She couldn't stop crying. She'd told herself not to hope, she'd *forbidden* herself from it.

And yet somewhere in the half-hour between when the cuddling stopped and the secret awful making out began, Liberty had disobeyed herself.

That was obvious.

These were the tears of disappointed hopes. These were the sobs of a fool who played a rigged game and lost, even while knowing she was bound to lose all along.

All is lost. That's how she felt, pinned there on the cold metal floor, shivering from the temperature of the metal, yet clammy beneath the insane heat of Justice's body.

It was like every blow she'd been dealt today started to hurt simultaneously. She could feel her bludgeoned heart beating hard and slow, as the tears continued to materialize.

Of all the pains inside her at this moment, one stood out the most. The girl Liberty loved, loved someone else.

Liberty wept, as only the broken hearted can weep. She couldn't stop herself.

All is lost.

— *3:15 p.m.* —

Liberty hadn't noticed at all, during her blind rage, how deep she and Justice had wandered into this truck.

This thing was like half the size of a semi and they were somewhere in the middle of it, closer to the end that *wasn't* the door.

Near the floor, it was dim.

The network of foreign objects and decrepit prop furniture surrounding their bodies created an artificial darkness, untouched by the light of the loading dock that bathed only the top half of the space in this truck.

Liberty looked left, shuddering as she further exposed her right ear to the sensation of Justice's breath.

It tickled.

Not in the fun way.

In the *God, please get me out of here* way.

She was eye to eye with a bunch of junk, which made her realize that she couldn't see anyone, and no one could see her.

"Hello?" Liberty called out, voice thick and warped from her crying. She doubted if anyone in the loading dock could hear her.

After all, she could hear *them* but only faintly.

With the show over, Liberty heard what sounded like lots of people nearby, moving and talking. She heard the creak of what could only be set pieces being rolled into the dock from the backstage area.

"Hello?" She tried to project her voice this time, but it was kind of hard with Justice's shoulder wedged into her throat. "Excuse me!"

Justice laid over her, like the world's most muscled and yet bony weighted blanket, out cold.

And her movements were restricted.

They'd fallen to the only part of the floor in this area of the truck they *could* fall to, a narrow walkway between a wardrobe and an upright Elizabethan settee of some kind.

Liberty wanted to shove him off her, but there was quite literally no place to shove him off *to*.

And attempting it meant Liberty had to...touch Justice, as if this situation wasn't horrifying and abominable enough.

Touching him just felt wrong.

She didn't want to, and she didn't like it.

And she knew if Justice wasn't unconscious, he'd feel the same way. But this was an emergency.

She could have a concussion, as hard as they fell.

He could...well, actually in Justice's case, the fall probably didn't knock free any screws that weren't already loose.

Not the point.

They needed to get out of there, and they needed to get out of there *now*. Which would require assistance, and Liberty was the only one capable, at the moment, of acquiring that, and to do so, she needed Justice off of her, so...

Very carefully, Liberty convinced her hands to go to Justice's shoulders.

She didn't have a good angle though. Liberty repositioned her hands so that they'd push his torso, but as soon as her fingers connected with his body, a chill zipped down her spine and she jerked them back.

Justice's T-shirt was so thin, she could...feel the line of his chest. *Ew, ew, ew.*

Hadn't someone invented a way to touch another human being without touching them at all yet?

Come on, science, keep up.

"IS SOMEONE THERE?" Liberty hollered as best she could. She couldn't do this. Touch Justice? *Yuck!*

If the roles were reversed, she would rather be incinerated in the thermosphere upon reentry from OUTER SPACE than have *him* feel *her* up as a necessary method of escape.

Liberty finally released the breath she'd been holding.

Oh, God, she could feel a panic attack coming, *rumbling* toward her like a train charging down the tracks.

Everything is going to be fine, Liberty tried to assure herself.

Embarrassing, but fine.

The truck shook a little beneath them, as something large was shifted inside.

Liberty's eyes went wide.

The theater people were packing up.

They were packing up the *prop truck* and they had no idea she and Justice were trapped inside.

EVERYTHING WAS NOT FINE.

Flung into panic mode, Liberty swallowed her disgust and resolved herself to shove Justice enough that she could move.

She attempted to shove his lower torso, which was less stocky than the upper half, but the angle still sucked, and even pushing as hard as she could, he barely moved an inch.

Attempting to shove near his waist was horrible for reasons she would never tell another living soul.

At least, he was wearing jeans, but every time she lifted him a little and failed, his waist slumped back onto hers.

It felt like a pelvic high-five. More like a low-five.

More like fuck no.

"Justice." She said his name in the same tone she'd use to eviscerate someone.

Nothing.

"*WAKE UP,*" she growled in his ear. More nothing.

"Justice Arnold Wendell Garrison, if you don't get the fuck up in the next ten seconds, I'll..." Threats definitely worked better when the intended recipient was awake.

Liberty sucked in a breath, ignored the way it made her feel, and finally resolved to put her hands to his chest.

She shoved *hard* and lifted his torso off of hers, but that's when she froze, looking up at his unconscious face.

The absurdity of this moment hit her all at once.

How the hell had it come to this?

Now that he was half-suspended sort of above her, Liberty needed to figure out what to do next.

She couldn't hold him and reposition the rest of her body at the same time, could she?

Liberty tried to shift, but there either wasn't enough room or the weight of Justice's lower half made wiggling impossible.

"HELLO?!" She tried again, but this time her voice was lost under the squeal of the box truck's door rolling closed.

Liberty's heart leapt straight into her throat, as she watched darkness swallow what little light there was to begin with.

"No! Wait!" She yelled in vain.

Distracted, she let her arms relax and in doing so, the top half of Justice's body flopped down, back onto her, this time in a worse way.

Justice's face connected with hers. They were cheek-to-cheek.

The box truck's door clucked until it finally clunked into place, locking them in darkness.

Liberty heard someone thump on one of the truck's outer walls, and a moment later, everything around them began to wobble slightly, as the truck suddenly juddered and rocked.

The truck was moving.

Liberty, with her face pressed so close—*too close*—to Justice's, had the wherewithal to utter but one syllable: "*Shit.*"

SCENE II.

— 3:45 p.m. —

LIBERTY.

For a few minutes, Liberty just laid there in silence, contemplating life.

What the hell else could she do?

She listened to the furniture creak. She tried to regulate her breathing to the roar of the road, flying past beneath the truck's wheels. She counted the cars that passed them by listening for the *whoosh* of vehicles driving by.

After a little while, Liberty acknowledged that this was the most impossible thing that had ever happened to her, and in light of that fact, all of this might very possibly be a nightmare that she would wake up from, if she waited long enough.

But then she adjusted a little and became painfully aware of Justice's body, still covering hers.

The soft skin of his cheek touched hers.

It reminded her of a dream she'd had once, after they'd stayed up too late one time in seventh grade watching old movies.

Nothing really happened in the dream, but it was in black and white. She and Justice were dressed like it was 1945, and they were dancing, slowly, cheek to cheek, as a bittersweet, tinkling jazz melody played around them.

I Got it Bad and That Ain't Good.

Yeah, that was it.

In her dream, they looked like stars of the silver screen.

Like the brown, tween-aged versions of Humphrey Bogart and Ingrid Bergman.

Liberty's dreams were always better than her reality.

And that one simple fact was what drew her finally to believe in what had happened to them.

If this was a dream, it was a terrible one. And Liberty didn't have terrible dreams.

Why would she, when she had reality for free?

No, this had to be real life.

Not even her subconscious could think up something as horrible as being trapped in a box truck with her arch nemesis.

Surely her subconscious didn't despise her *that* much. Liberty took another deep breath.

She was seven out of ten panicked, but she refused to let that stop her from taking command of this situation.

The answer here was simple.

She'd simply call for help. She'd call her school, the school would call the theater people, the theater people would stop driving long enough to set them free, and this entire adventure would be over before it even began.

Liberty reached for her phone, usually at her hip, and then remembered that she didn't have it.

Her phone was in her locker, exactly where she'd left it in order to avoid messages.

Right.

Okay, eight out of ten panicked. But everything was still fine.

Surely, Justice had his phone.

No teenager would be caught dead without one. His phone was in one of four pockets in his jeans, without question.

So now all Liberty had to do was stick her hand in his... *goddammit.*

JUSTICE.

Sometimes Justice awoke with a "Huh?" as though the morning had literally called his name.

This morning, he was awakened by a hand on his left hip.

The sensation disappeared, and he almost slipped right back into sleep, but then the same sensation happened again on his other side.

He scrunched his already-closed eyes and opened them a little. What time was it? Why was it still dark outside? Why was a hand traveling across his butt, almost like it was trying to brush some lint off the back of his jeans?

Groggy and confused, Justice inhaled sharp, grumbled something unintelligible, and then yawned big and wide.

And then, Liberty's voice—way, *way* too close to him—said, "Could you try to keep your dank breath off my face?"

"WHAT THE FUCK!" Justice shouted at the same time he started moving and Liberty started yelping, "Ow, ow, ow! Your knee is digging into my *thigh.*"

Justice froze, his heart galloping. What in holy hell was going on? Why was it so dark?

Why was Justice *on top of...*

"*Liberty?*" Surprise and uncertainty were evident in his voice, even though he knew it was her. "Why are—When did—What is happening? Tell me what is happening."

When he tried to move again, Liberty poked him in his side hard enough to rupture his appendix. "*Ow!*"

"Are you trying to permanently bruise me?" She snapped. Liberty sounded pissed, but she also sounded afraid.

Something was wrong.

"What is happening!" He demanded.

"We're still in the truck," Liberty finally said. "You fainted and it's... it's a long story, but it will be fine, as soon as we call for help—"

"We're in a..." Justice looked around, eyes slowly adjusting to the darkness.

With difficulty, he made out the faint line of Liberty's body, reclined (he gulped) beneath him.

Justice could tell his knees were bent just barely on either side of her waist.

And a second ago, they'd been digging into her thighs...

They were in a narrow, little crawl-space—DID SHE JUST SAY THEY'RE STUCK IN A TRUCK?

Memories blinked into color behind his eyes.

Him running all over campus trying to find Magdalena. Him getting his things from the loading dock.

Liberty, athletically retarded as she was, tripping on his board and sending it flying into...into...

"The *prop truck?*" Disbelief tight in his throat, he put the pieces together.

Justice felt his body sway.

He heard something creak nearby.

Liberty had neglected to mention one very important detail in her account of where they were.

They weren't just trapped in a truck.

They were trapped in a *moving* truck, as in a truck that was *going somewhere.*

"We've been accidentally kidnapped?" His stomach dropped. "Fuck, we're being SMUGGLED!"

"We *are not* being smuggled."

"You don't know that."

Liberty didn't respond right away, probably because she knew Justice was right.

His heart pounded, deep and resounding. Like the bass in a rap song.

"Do you want to fill me in on *how* exactly you got us *trapped* here, like a pair of stowaways?"

"First of all, stowaways don't get trapped. They voluntarily secretly infiltrate a moving vessel. Second of all, I didn't get us trapped anywhere, you dick!"

"You pushed me," Justice remembered. That was the last thing he remembered. Why was that the last thing he remembered?

"Because you *tripped* me!" Liberty growled.

Was she talking about what happened with his board? Did she actually think that was intentional? She really thought Justice just left his skateboard sitting around, waiting for her to run in and trip on it?

"Oh, like it's my fault you're bad at running."

Liberty proceeded to give him another vicious jab of her unreasonably strong fingers.

"Would you stop fucking poking me!"

"Gladly." He could almost hear her fake-smiling. "And if you could *get off of me,* at your earliest convenience, that would be swell."

"Swell? *Swell?*" Justice muttered, maneuvering in the dark to get them out of this position. "You sound like a commercial from the fifties."

"Bite me." Liberty sat up on her elbows. "We've got bigger problems."

Justice felt another poke coming on, but didn't know how to defend himself. If he blocked with one of his hands, a vicious poke could knock him off balance and then he'd fall further on top of her.

He couldn't exactly see, but the outline of her face looked to be directly below his.

No fucking thank you.

"Just tell me how we got stuck in here!"

"You *fainted!* Okay?" Liberty huffed a breath. "Because apparently you're still ten."

A searing twinge of embarrassment stabbed the back of Justice's neck. Before he could recover or blindly deny it, Liberty surged on with this horrifying account of what happened, annoyed as hell.

"You saw the blood, you fell on top of me, I couldn't get up, and no one heard me when I called for help."

The gravity of their situation slammed into Justice so hard, he couldn't think straight. All he could do was avoid the truth for a few more seconds.

"I did not *faint,*" he challenged her.

"As if there is any other reason *in the world* why you would be on top of me."

Justice let out a frustrated breath, prompting Liberty to growl at him, "What did I just say about breathing on my face?"

He ignored her. He was puzzling through their most immediate problem.

There was no room, which meant the only place for Justice to go was back. There was more room by their calves and feet. As quickly and carefully as he could, he began to crawl in reverse. He kept crawling backwards until they were free of each other.

Liberty took an overdramatic breath, like she'd been underwater for ten minutes.

"Sweet Joey Ramone," she croaked. "Air. Glorious, weird theater people air, but still."

Justice's mind raced through everything he remembered about their afternoon.

He didn't remember fainting, but when the memory of Liberty's bloody nose came to him, he shivered involuntarily. Nausea rocked through him, just thinking about it.

If blood was involved, his fainting was unfortunately a very real possibility...

But then, Justice remembered how he'd woken up.

"You grabbed my ass," he recalled aloud.

"I DID NOT!" Liberty about screamed.

Her voice got all shrill when she was embarrassed.

She actually blushed sometimes, too. Her cheeks turned a dusty rose color. Justice never could get the hue exactly right.

"I was *looking* for a cell phone," she defended herself.

"Yeah, that makes sense." How dumb did she think he was? "You were looking for *your* phone in *my* back pocket?"

"I wasn't looking for my phone. I was looking for your phone!" She insisted. "Mine's at school. In my locker. I was going to use yours to call for help."

That was actually a great idea.

Justice dug into his pocket to do the honors himself, but that's when he realized something unfortunate.

He didn't have his phone either.

"WHAT?" Liberty wailed, when he told her.

"That's why I was backstage in the first place," he shrugged. "I left my stuff there this morning, and I needed it so I could text Mags and—" Justice stopped himself before he finished his sentence.

He was worried that Liberty, as smart and insightful as she was, might figure him out right then, right there.

She'd spotted better hidden truths than this one. But Liberty went quiet at the mention of Mags.

Maybe she was lost in the reality of their situation. Justice definitely was. They were trapped in the back of a box truck with no windows, no doors, no cell phones, and no way to get anyone's attention or signal for help.

They were being taken somewhere.

Oh God. They were being *abducted.*

What if they got sold into a human trafficking ring? This was bad. This was *really* bad.

"So...what do we do?" This time, when Justice asked the room, even he sounded scared.

"Nothing," Liberty sniffed, voice thick with emotion. "We're fucked."

— 4:00 p.m. —

LIBERTY.

This isn't happening, this isn't happening, this isn't happening, this isn't happening.

Liberty was back to denial instead of acceptance.

She knew one thing. Acceptance was a whole hell of a lot easier before Justice woke up.

Liberty tried to think of something else, *anything* to distract herself, but all that came to mind was a sliver of Magdalena's tongue disappearing between Adam's salmon-pink lips. Her stomach clenched, like she might hurl up her shriveled heart, right there in the darkness.

The truck had been thunking along steadily for a while without any stops or turns. Liberty suspected they were on a highway, and that wasn't good.

They lived in Western Massachusetts; getting on a highway usually meant going to another state.

Or Boston, which might as well have been another state with its ugly layout and ridiculous road signs and panic-attack-inducing traffic.

Either way, if they were on a major highway, wherever they ended up, Liberty thought it was likely they'd be at least an hour from home.

But that was a total guess that she'd pulled straight out of her ass. She wished she knew what time it was, but alas, there weren't any Accidental Kidnap Clocks at her disposal.

That old saying, *time flies when you're having fun,* was also true in reverse, she found.

Time fucking crawls when you're miserable.

The worst-case scenario was that the What You Will Shakespeare Company had a show to do in frickin' Florida and they were going to road- trip down the East Coast without opening their prop truck one single time.

By the time they rolled into the sunshine state, Justice and Liberty would be a pair of rotting corpses, having died either from starvation or a double homicide brought on by three years' worth of provocations and twenty hours of close confinement.

Liberty squeezed her legs to her chest a little tighter and rested her head on top.

The most likely outcome is that you're going to be fine, she rationalized. These people are thespians, not black-market organ sellers.

Aside from his accusing her of copping a feel (*AS IF)*, she and Justice hadn't said much to each other since they'd gotten vertical.

And that was both okay but also not.

A few times, it got so quiet in the truck, Liberty almost convinced herself she was alone.

That she was the one trapped, all by herself. And in some ways, she realized, she was.

If you were trapped somewhere with someone you hated, you *would* be alone. And that's because so long as that other person isn't in your corner, you're on your own.

That's how Liberty felt, *on her own.*

Except worse because she was on her own, under great duress, *and* in the presence of Justice—a guy who didn't need any more leverage against her.

He didn't need any more ammo than he already had. And yet, life saw fit to give him more.

Now, assuming they survived this cruel twist of fate, the next time someone called Liberty a bigot, Justice could throw in, *One time, she groped me.*

And *away* the rumor mill would go.

Hell, Justice would probably turn this entire thing into a story about how devious and horrible she was. How she'd trapped him by throwing his skateboard into a box truck, making her own nose bleed so he'd faint, and then copping a feel while they were trapped together.

The story sounded ridiculous in her mind.

She wished she could laugh, but the tears had returned and were spilling down her face.

Today felt like rock bottom, except that rock bottom had a trapdoor. And now Liberty was even hesitant to accept that *this* was the worst her day could get.

If today had taught her anything, it was that *things can always get worse.*

JUSTICE.

It had come to Justice's attention that Liberty was crying, which meant that they were in *deep shit.*

Liberty used to love problems.

She loved to jump into leadership positions and use her creative academic mind to figure things out. Liberty usually leapt at the chance to take charge, but not today.

Today, she was solemn and quiet in the darkness encapsulating them both. She seemed dejected almost.

Her silence scared Justice.

If she was scared enough that she didn't even have the energy to insult him, then she was really scared.

And Liberty being really scared always gave him the impulse to really cheer her up. Her silent tears only made things worse.

Great. Just fan-freaking-tastic.

Justice forced himself to sit still and stay calm.

Earlier in the day, when he and Washington had helped the theater company people unload, they'd met a few of the company members.

Everyone they met seemed great, not like child traffickers at all. Everything was probably going to turn out all right.

Liberty sniffed, congested from tears. The sound stained his memory like ink.

He was thrown back in time to the day of Liberty's thirteenth birthday party. She ran away from the gathering mid-song, and by the time he'd carried her back to her house, most of her family members had departed.

Justice remembered putting her down on the sidewalk. They'd stood there together, by the Marshalls' red mailbox, looking up at her house.

Liberty noticed her dad's car was still in the driveway. Justice watched her look at that Lexus like she wanted to set it on fire.

"You ready?" he'd said.

Liberty didn't answer him, but she led the way to her front door. He still remembered how Liberty gingerly turned the doorknob, like a burglar sneaking in.

She didn't want anyone to know she was home. Once they'd entered her foyer, she seemed lost.

Standing there with chrysanthemums in her hair, in a pink dress that would have looked ugly on anyone else.

She looked like a little kid who'd misplaced her parents.

But then they heard Don and Jeanine down the hall. Arguing.

Their voices bounding down the hallway toward Justice and Liberty.

Without a thought, Liberty grabbed Justice's arm and yanked him into their coat closet.

That was the last time they'd been confined together in a dark place. He remembered them sitting on the floor in the dark, old peacoats and windbreakers hanging above their heads, listening in silence as her parents showed up in the foyer, bandying sharp words like swords.

"Did you come here to play comedian or to celebrate your daughter?" Jeanine spat.

"I'm not allowed to talk to my own family at a social gathering?" Don countered.

"You HUMILIATED her! *On her birthday.*" Their footsteps marched toward the front door. "All I'm saying is don't be surprised if you don't win Father of the Year this year. Or any year."

"I would apologize if she were here, but she's not. What do you want me to do?"

"This isn't about *me,* Donovan! This is about Liberty." Silence followed Jeanine's remark.

But Justice stopped listening after that because he heard Liberty sniff beside him.

She was crying all over again, and after he'd done all that work to cheer her up the first time.

Honestly, he didn't know what to do.

He didn't know what it was like to have a dad like Liberty's. He only knew what it was like to have his dad.

And his dad—an idea came to him.

Using his forefinger, he began to draw shapes on Liberty's knee.

"*What are you doing?*" she hissed.

"You're supposed to guess," he whispered back. "What do you

think it is?"

He drew another shape on her knee, a compass. She guessed right. He created another shape and so it went, until the arguing calmed down and her dad left and Liberty was ready to face her mom and whoever was left.

Being trapped in a box truck with Liberty was sort of like being in a closet with her, only not at all.

Hearing her sniffle clawed at him. It was a sound he hated.

He didn't mind the thought of Liberty in pain, but having to *hear it* made him crazy. He desperately wanted it to stop—he needed it to stop.

Justice tried covering his ears.

It was dark, so she couldn't see him.

But with his ears covered, the rumble of the truck was distorted in his head.

It made him feel like he was in the belly of a whale, a scenario which was actually in the top three on his Ways I Don't Want to Die list. So he removed his hands and suffered for several more minutes at the sound of Liberty's soft, soft sobs.

And finally, when he couldn't take it anymore, he studied the outline of her in the dark. She was sitting with her back against the wardrobe.

Once he was sure there was enough room for him and he'd asked himself *Are you sure about this?* a good twenty-seven times, he moved himself closer until he was sitting with his back against the wardrobe, too.

"What are you doing?" Liberty asked almost immediately.

Justice couldn't bring himself to respond because he didn't actually know *what* he was doing.

All he knew was that Liberty's warbly, depressing voice sounded so much like her younger self that he felt like she was jabbing him right in his heart.

It absolutely didn't make any fucking sense, but he lifted the forefinger of his right hand and gently touched what he hoped to God he'd correctly identified as her knee.

What he wasn't prepared for was the way it *felt* to make physical contact with her, to...touch her, *skin on skin,* after three years. Maybe Liberty felt it, too, which is why she swatted his hand away after a few seconds of silent shock.

That small rejection was enough to make Justice crawl away and hate himself forever for doing something so ridiculously cringey and gross, but he forced himself to try again. Because...

If he crawled away without trying again, Liberty would just keep crying. And who knew how long they'd be stuck in here together?

He didn't want what little of his sanity was left to be whittled away by her stupid tears. This was about preservation, about *survival.*

Yeah.

Justice liked the sound of that. He was doing this for *survival.*

Again, he took his forefinger to her knee, and this time drew a shape before she could swat his hand away.

Once he'd finished, Justice didn't move and Liberty didn't either. He didn't say anything, nor did she.

And she didn't destroy him and he didn't spontaneously contract a terminal illness from touching her, so all evidence pointed to...so far so good.

Liberty sniffed, harder than she had before.

Oh, for fuck's sake.

Had Justice somehow managed to do the one thing that would make her feel worse than she already felt? No, no, no, no, no, no, no, no—

"Trapezoid," she sniveled.

He was so shocked that she remembered this game that he almost forgot that he had, in fact, drawn a trapezoid.

She was right.

Before he lost his nerve, he drew another shape. This game was actually better than he remembered, and that was because the last time they played, Justice knew a hell of a lot less about drawing. He could draw way more things now than he could then.

So for the next shape, he decided to make it fancy.

"A rose," Liberty guessed, when he'd finished.

Justice thought he might actually trip her up with that one. He'd drawn a shitload of petals, plus thorns on the stem. He kept drawing pictures and she kept guessing, and finally, Justice resorted to drawing letters, spelling words and sentences.

"E...V...E—*Evening? Ever*—R...Y—*Everything.*"

Liberty was guessing faster than he was writing now, literally finishing his thoughts before he was done with them.

"Is...G...O...*Going... Tobe?* Wait. No. Everything is going *to be*—" She stopped guessing as Justice spelled *OK* on her knee. After a few moments had gone by, she murmured, "You don't know that."

"Yes, I do," Justice replied, surprised by the sound of his own voice. He'd never admit it to her or anyone anywhere, but no matter how they felt about each other, he still believed in their team magic.

Justice still believed that if the two of them were together, even if they ended up killing each other, they'd do it in style and everything would somehow work out in the end.

If they were together, for better or for worse, he really believed that everything would be okay.

— 4:20 p.m. —

Well, now, shit was weird.

In all Justice's thinking about whether he should have started a game of Draw-Skin-Guess, he hadn't given one single thought to what he'd do *after* he and Liberty were done playing.

They were sitting shoulder to shoulder, and he'd just spent the past several minutes touching her knee.

What did that mean exactly?

What he wanted to do was move away from her again, but he felt like an asshole considering that.

And it was because...

Jesus H. Christ...

It was because he didn't want to hurt her feelings or do anything that might make her sad again, okay?

He didn't want to make her sad because then he'd feel compelled to cheer her up, and they'd have to do this whole song and dance over again, and he didn't want that.

Which ultimately meant...that maybe Justice needed to be more than civil with Liberty right now. Maybe he actually needed to be, you know, kind of, like... nice?

Justice hoped she couldn't feel him shudder on the inside.

Being nice to Liberty felt like the slipperiest slope in the world. Because once you were nice to her, you started to care about her, and once you started to care about her, she'd find a way to crush your heart into a bajillion pieces.

Justice had been down the road that started with being nice to Liberty, and he had no desire to travel that road again.

An hour in solitary confinement with her and he was already losing his goddamn mind.

Someone, anyone, please. Send help.

"Oh, shit," he unintentionally thought aloud.

"What?" Liberty replied.

"Mags and I were supposed to meet up after school, and now she'll think I stood her up and I have no way of telling her the truth, not that she would believe me, let alone that I want to—" He rambled his way through the truth, barely stopping himself in time.

In the end, it didn't matter, though, because Liberty finished his sentence. *Damn her.*

"That you want to...go out with her?"

Justice didn't know how he expected Liberty to sound in the nightmare scenario where the two of them ever talked about his love life again, but he definitely hadn't expected her to sound so down about it, so morose.

Hateful? Disgusted? Nasty? Sure.

Sad though? About *his* love life?

His love life should have been the only thing about him that she genuinely didn't give a fuck about.

Why did it sound like she did?

But then Justice remembered the stupid play. Liberty and Magdalena snuggled up together.

The look on Magdalena's face. Justice recognized it.

He used to make that face when Liberty was around, too.

That same twinge from earlier rocked through him, that discomfort at the idea of them being together, so he said, "Why? You trying to date her, too?"

"No." Liberty was quiet a long moment before she added, "Never." There was pain in her voice.

It was the kind of *never* that came with a story, and Justice's curiosity was *high*.

The worst part of this moment was that Justice knew exactly what to do to get the information from Liberty that he wanted.

It was simple, yet terrible, and somehow he already knew she'd agree. He couldn't believe the word was about to fall from his mouth.

"Trade."

Justice closed his eyes when she said, "Terms."

He hated that he knew her so well. And he hated that in some ways she was so consistent, she was exactly the same person he remembered, and in other ways, she was so drastically different that—never mind.

It's called being two-faced.

"If you tell me how you feel about Mags, I'll tell you how I feel about her." The words were out of his mouth before Justice could stop them.

Christ. Were they really doing this? There was no way she'd agree to this, right?

He couldn't possibly be *that* right about her—

"Deal." Liberty readjusted beside him. Somehow they were sitting closer together when she was done. "But you have to go first."

Fuck. Justice dragged a hand down his face.

He was already regretting everything about this.

Every. Single. Thing.

"Take it or leave it, Garrison," she goaded him when he didn't reply. He blew out an exhausted breath.

"Fine. Me first." Why had he been so dumb as to offer up the answer to a question he didn't really want to answer? "Mags. *Mags.* I...you know, I...Well, obviously, I like her."

"Eloquent."

"No commentary allowed." Justice braced for the itchiness of... emotional exposure...and forced himself to press on. "I guess it started freshman year. Model UN. I had no idea who she was. She didn't hang out with anyone except you. I know that you...uh, you have good taste in friends."

That was true.

Liberty had good taste in friends, even though *she* wasn't a good one.

"So I figured she was probably okay, and then we got paired together to represent India that one time, and I found out that she's awesome. And I've just thought she was awesome this whole time basically, so yeah. Why not take things to the next level and be, you know, awesome *together.*"

Justice was so glad he couldn't see Liberty's face.

He was so glad she couldn't see *him,* after the way he'd fumbled so atrociously just now.

The post-atrocity silence was too much, so hurriedly, he tacked on, "Now, you."

"How do I feel about Mags," she breathed. "She's...she's...I guess that...I think she's great. The end."

Justice made a buzzer noise. "Foul. Unsatisfactory answer."

"You can't call a foul if you don't previously set answer guidelines first," she told him.

She was right. That was in the Trade Bylaws they'd established as kids. Damn her for remembering the rules and using them to her advantage.

How was Justice supposed to argue with her? He was the one who'd come up with that rule in the first place.

"Plus," she added, "it's my turn."

"Your turn to what?"

"Initiate a trade."

SCENE III.

— 4:50 p.m. —

LIBERTY.

Justice was dumb as hell for opening up *this* can of worms.

If he remembered anything about Liberty in middle school, he should have remembered that she came with questions.

Lots of them.

Now that she knew he was open to trading information... Well, let's just say there was some info she wanted.

This moment was so strange because she never thought it would happen.

The demolition of her friendship with Justice was like moving out of a childhood home. Their friendship held fond memories that would remain cherished in a deep, dark, untouchable corner of her heart, but had she ever expected to return to something like friendship with Justice ever again?

No.

It was like walking, once again, through the halls of a childhood home only to find it wasn't that different from how she remembered it.

Sitting in the dark, shooting the shit with Justice, was exactly how she remembered their friendship.

It was nostalgic and comfortable somehow... She hated it.

But it was also like...finally scratching a three-year itch.

Maybe if she asked him a few of the things that she'd sometimes, over the past three years, been *dying* to ask him, she could stop caring about them and move on.

Completely. For good.

There would be no better opportunity than this, she supposed. So she sucked it up.

Should I go chronologically or alphabetically? She wondered to herself. She couldn't believe they were actually doing this, but at the same time, very few things that had happened to her today could be classified as *believable.*

Liberty needed to be deliberate, intentional, and cool as fuck. She didn't want to spook him into shutting down.

Let's give ourselves some room...

"I'll trade you ten personal questions," she announced. "I'll ask you ten, and you can ask me ten." She sucked in a nervous breath. "Do we have a deal?"

The one thing she hadn't considered: Why in the world would Justice be interested in asking her anything about herself? If he was interested in Liberty's personal life, he wouldn't have done such a thorough job of removing himself from it.

This couldn't be a very tempting deal for him, she concluded, which was why she was nothing short of *stunned* when he said, "Deal."

After she'd pulled her eyebrows out of her hair and picked her jaw up from the floor, she stammered out, "Any parameters you'd like to instate?"

Justice was quiet a moment.

His shoulder felt giant beside hers. Liberty thought Justice slightly resembled a bear in the dark.

"Sky's the limit," he finally said.

Liberty snapped to look at him, but she couldn't see his face. *You don't mean that,* she wanted to say. *You just don't want to look like a wimp.*

But she didn't say any of that.

She'd asked for Justice's boundaries, he didn't specify any, which meant...Liberty Marshall could ask Justice Garrison anything she wanted and he'd answer.

Oh, the power she held in her hands.

"All right. Well, I've got parameters," she jumped in, clearing her throat. "No lies."

"Obviously."

"No technical answers."

"Fine," Justice agreed. "But on one condition. I get to go first again."

"Okay." Liberty, heart stuttering in her chest, had no objections to going second. That would give her time to convince herself this was happening. "The floor...is yours."

Anticipation buzzed inside her like a swarm of slap happy bumblebees.

And then, she proceeded to wait in silence for Justice to pose his first question. One minute passed between them in silence. Then, another ten more.

Before they started trading information, Liberty had been eager for this truck ride from hell to end. But now that she had an opportunity to learn some things she wanted to know, she felt anxious that they would arrive wherever these theater people were headed too soon.

Liberty understood that this chance to ask Justice questions had been sponsored by the fact that A) they were trapped and B) they were trapped somewhere dark.

If they weren't trapped, this wouldn't be happening. And if they were trapped somewhere with light, this equally wouldn't be happening.

Seeing each other's faces would've deadened any possibility of their being vulnerable.

There were no guarantees they'd even be able to go through with the vulnerability they were attempting right now.

In the time it took Justice to formulate his first question, she wasn't sure he wouldn't abort this entire scenario any second. Liberty was still shocked that he was voluntarily sitting so close to her and had been for so long.

The suspense of what he was going to ask her and her rising anxiety that, at this pace, they'd be free of this truck before she got to ask her questions collided the same second Justice finally came out with:

"How's Judge?"

Liberty was speechless for a moment.

It took him *ten whole minutes* to come up with a generic-ass, no- effort-necessary question about *her dog?*

On the other hand, Liberty wasn't surprised that Justice might be curious about her dog. Justice and Judge went *way* back. And even though he'd found plenty of things to hate about her, there was no possible way Justice could find anything to hate about Judge.

Judge was a dog. Judge was perfect.

The only things he was guilty of were the occasional fart when he walked and wanting to be everyone's friend.

"Uh, Judge is fine. He's seven now. Which is forty-nine in dog years, so basically, I think he's going through a midlife crisis. But other than that, he's okay."

"Was he sad when Burt died?" Justice asked next. Again, he'd surprised her.

How did *Justice* remember that Judge used to wait on her front porch for the mailman every day?

"What?" Justice asked, guessing at her shock. "Burt was our mailman, too."

Sometimes Liberty forgot that she and Justice lived on the same street. She never, ever saw him, even though they lived their lives so near one another.

"He still waits for him actually," Liberty finally answered. "Every day. Judge still waits on the porch."

Justice paused. His silence sounded like he was smiling, but maybe Liberty was imagining that.

Liberty pushed on. "You've already used up two questions. Eight to go."

Thank God, Justice didn't take forever to think up question three. "Do you... are you still in contact with George?"

Justice was just *full* of surprises all of a sudden. "George... Monsouri-Amand?"

"Yeah. G. M. A."

It was very clear in Justice's voice that even after three years of not seeing or speaking to George, Justice still very much disliked him.

"George and I talk all the time," Liberty admitted, remembering the parameters she'd set.

No lying. No truth-bending.

"Somehow—I don't know, the distance made our friendship stronger. He, uh...Um." Liberty babbled on, trying to swallow the anxious little lump in her throat, but it wouldn't go down.

"He *what?*" The chill in Justice's voice made her even more nervous.

Damn it.

"He's really different now, definitely not a bully anymore. I think he was always a good guy in his own way, and now he's a good guy in lots of ways, if that makes sense."

"*Sure he is,*" Justice huffed under his breath.

"See for yourself when he gets back," Liberty fumbled on, trying to sound positive. "He texted me earlier that...he's going to do senior year with us at PSM."

The words were out before Liberty could carefully consider whether she should have said them. She didn't wonder too long, because Justice suddenly stiffened in reaction.

"You must be thrilled."

"What?" Liberty bleated.

She *was* excited George was coming back, but what was that edge in Justice's voice?

Instead of explaining himself, Justice made them sit in silence a few more seconds before moving onto his fourth question.

"Have you...have you ever, past or present, liked him?" Justice inquired. "I mean, like, *liked him* liked him."

Liberty choked on her own tongue.

Even when she and Justice had been tight, he had *never* asked her, point blank, if she had a crush on anyone, *ever.*

Her whole face felt hot.

Holy shit, she never in a million years expected that he was going to ask her *that.*

Even more than before she wanted to know what was going through his mind. There's no way he'd been wondering about her and George since... way back when? Right?

Liberty thought she was alone in the Questions I've Always Wanted to Ask You department. Could it be that Justice had things he'd always wanted to ask her, too?

Was this question, about her and George, one of them? Could that possibly be?

"No," she said, breathless somehow, even though she had no reason to be. "In middle school, he and I were friends, and we're still friends now. That's all."

"You never liked him?" Justice pressed.

Was that *relief* Liberty heard in his incredulous voice? Confusion?

Angst? Where the hell was he coming from here?

"Ever? *Ever?* Not even a little tiny bit?" He clarified.

"No," she repeated. "Never."

How could he be surprised?

Better yet, how could he have ever thought to begin with that Liberty might like George at all, when she'd so very clearly been in love with Justice?

At the time.

In the past, she meant. Not like, now.

This time, Justice seemed speechless. Or at least, he got very quiet and didn't say anymore for a while.

"That's five questions down," she whispered. "Five to go."

"I know, I know," he snapped. "Stop rushing me."

Liberty closed her mouth and waited for his next inquiry.

This time she tried to prepare herself for another left-field question. She still could not imagine that anything going on in her life could be of interest to him, but maybe he'd say the same thing about her, and she did have a list of things in her mind that she wanted to ask him.

"How's your mom?" He asked.

She cringed. Hard.

Just the memory of that morning was enough to make her recoil in shame, let alone voicing out loud that such a horrific thing happened.

"I'm sorry about this morning," she blurted out, hands hiding her face.

When she didn't say anymore, Justice nudged her shoulder with his. "Answer the question."

"Sorry. Yes. She's..." Liberty was forced to give her mom some real thought, which she hadn't today really, at all.

How was her mom?

Liberty had been so wrapped up in her own crap all day that she hadn't given one single thought to what it must be like for her mom...

A nurse, who's seen probably hundreds of patients die, who's spent way too much time in hospitals—to see her own dad in one, with a *tumor,* on what could be a day very near his last day on earth...

Her mom never showed it. She never saw her mom break down or cry. But today, she must probably feel...scared and sad. But Liberty didn't want to tell Justice all of that.

"My mom's fine," she hedged. "She's busy as usual. She's been promoted a few times at the hospital now. She's basically head nurse in charge, I guess."

Liberty wished she had better things to say about how her mom was, but life was cruel that way sometimes.

Sometimes there was nothing better to say.

"How's your dad?" Justice asked next.

She definitely should've seen this question coming, but she hadn't. And now, tears climbed up to the rim of her eyes.

Justice knew just a little too much about her. All those endless hours of talking and laughing with him were coming back to bite her in the ass. Hard.

"He moved to New York." Liberty squeezed her eyes shut, like that might make this moment move faster. "Two years ago. He actually...he offered to let me come live with him if I wanted. You know, go to school in the city."

There were some days when Liberty felt like turning him down had been the wrong choice.

Other than Magdalena, what did Green River have that was superior to New York City?

"Why'd you turn him down?" Justice muttered, maybe thinking the same thing she was.

"Mom needs me." Liberty surprised herself with that

response. It sure didn't always feel like her mom needed her. But Liberty knew that she did, deep down. "If I wasn't around, she'd probably forget to eat. So..."

"Was it...was it your idea that you and I work together on DJing the parade?"

Liberty actually laughed at that, and then she stopped herself. She could tell that Justice was taking such pains to be cordial with her. The least she could do was not laugh in his face for saying something stupid.

Justice couldn't help saying stupid things. It wasn't his fault.

"No," she assured him. "That idea was an Adam Grosch original."

"I should've known."

Liberty shoved Adam out of her mind. Thinking of him only made her think about... Gross.

Repress it already, she commanded her brain. *What are you waiting for?*

Justice seemed to approach his last question delicately. In a guarded fashion.

Liberty had no idea what *that* was about.

"Earlier. During the show. When I asked you where Magdalena was, did you know...she *wasn't* talking to Mr. Tanaka?"

What a strange, horrible question.

Damn it, Justice.

Forcing her to think about...*God.*

Wait. Did...Justice know where Magdalena and Adam actually were during the play? Or was that terrible information hers to keep?

"No," she told him. "I had no idea. Magdalena just said she'd be right back, something about Mr. Tanaka and a budget question. I...I don't know where she went."

"And earlier," he continued, more confident now. "When you

ran into the loading area, where were you coming from? Why were you running?"

"I'm sorry," Liberty was happy to say. "You've run out of questions. Thanks for playing and try again next time. It's my turn."

Did Liberty imagine it, or did Justice just gulp?

— *5:15 p.m.* —

JUSTICE.

Justice felt like an idiot for starting this game.

Liberty was really good at questions, which is why he'd forced her to let him go first.

He could prepare to ask her questions way faster than he could prepare himself to answer hers.

Dear God. What had he gotten himself into?

Honestly, Justice was still reeling from what he'd learned about Liberty in the last half hour, or however long it'd been.

He was beside himself.

Justice spent their final weeks and months of eighth grade *convinced* that Liberty liked George. He'd been absolutely sure of it, and not just him.

Washington, too.

When Justice used to confide in Washington about his feelings toward you-know-who, Washington would always tell him how Liberty was falling for George.

She was developing feelings for George every day, blah, blah, blah. Justice would ask Washington, *Well, what did she say?* And Washington would give a full account of all the things she'd said about liking George, but being afraid of damaging their friendship, that she was crazy about him.

Back then, Justice never asked Liberty anything about her love life. He didn't want to give his own feelings away...

It's not like he was exactly subtle or anything. But better late than never, right?

He asked Liberty himself, today, after all this time, and she'd... denied it. All of it. Even after setting the parameter at the beginning of "No lies."

Liberty had Justice fucked up.

"Um," Liberty cleared her throat. She'd gone so quiet while she was thinking of her questions that Justice had momentarily forgotten she was there.

Oh, wonderful. Let the ass-kicking begin.

"Okay. My first question is...how's Hope?"

Justice let himself breathe. An easy one. Liberty was starting out slow. He couldn't let her take him by surprise.

Don't get comfortable, he reminded himself. *There's a greedy, evil investigative journalist inside that girl, just waiting to jump out.*

"Hope is no more of a spaz than usual," he supplied, thinking of his sister.

She was about a forty-five minute drive away from them at New Arlington College.

"She's finishing up her first year at NAC. Right now, she's thinking she'll major in dance. But she definitely likes food too much to make it as a ballerina. She's minoring in music studies."

Justice bet *that* little tidbit would make Liberty smile. She and Hope were the sisters each of them never had.

It was revolting.

And also kind of sweet in a two-desperate-girls-bonding sort of way. "All of her friends suck. She brought this guy home for Thanksgiving who would not shut up about Nietzsche. I wanted to stuff his head up the turkey's ass."

Liberty giggled. Actually giggled.

There was a sound he hadn't heard in years. It was a sound that refreshed him, like ice cold water in the summer heat. She was already lulling him into a false sense of security, even now.

"How's Mama Garrison?" Liberty asked next.

Here we go.

Chelsea Garrison, Justice's whirlwind of a mother, used to *love it* when Liberty called her Mama Garrison.

Justice couldn't do anything about the annoyance that cropped up inside of him, like weeds, whenever someone mentioned his mom.

It's not like Justice and his mom had a bad relationship. It's more like...they didn't really have one at all.

"She's fine," he shrugged. "She's flying to Hong Kong right now, I think. Or maybe she's flying back. I always get her flight schedules mixed up. She's usually around a few weeks at a time, and then she's gone for a few weeks. You know, usual flight attendant stuff."

"You must miss her," Liberty said next, which felt like she'd taken a kitchen knife and lodged it between his ribs.

She said it all melancholy and sincere, as though she actually cared if he was in pain.

She didn't. Justice couldn't let himself forget that. Not for a second. Liberty didn't actually care about him. She was just trying to butter him up.

You must miss her. Bullshit.

"And how's your dad?" Liberty just kept coming with the punches, didn't she?

"Theodore's in Boston now," he told Liberty.

Theodore Garrison, as Justice liked to think of him. It made him feel empowered, as though he and his dad stood on equal footing.

"He, uh...met this woman. A psychologist named Robin. They got married last summer. *Eloped,* actually, in Turks and Caicos—" Justice felt like his whole mouth was made of lemons. That's how bitter he felt talking about this.

How could he not?

His dad had been his first best friend, before Washington,

before Liberty. It was Justice and his dad. And then his parents got divorced, and his dad—all because he was mad at Justice's mom —*left him.*

He left him and his sister and moved two hours east to Boston, one of the worst cities on earth, to start a new life, without them.

And he'd done a good job.

Because now he had Robin. And now he and Robin—

"They're, um...he, my dad, he's pregnant. I mean, they're... *they're* pregnant. With a baby. An actual human child. Who will, God willing, be born sometime this winter."

"What?" Liberty responded, like this was a good thing. "You're going to be a big brother?"

OH, GOD.

Justice hadn't even *begun* to think about that!

No, no, no, no. He did not have the bandwidth to talk about this any further.

"What's your next question?" he asked, trying not to seem too eager to move on, even though he desperately, desperately was.

"Um..." Liberty did this thing with her voice when she was nervous to ask a question. It was hard to explain, but Justice always knew it when he heard it. "How's...Washington?"

Washington? Why was she asking about him?

"Washington is...Washington, I guess. He's loving costume design. He still hates pickles. He's not very different. I liked the way he dressed in middle school better."

For some reason, Justice got the feeling that he was not answering this question the way Liberty wanted him to.

That put him on edge.

What was she getting at here?

Even in the darkness, he could tell that she was fidgeting.

Another nervous tick of hers. She played with her own fingers when she was nervous.

What the hell was she trying to ask him?

All this beating around the bush made him feel uncomfortable. "What is it?" he said.

"What is what?"

"Your next question." He exhaled hard, not wanting to call her out too directly. But if she kept pussyfooting around, he was going to have to—

"Have you ever, past or present, had feelings for..." She paused, which may as well have induced a heart attack.

What the hell would he do if the end of her sentence was *me?* Was she asking, after all this time, if he'd ever liked her?

And if she was, what was he going to tell her?

He'd agreed not to lie, but if he didn't lie, then he'd have to tell her the truth, and he couldn't do that.

Not when he'd already arranged to take the truth to his grave. But when Liberty finished her sentence, *me* wasn't at the end of it.

Dewey was.

"Have you ever, past or present, had feelings for Dewey?" She found the will to ask.

Justice just sat there in silence for a while.

This was a question he didn't know whether to laugh at...or *die laughing* at.

"What the hell?" A chuckle lurched from his throat. "What are you even talking about right now? What are you saying?"

"Answer the question," she urged.

"*No*, Liberty."

He couldn't remember the last time he'd said her name *to her*. Her name tasted funny on his tongue. He was out of practice, saying it.

"I have never had, nor do I currently have, feelings for Washington, on account of the fact that I'm *straight* as a desert highway, which I always thought was, you know, evident."

"But you were his first kiss," Liberty said next, which made Justice want to crawl into a hole and die.

Would no one ever let him live that down?

Yes, *okay*? He'd been Washington's first make out. And yes, it was fine. No, he was not repulsed by kissing a guy. Far from it. It was whatever. It was fine. Everything's fine.

"And you two are inseparable."

"Your point?" Justice prompted.

"I always thought—" She dropped off mid-sentence again.

"You always thought *what*?"

This was clearly confusing to her, but he hadn't the faintest idea why. Wait a minute.

There was no way she'd been thinking he'd had feelings for Washington this whole time, was there?

Did anyone else think that? Like Magdalena? Oh, beautiful. Excellent. Bravissimo.

Today was outdoing itself.

"You've got five questions left, you know," he informed her, eager to move on and get these questions over with before she could ask him anything else he didn't want to answer.

"Are you planning to ask Magdalena out, sometime in the near future?" Was her next question.

Justice sighed, letting his eyes fall closed. He wanted to tell her yes. But why was he hesitating now? Why didn't he feel sure?

He'd been so motivated that afternoon to do it, to ask her, to let her know how he really felt about her, but today had taken the wind out of his sails in a big way.

He didn't know what he'd feel like doing when they eventually got out of this situation and went home (if they got out of this situation and went home).

"Maybe," he decided aloud. "Maybe I will, maybe I won't."

"Foul," Liberty announced. "No technical answers. I ask you a yes or no question, you have to give me a yes or no answer."

Justice knew the rules. Now, he had the opportunity to amend his answer to a yes or no. If he wanted to stick with his original answer, the foul would be sustained and Liberty would get to ask him eleven questions instead of ten.

The kicker: Did he want to brave an eleventh question over this ridiculous one?

"Then yes," he amended. "I am planning to ask her out soon."

The atmosphere between them changed when he said that. The air between them became solemn all of a sudden. Clearly, this was and also wasn't the answer Liberty was looking for.

Score, he congratulated himself. He'd managed to catch her off guard, the same way she'd been catching him.

"Amendment accepted," she said after a moment. "Next question. Why did you ask me if I still talk to George?"

Oh, *hell.* This wasn't fair at all.

She got to ask him *about* his questions, but he wouldn't get the chance to ask her about hers? Damn it.

Now he had to answer for his own inquiries? Today just got better and better.

"Curiosity. Next question." He didn't expect Liberty to let him get away with a one-word response, but she did. Probably because her next question was...(and Justice seriously should've seen this coming):

"Why did you ask if I'd ever liked George?" Fuck, fuck, fuck.

What was he going to tell her? *Way to go, Garrison.*

Unfortunately, it seemed like his best bet here was probably... the truth. Couldn't he just die instead?

That would probably be less mortifying. "Because I thought you did. Back in the day."

"You did? You thought I liked *George?*" She clarified. "Why?"

For fuck's sake. What was he supposed to say now? *Washington told me so? The two of you seemed close, so I just assumed? I was nuts about you at the time and maybe a little jealous of your friendship with him?*

"He was horrible." The tension in Justice's jaw made it hard to speak. "George was horrible in eighth grade, and you were the only one who treated him like he wasn't."

He squeezed one fist and then released it.

"I always thought that the reason you were nice to him was because you, for some baffling reason, maybe, liked him. Why else do we overlook another person's flaws?"

"For political gain." Liberty quipped, but her mind seemed far away, like she was on autopilot.

Like she was saying one thing, but deep in thought about something else at the same time.

All she was doing was confusing Justice further.

If she really didn't have any feelings for George, then it made sense that she'd ask Justice why he thought she had. If liking George really was a preposterous notion, then it made total sense that she'd be asking these questions about his questions.

And if she was lying, if she actually did like George, wouldn't she want to stay off the subject? Why would she willingly use not one, but *two* of her questions to go back to the subject of GMA?

Other than to mess with Justice's mind, of course, something she very clearly took much pleasure in.

In some circumstances, Justice couldn't figure Liberty out. *At all.* And instead of dwelling on that, Justice wanted to move on. So he said, "Last question. Let's get this over with."

SCENE IV.

— 5:30 p.m. —

JUSTICE.

In the moments of quiet while Justice waited for Liberty to pose her final question, he remembered her words from earlier: *You must miss her.*

The anger was still there inside him, but he could tell now that part of the reason he was angry she'd said that was because she was right.

She understood him.

Even after three years of virtual silence and complete distance from each other, she understood how he was feeling. She didn't care about him, but she saw straight through to his heart, *still,* and that sucked.

That was a horrible feeling.

Knowing deep down that the person you despise most was also the person who understood you the best.

That's how Liberty used to make him feel: *Seen.* Heard. Understood. That's how he used to feel about her. He just wanted to see her all the time and listen to what she had to say and understand what was going on with her.

It was all so simple, and that's probably what should have tipped him off that it wasn't real.

Nothing *that good* could really be that easy. Nothing worth fighting for ever was.

It was wild to think that this time three years ago, Justice was somewhere *dying* to go out with the same girl who was sitting beside him now.

The crush that crushed all crushes, as he used to think of it. If his middle school self could see him now, he'd probably advocate for Justice to pick up where they left off...

Now, *there* was a thought he'd never considered.

What would it be like to be with Liberty now?

Present-day Liberty.

Whatever he thought dating her would be like in middle school, now it would probably be completely different, right? What would they even do? What would they even talk about?

For no reason at all, he tried to contemplate it in his mind, but he came up blank. He couldn't envision anything when he thought about being with her now.

Probably because being with her now is the last thing he would ever, *ever* be interested in.

That's just the way Justice was.

Once bitten, twice wise.

"My last question is," Liberty began, after keeping him in suspense for several minutes. "Justice..."

His heart flopped when she said his name.

He couldn't remember the last time he'd heard his name on her lips. Why were first names so intimate? *Yuck.*

"What happened?" She shifted beside him, squeezing herself a bit tighter. "Why did we stop being friends?"

That question made a faraway bell ring in the back of Justice's mind. A memory from middle school.

Him getting home from school. Both of his parents were home, for a change. The divorce had been in progress for weeks. Everyone was tired and heartbroken and stressed.

Hope stayed out of the house as much as she possibly could, and Justice liked to hide in their attic and play video games until everyone went to sleep so he wouldn't have to face either of his parents.

He couldn't forgive his mom for abandoning his dad, and he couldn't forgive his dad for breaking up their whole family over it. Justice and Hope felt like their mom abandoned *them*, too, but they weren't trying to divorce her and find a new mom.

They were just going to put up with her for the rest of their lives, and the least their dad could do was be there to support them through that.

Instead, he was ready to bail.

Instead, Justice's best friend was ready to bail on him, their life, their traditions, everything.

How could Dad do it? Justice still wondered.

That day, he walked in and he knew his parents were fighting because both of their cars were home, yet the whole house was virtually silent.

Ironically, the house was at its quietest when things were bad between them. When they were happy, the house was full of music and laughter.

They were there to greet Justice when he arrived, but that day, he walked in, and all he heard was nothing.

On his way upstairs, he heard them in the study, talking in strained voices, and usually he ignored them when he knew they were fighting.

It only made him scared and angry to see it, but that day, he drifted toward the study and eavesdropped.

The door to the study wasn't closed all the way.

They'd probably left it ajar so that they'd hear when Justice got home and be able to stop fighting in time and pretend like they hadn't been fighting at all.

His parents loved to pretend with him, as though that's what he needed: two profoundly unhappy people to lie to him every single day about how profoundly unhappy they were.

"Just…" It was his mom's voice, even and sincere. "Just tell me where we went wrong," she said. "What happened here?"

"Chelsea, no one gets married to someone so they *don't* get to see them every day."

"You hate that I'm a flight attendant," she concluded.

"No, I hated that you were never home," his dad explained. "Getting on the phone with you and having more than a five-minute conversation was harder than getting into college."

Justice heard his mom sniffle, like she was crying.

It hurt him to hear that, but he was also numb to his parents' pain. They'd put him through so much with this divorce that he found it hard to be compassionate toward either of them.

"And when you were home, all you could think about was leaving again. And you were never happy to see me, and I thought, maybe there's someone else. Any normal person would be suspicious, right? You spend more time away than at home." His father's voice thickened.

Maybe he was about to cry too.

"I'm supposed to believe you were never lonely all those nights in hotels halfway around the world?" He railed on. "Because I was *here*, with our *kids*, and *I* was lonely."

"Of course, I was lonely! Because I missed you, all of you, so much. I love—"

"STOP TRYING TO MANIPULATE ME," Dad fired off. "I know you think it'll work this time. A few tears, some sweet words. Throw me a bone and I'll fall back under your spell? How stupid do you think I am? You're not a wife or a mother. You're a *pen pal!* And not a very good one at that—"

"Justice?" Liberty's voice brought him back to the present moment. There were tears in his eyes, which he swiped at as discreetly as he could. His mouth felt wired shut with all the tension currently constricting his body.

"What was the question?" His words were hard and robotic.

"Why did we stop being friends?" Liberty repeated, much less confident than before.

Justice tried to think about her question. Really, he did. For about ten seconds.

But then he stopped because this question, her last question, was *proof* that she'd been messing with him all along. Nonsensically, Justice started laughing.

It was funny. *Why did we stop being friends?*

As though she didn't know. As though she'd forgotten. As though the answer to 2+2 could be anything other than 4.

"Why are you laughing?" she asked after a minute.

"I'm sorry, you've exhausted the allotted number of questions —" He did a weird thing with his voice when he said that.

He felt weird. He felt tight and loose at the same time. Tense, but a little wild. He didn't know what he might say next.

"Are you going to answer my question?"

"Yes, Liberty, of course. The reason we stopped being friends is because I discovered what a conniving, manipulative, hurtful, thoughtless, homophobic liar you are, and I don't keep people like that for friends."

"Justice, what are you talking about?" He heard her voice wobble. So much for not hurting her feelings.

Oh, well.

Justice suddenly got to his feet, carefully using the wardrobe behind them for support.

"No further questions."

— *6:00 p.m.* —

LIBERTY.

Liberty knew this temporary unspoken truce they'd formed would explode eventually; she'd just been hoping it would happen *after* she got an answer to the question that had been haunting her for several years.

But Justice stood up, and now he was gone.

Not really, but sort of.

He maneuvered his way around the wardrobe into another area of the truck, leaving Liberty there alone with her feelings to stew and stew.

Maybe he wanted to get away from this conversation, but he couldn't get away from *her*.

At least, not without a fight.

Liberty stood, too, and put both hands gently on the wardrobe. She moved slowly around it, following the sounds of Justice cursing as he tripped over things and bumped into others.

"Just talk to me!" she yelled into the void, the way she'd wanted to for such a long time.

"You *wish*," Justice shot back.

"Do you honestly think I'd be asking you about this if I didn't want an honest answer?" Liberty's eyes had adjusted to the dark, but it was only a few notches from pitch black in here, and seeing what was on the floor around her feet was still a challenge.

"Ah, but you're not honestly asking, are you?" Justice said. "You're trying to manipulate me. It's one of your many talents!"

A loud clang was heard as Justice must've slammed into something. She heard him groan in pain. "Ow, fuck."

"Are you okay?" She called.

"Would you just STOP?" He shouted a moment later. He let out a mirthless sound. "If I died, you'd probably throw a party."

"Why do you think that?" She meant to sound powerful, but she just sounded hurt.

Liberty could make out the rack of clothing she climbed through when they first got into the truck. She pushed the clothes apart and carefully ducked through the rack to get to the other side.

"Didn't I just tell you to stop?" Justice's voice was louder and clearer now. She must be closer to where he was.

She couldn't see him for shit.

"*Stop what?*" She snapped.

"PRETENDING LIKE YOU CARE!"

"I DO CARE!"

She did? Had those words really come out of her mouth?

"You must think I'm the *dumbest guy alive—ow!*"

"You're certainly in the running." Liberty cautiously stepped over an unidentified blob in the dark. She could see something moving a few feet away from her, on the other side of a bunch of junk.

That had to be Justice.

(*Please let that be Justice.* Liberty didn't have time for this to turn into a horror movie.)

Liberty maneuvered toward the moving shadow as best she could. The shadow started to look more and more like a boy the closer she got. She shimmied around a stack of boxes maybe? There were about three feet between them now.

"Well, guess what, Liberty Marshall?" Justice was still yelling like she was on the other side of the truck. "Fuck you!"

"I'm right here," she said at a normal volume.

It took Liberty exactly one millisecond to realize she'd made a mistake. Because she'd accidentally, without realizing it at all, snuck up on Justice Garrison.

One does not simply sneak up on Justice Garrison.

Justice is not the type of person who gasps or screams when

he's scared. If you catch Justice by surprise, he spazzes out. He makes a Scooby- Doo noise, flails his arms, jumps back—and one time, when someone surprised him, he punched them in the face, involuntarily.

Like a sneeze.

Liberty had half a second to cover her face before he involuntarily body checked her or something in surprise.

Right on cue, Justice yelped and said something that sounded like, "*Wuhthufudiyuhcowhuno!*"

One of his arms shoved her shoulder, knocking her off balance, but she grabbed his arm to keep from falling, and that seemed to spook him worse, so he tried to back up, but he bumped into something, so he jumped forward, knocking into Liberty, and sending them both sprawling.

This is the end, Liberty thought.

They were surely about to fall into a box of weapons or some-thing, and she was going to be accidentally impaled by a sword and on the news, people would talk about the strange circum-stances under which she'd perished—

They fell into something sooner than she expected, and what they fell into creaked under them...was it a bed?

There was a moment of stunned silence, each of them shocked that they were both alive and unharmed, before it occurred to Liberty that their limbs were partially tangled from the fall.

Justice must've realized this at the same moment, because suddenly they both scrabbled backward, trying to put some distance between them.

"Jesus, Justice... Look. There's nowhere you can run and there's nowhere you can hide, so you might as well just tell me." She could feel that current of courage pumping through her veins. "What did I do to make you hate me so much?"

"I refuse to dignify that question with an answer," he replied, like a pompous *ass.*

Annoyed now, Liberty deftly rocked forward on the bed (or whatever they were now perched on) and, with perfect accuracy, delivered a swift but devastating flick to Justice's forehead.

"Tell me," she pressed.

"OW!" He cried. "Did you just *flick* me?"

She could tell he was angrier than before, but his anger didn't scare her. And what was he realistically going to do?

Without warning, Liberty felt a whopping slap on her right shin. The sound of the slap echoed through the truck. She winced, but she didn't make a sound.

Her shin hurt, but that wasn't the worst of it.

It was how angry and frustrated and childish Justice made her. Was it really so hard for him to answer *one question?*

Instead, he'd forced her to face the fucking obstacle course that was this truck, he'd been insulting her nonstop, and now he clearly just wanted to make her mad.

And it was working.

Liberty hated to admit it, but it was working, and what she was about to do she doubted she'd be proud of.

Adrenaline gushed through her veins, and without another thought, she launched herself at him—the way she had so many times as kids—hooked her arm around his neck, and noogied him into submission.

"Just...tell...me!" she growled, as he swatted at her unsuccessfully. This was so much easier when they were kids, because Justice used to be a scrawny little string bean.

If she'd wanted, Liberty could've picked him up by the ankles and swung him like a bat then. But she'd forgotten, before she launched her present attack, to factor in that Justice was bigger than her now.

He possessed the strength to pick her up and toss her off of him like it was nothing. Liberty hit the bed again and bounced, thank God.

"Trade rules," she tried. "Foul. Technical foul."

"Just because you didn't like the truth doesn't mean I didn't tell it," he defended himself.

"Justice—"

"Liberty, I'm not going to fight you."

"I think you are," she goaded him. "Because if you don't fight me, I'm going to kick your ass, and I don't think you want that on your conscience."

Justice didn't say anything, and Liberty knew that was because he was considering it. Justice hated her, and she was giving him the chance to prove it.

It was an opportunity his pride would never let him pass up, even if he desperately wanted to.

"No blood," he yielded after a moment. "No biting."

"No dislocating, no choking," she added.

Justice scoffed. "No tickling or licking. No wet-willies of any kind."

"Are we doing Boston rules or Chicago?"

"Strictly Chicago, best three out of five." She could tell that he was holding his hand out to her in the dark. "Take it or leave it."

She shook.

"Let the beat down begin." She smiled in the dark.

It'd been too long since she'd wrestled anyone, let alone Justice.

They'd done this all the time as kids.

Liberty used to watch little boys roughhouse and climb trees and fall down and feel so envious. She wanted to do all of those things, but before she had any male friends, she didn't have any opportunities.

Washington had always been too dainty to wrestle, and Justice, even though he was way more of a lover than a fighter, was easily provoked.

Plus, Liberty almost always won, and few things were as

important to Justice as redeeming himself when he felt he'd failed.

Man, she'd fantasized about punching Justice in the face so many times since starting high school, but she never imagined she'd get her wish.

Chicago rules meant a direct blow to the back counted as a win. Three wins and the wrestling match would be over. The object, of course, was to keep Justice away from her back, while coming with a vengeance for his.

Quickly they both moved to their starting positions on either side of the bed.

"On three." Justice cracked his knuckles. "One, two... THREE."

They lunged for each other at the same time, making the bed squeal beneath their weight. Justice yanked her hair to throw her off, but Liberty was undeterred.

She threw both of her arms at his chest and, with the kind of skill that only practice provides, she gave him a purple nurple that would've been worshipped by bullies everywhere.

Justice doubled in pain, exposing his upper back and Liberty smacked his deltoids hard and fast.

"Point," she chirped triumphantly. "Reset." They moved back to their original positions.

"You *cheated,*" Justice accused, malice dripping from his tone. The sound made Liberty smirk.

She shrugged. "Purple nurples are legal unless designated otherwise before the match."

"It's a total double standard! You can grab my chest, but if I grab yours, I'm a lech."

"Hmm, sounds like a personal problem," Liberty mused. "Why don't you take it up with the patriarchy and stop stalling?"

"One... two..." This time when they rushed at each other, their faces collided and they smacked foreheads. Both of them reeled back from the unintentional blow.

"*Fuck,* that hurt. What's your head made of? Titanium?" She touched her already sore forehead and winced.

Justice used their mutual confusion to slap her back.

"Point. Reset," he grumbled. One to one. It was still anyone's game. "Count it off."

Back in their starting positions, Liberty took a moment to remark, "I can't believe that you'd rather wrestle me like a child than just tell me what I did to make you hate me."

"Why, so you can play the victim? And act like none of it ever happened?" Justice countered. "I'm not going to let you gaslight me ever again."

"*Gaslight* you?"

"Count it off," he insisted.

"One," she breathed. "Two... three!" But this time when Liberty threw herself at him, she felt off-kilter. What was he talking about? *Gaslighting him?*

When had she ever done that?

With her mind racing, she forgot to pick a strategy for winning this set. She was unprepared when Justice caught her by the waist and yanked her to him, so that they were chest to chest.

Both of them were standing on their knees, only centimeters separating their faces.

Against her torso, Liberty could actually feel his heart beating. *Racing* was more like it.

Her nose could sense the presence of his nose so near hers, even though their noses weren't touching.

It felt like her heart had stopped beating altogether.

Every inch of her skin suddenly felt alive to the surprise of this moment. Her mind was completely blank except for one impossible question: *Was Justice Garrison about to kiss her?*

If so, WHY?

If not, why was he holding her like this?

Why was she letting him?

If he kissed her, then what? Did Liberty...want him to?

This moment was too confusing to make sense of.

Justice removed one of his hands from her waist and very gently touched the back of her neck, which Liberty felt all the way in her toes.

She couldn't breathe. She couldn't think. She couldn't reason. She couldn't even move.

And then, with that same hand, Justice gave her back one big, good pat square between her shoulders. The force of it pushed them even closer together.

She couldn't even tell if her own eyes were open, it was so dark. She definitely couldn't tell if any of this was real or not.

"Set point," Justice murmured, confusing her further. "Doesn't feel so good when someone plays with your emotions. Does it?"

The hand still left on her waist suddenly shoved and she fell back toward her starting position. It took her a moment to realize what he'd done.

He'd feigned like he was going to kiss her, for the purpose of winning the set.

No, for the purpose of making a point, but what point was he trying to make? Was he trying to tell her that *she'd* played with his emotions once and hurt him?

Liberty couldn't make any sense of it, and her brain was still half dead from the almost-kiss.

She again felt gratitude toward the darkness.

Thank God Justice hadn't been able to see her face.

Who knows what she must have looked like, kneeling in front of him, waiting to be kissed, like a sitting duck waiting to be shot?

What an idiot.

She'd momentarily forgotten how to speak. She sure as hell didn't remember how to count.

It was like her brain had just restarted itself, and right now it was buffering. But before either of them could say or do anymore, the truck dipped into a turn, throwing them both off balance.

Justice, still standing on his knees, didn't have time to catch himself. He fell right over and off the bed onto the floor. The sound of him hitting the ground was followed by Justice crying out in pain.

The sound made Liberty's heart go sideways.

The sound of him hurt made Liberty's fury, stress, and confusion crumble away, like loose rocks off a cliff.

"Justice? Are you okay?" She scrambled off the bed after him, trying to understand how he'd fallen and help him up at the same time.

She was annoyed at how easy it was to fall into caring about him. Making sure he was all right was the decent human thing to do, but it very stupidly resonated with the part of herself she'd stuffed into a box and left buried under stacks of old records in her bedroom closet.

"Hey," she said, when he didn't respond. "*Justice.*"

"I'm fine," He muttered. "I think I...cut my chin."

She heard him suck his teeth in pain. She found his arm and started to help him to his feet.

He didn't bother resisting.

Liberty could see now that they were right next to the box truck's door.

They'd made it to the far side of the enclosure.

Liberty couldn't see Justice or the cut in question, but that urge to help him was clear and strong.

Finally, amazingly, the truck slowed, easing to a stop.

The truck shuddered and went still as the driver cut the engine. And if they heard Justice and Liberty banging on the walls in here, they'd be bound to open the back and check it out, right?

They were saved!

But before any saving took place, abruptly, Justice wretched.

The unmistakable sound of unleashed vomit followed, and Liberty, suddenly, *horribly,* felt wet in multiple places. Almost in sync, the truck door slid open, clucking and creaking as it went up above their heads.

After hours of near pitch black, the afternoon light blinded them like they'd just emerged from a cave.

Liberty was closer to Justice than she realized. He did have a cut on his chin.

And there was barf all over him and all over her.

And outside, staring at them with frozen, baffled, open-mouthed faces, was the crew of the What You Will Shakespeare Company.

Justice and Liberty had clearly arrived, but where?

SCENE V.

— 6:45 p.m. —

JUSTICE.

Puking always took something out of Justice.

(Besides the obvious.)

It immediately exhausted him.

He let the sun warm his stinging face as he awaited the return of Jack Elby, the leader of the What You Will people, who'd taken up the quest of finding Justice a Band-Aid, a cup of tepid water, and a toothbrush kit. *Bless him.*

While he waited, Justice watched the other crew members unload the truck. They had a system going where some of the crew would heft things out of the truck and other crew members would move the items toward a dirt path up ahead.

Justice didn't know where it led, but it seemed important.

His view was suddenly obscured by a round person, and when Justice saw that it was Jack, he gave the man a better look. He actually resembled Benjamin Franklin.

It was a little scary, honestly. Like talking to a picture in an elementary school textbook. The age range of the cast and crew appeared to be thirty on up to *old*.

And Jack Elby was clearly the *oldest*.

"It appears that you and your classmate stowed away," he observed, after Justice had gargled the water and tried to spit it out without being too disgusting.

"It was an accident." Justice shook his head, in kind of a daze. He could hardly believe it himself.

One minute he and Liberty were wrestling. The next he was teaching her a lesson, the next he'd fallen and gotten hurt, the next he'd puked up all his vital organs, and now he was here, *outside*, in the light day, something he hadn't been sure he'd ever again see.

The whole thing felt more like they'd stumbled into an alternate dimension, and now that they'd stumbled out, Justice felt lost.

"So we gather," Jack agreed. "I can tell you that there's no standard procedure for this particular situation. We've contacted your school to let them know what happened. Keeping communication lines open and whatnot."

Did he just use *whatnot* in a sentence?

"Since this event technically took place after school hours, your school thought it would be best to let your parents handle pickup." Jack cleared his throat. "On another occasion, one of us would take you both back, but we're due to perform at nine, so we can't leave."

"Nine?" Justice looked at the sky. The sun was clearly on its way down, but it didn't seem low enough in the sky for it to be anywhere near nine o'clock. "What time is it now?"

Jack checked his watch. "Quarter to seven." Justice almost did a spit-take with his water.

Was Jack Elby trying to tell him that he and Liberty had been trapped in that box truck for over *three hours?*

He couldn't wrap his brain around that at all.

"That's soon," Justice finally said, noticing the parking lot again. Did all the trucks and trailers out here belong to other performers, too?

"Indeed." Jack cracked a Coke can open and slurped back a few swallows of soda.

"Where are you all set to perform?"

"At the Rhode Island Shakespeare Festival," Jack answered.

Justice lifted his eyebrows. "Oh. Wow. Yeah, okay."

"I lent my cell phone to your friend—"

"She's not my friend, but please continue."

"—so that she should call her parents. I suggest you do the same. And after that, I think we should get you a change of clothes. I assume it may be a while before someone comes to get you."

"Why's that?" Justice had missed something.

He wasn't sure what.

"Rhode Island is a three-hour trip from Green River."

"But we're not in Rhode Island," he pointed out. "We're…"

Slowly, Justice realized that he'd been accidentally kidnapped to Rhode Island and that all hope of this wacky adventure ending imminently, let alone his asking Magdalena out today, should be abandoned.

"Oh, for fuck's sake." Justice set his cup down and stood. He needed to go for a walk, maybe blow off some steam, kick something and pretend it was Liberty.

But standing up reminded him that his shirt was covered in dried puke.

Yuck.

Justice didn't think twice about carefully pulling his t-shirt up and over his head. He spotted a nearby trash can, balled his shirt up, and shot it like a goddamn all-star.

Justice for the three. The shirt went in. *It's good.*

When he turned back toward Jack, he froze.

Behind Jack's head, Liberty was passing by and when she saw Justice, she froze, too. But she wasn't looking at Justice's face. She was looking at his body.

Was she? She was. *Well, why wouldn't she be?*

Justice went back and forth with himself about whether Liberty was checking him out. He waited until she finally met his eyes before looking away.

Yeah, she was definitely *checking me out,* he decided. What's more, he liked it, but that wasn't the point.

"What was that you were saying about a change of clothes?" Justice refocused on the catastrophe at hand.

Jack stood, too. "This way."

— 6:50 p.m. —

LIBERTY.

With Jack Elby's cell phone in hand, Liberty paced in the grass. Standing in the prop truck's shadow, the air felt cooler.

She paced partially because she didn't know what to do and partially because her thin sweater did nothing to protect against the crisp April breeze.

She kept at it until she paced right into someone.

"I'm sorry," she and the someone said at the same time, backing apart.

Justice threw up on her, but Liberty didn't feel like crying about it until she bumped into someone and got dots of puke on *them.* Could this day get any more horrendous? Could today possibly make her feel worse than she already did?

The someone was one of the actors.

A thirty-something named Ashley Baker, who played Beatrice in *Much Ado.* Liberty knew this from anxiously flipping through the program while panicked and bored earlier at the play.

"You're…" she murmured, momentarily distracted by how lovely Ashley was up close. Ashley looked at her now puke-a-dotted jeans and tried to dim the horror on her face.

Guilt rocked through Liberty.

Ashley said, "Hi there. You must be one of the stowaway kids. Jack asked me to come over here to see if you needed any help."

"I'm sorry about your…" Liberty choked on the words.

That's when she realized she was crying, bitter, frustrated tears. "I need to call my mom," she explained. "But this morning, we… and Magdalena put her tongue in that guy's face and then…then… Justice puked on my favorite pair of Docs," she blubbered through.

Her anxiety was back up and threatening to overwhelm her. The gravity of their situation this afternoon was catching up with her. This was *serious*.

"Why don't we start with introductions?" Ashley patted her shoulders reassuringly. "What's your name?"

Later, when they were seated beside the prop truck, legs outstretched, Ashley admitted, "I don't get it."

Liberty was busy admiring the picture of their shoes side by side, Ashley's Barbie-pink converse and her own rainbow Docs. (She'd kicked most of the puke off them. Still, their former glory had not been restored.)

"Don't get what?"

"Why you're so nervous to call your mom?"

It would probably be faster to list all the reasons she *wasn't* nervous than to list all the reasons she was, but she wanted to tell Ashley something…

"My grandpa was hospitalized this morning, and also, my mom and I…" Liberty clenched her teeth to keep the reflux of this morning's anger down. "We got into a fight."

"A fight?"

Liberty let out a colossal sigh. "You know how some families have traditions? Mine doesn't. The closest thing to a tradition we've got is that we go out to Cape Cod every May, just me and Mom. And this morning, she told me she decided to postpone our trip. Without even asking me about it."

Ashley nodded. "Did something important come up?"

"*NO.*" Liberty's morning anger was back. "She decided to postpone it because my grandad wants to buy...*a boat.*"

"You mean...the currently hospitalized guy?"

"*Yep.*"

"What does a ninety-five-year-old man need with a boat?" Ashley asked.

Liberty threw her hands in the air. "He and my uncles want to go fishing this summer?"

"And they need to *buy* a boat? Why can't they *rent* a boat?"

"*Thank you,*" Liberty agreed, grateful to be understood perfectly for the first time all day.

"My mom doesn't even *like* fishing. The only reason my grandpa asked her to come with him is so there'll be someone there to wait on him hand and foot."

"What about your uncles?"

"*Your uncles aren't good at the messy stuff,*" Liberty mimicked her mother's voice. "That's what she told me."

Liberty let her anger simmer down as the wind picked up.

"My mom is always working crazy hours at the hospital, helping strangers left and right. Caretaking is what she does *professionally.* She shouldn't have to be a caretaker in her personal life. And especially if that means missing out on the one semi-tradition our family has..."

Liberty hated the way she felt and sounded so petty.

"I think she might be scared of losing time with Grandpa, but honestly she's missing out on time with *me.* One more year and I'm gone forever and she's just...throwing away memories we could be making, all so that she can be my grandpa's handmaiden."

Liberty blew out a breath, and ranted on. "I mean, the guy is almost a hundred. She's had forty-eight years with him. She's barely had seventeen with me. You'd think that our relationship might take priority."

Ashley smiled in a way that made it clear she didn't agree with Liberty, but still understood where Liberty was coming from. "Something tells me you might vibe with King Lear."

"Huh?"

"Never mind. I absolutely get that you had a fight, but your mom just got a call from your school saying that you accidentally stowed away to another state. She'll want to hear your voice," Ashley insisted. "She'll want to know you're all right."

Liberty nodded, this morning's anger and this afternoon's shame still hot beneath her skin.

"Give her a call," Ashley said. "When you're done, follow the signs to the guest service center." She pointed to a few signs beside the dirt path up ahead. "We'll see what we can do about getting you a change of clothes."

"Thank you so much." Her gratitude was immense. "Oh, wait!" Liberty remembered to ask, "What...town are we in?"

"Liberty."

"Yes?"

Ashley shook her head. "No, the town. We're in Liberty, Rhode Island."

ACT III.

SCENE I.

— 7:00 p.m. —

JUSTICE.

Justice accompanied Jack Elby down a well-beaten yet unruly path, following signs for a "guest services center." Justice eyed the woods as they walked.

Even for a Western-Massachusettsan, this felt remote.

Thankfully, the place turned out to be a squat circular building, clearly populated with droves of people.

Inside the center was what could only be described as a makeshift backstage area. Vendors and performers were scattered around the room, rehearsing scenes and fidgeting with dingy but freshly pressed costumes.

The room smelled like his grandparents' hall closet.

When finished primping or playacting, the performers exited a door to Justice's right. A sign just outside read "To the Faire Grounds," with a red arrow painted beneath.

Watching everyone—dressed in their Elizabethan wear— somehow eased the trepidation within Justice. Which was an unusual reaction for him, given that all these people were pretending to be medieval Europeans.

Honestly, he might have felt more threatened by this situation, if everyone around him didn't look so stupid.

Hope had forced him to watch *Shakespeare in Love* with her at least ten times over the years of their unfortunate siblinghood, and usually, movies set in medieval Europe always made Justice feel strange.

There were never any brown people in them. He always wondered where black people were in those times. Then he remembered the way his peers glanced at him when they learned about slavery in school, and then he promptly imagined the worst.

This entire operation was clearly a Renaissance fair type of deal, and just like the movies, there wasn't a single person around who looked like him.

Except Liberty.

For one second, he felt comforted that she was stuck in this weird adventure with him, but then he remembered the hatred in her eyes as she'd uttered the words that devastated their friendship, the ones that made them the enemies they are today.

And then he remembered how it'd felt to hold her close in the dark, the uncomfortable heat.

Then, her eyes on his body. Comfort over.

"This way!" Jack gave a shout.

This Elby guy led Justice toward a part of the room where echeloned clothing racks stood, each one belonging to a different theater group. The racks were occupied by the kind of dark protective clothing bags that often reminded Justice of body bags.

If dead bodies didn't smell, it would be an excellent way to hide one in plain sight, Liberty had once told him while they sat sketching and scripting their middle school comics.

She had such a morbid brain.

One day she's going to direct horror movies or trippy punk rock music videos, Justice always thought.

Jack grabbed the fattest of the non-body bags. It was thickly stuffed and when he unzipped it, two smaller bags were slumped inside. He retrieved one and slung it into Justice's unprepared arms.

"Come along," he said, moving again, this time toward a longer part of the room with curtained stalls erected in two straight lines. Full-length mirrors were stationed nearby, along all the walls in this place, like a fun house.

At the stalls, actors glided in and out of curtains putting things on, looking in the mirrors, and pulling things off. Flashes of undergarments made Justice drop his gaze to the bag in hand and follow Jack blindly. He bumped right into the man, for lack of watching his step.

"Go on then, lad." Jack motioned toward a larger stall than the others.

"What?" Justice bleated, mind going blank.

"When you pull everything out, it's important that you put things on in the right order. First, the stockings. Then undershirt, trousers, doublet, belt, shoes last," he ran through the instructions quicker than Justice caught on. "When you come out, check in with Ashley Baker."

Jack settled a reassuring hand on Justice's shoulder and then rejoined the throngs of theatrical chaos.

"And he's gone. Okay." Optionless and in need of a moment to himself, Justice ducked into the stall, hung the bag, and tied the curtain closed as well as he could.

He didn't want to be flashed almost as much as he didn't want to flash anyone, contrary to popular (and necessitated-by-puke) belief.

It was quieter in here, and Justice had a moment to think.

The mirror in the stall reflected him, and when he looked into his own eyes, he dropped into Motivation Mode.

That was the mindset he needed right now.

Motivation Mode helped him win soccer matches, convince his parents to buy him skate stuff, and ask people out.

"Okay," he told himself. "So Liberty got us kidnapped and now we're at the...Medieval Madness festival or whatever. But that's fine. Justice, you can handle this."

He braced himself against the mirror, looking deeper into his eyes. "You. Can. Do. This. Mom's out of town. Dad and Robin are in Boston. Call Hope. She'll come get you. Will she ever let you live this down? Of course not, but that's okay. All you have to do is survive a few hours at a fair."

He sucked in a breath. "It will be over before you know it, but first, you've got to get changed. Okay."

Justice grabbed the clothing bag, unzipped it, and took stock.

A strange long, thin blue scarf. Puff pastry shorts. An intricately threaded enormous jacket thing (also in blue). A billowy-sleeved cotton shirt. A thick leather belt. And men's Elizabethan Jesus sandals.

Justice grabbed the billowing shirt first. He held it up to himself in the mirror. "What...is this supposed to be a man blouse?" Next, Justice examined the weird scarf, only to discover it wasn't a scarf at all.

It was a pair of tights.

Blue tights.

Many minutes later, Justice still hadn't made any progress in the pursuit of changing clothes. And the stress was getting to him. Justice had been reduced to shit-talking, backed up with absurd excuses.

Justice faced the Shakespearean ensemble he was supposed to wear, attempting to psych himself up. It was Motivation Mode against the Mortification of Wearing Blue Tights. Mortification was winning.

"I can put you on," he threatened the outfit. "You think I can't put you on? I totally can. It's just that these are my favorite pair of...puke pants and..." He faltered in defeat. "I am talking to literal clothes on a hanger."

After another good, long pep talk, he'd made a modicum of progress. In his hands were the blue tights. What was formerly on the hanger was now in his grasp (which was a win), but he honestly had no clue where to go from here.

He knew that the tights went on his legs and that they were stretchy. They had to be. Otherwise, they'd only fit someone like an unnaturally twiggy fourth grader.

He lowered them to his feet, gave up, and then tried to get himself together.

Again.

LIBERTY.

Hi, Mom. I know you probably received a troubling phone call from school saying I'd been accidentally smuggled. Just calling to say that it's true and if you wouldn't mind coming to pick me up, that would be excellent.

Even in her head, that sounded really shit.

For fifteen minutes, Liberty had been laboring over what to say when Mom picked her up.

It shouldn't be this complicated.

Ashley Baker was right. Her mom was probably beyond panicked. She'd probably already spent her day worrying about Grandpa, and now she'd be extra panicked because of Liberty. She probably did want to speak to Liberty and make sure everything was all right.

But why couldn't Liberty make herself believe that?

Maybe because Mom chose a *boat* over their ten-year tradition that morning?

Maybe because Mom was a nurse and the needs of the sick almost always came above Liberty's?

Trying to shove the useless thoughts from her mind, Liberty glanced down at the phone in her hand only to realize she'd accidentally hit the call button already.

The call was in the process of connecting.

Shit, shit, shit. She didn't know what to say, and whenever Liberty was truly unprepared, she started to cry.

She started to hang up, but decided to be strong and hold the phone to her ear instead. The call connected.

"Mom?" Her voice quivered. Goddammit. Mom's worried voice trickled into her ears.

"Hi. You've reached Jeanine Marshall, head nurse at Bellgrave Memorial Hospital. If you're a patient and this is a medical emergency, please dial 911 for assistance. If this is a work-related communication, please relay it to Fiona Cartwright, extension 2247. I'm currently dealing with a family emergency. Leave a message and I'll get back to you as soon as I can."

Mom, this is Liberty.

Accidentally left my phone at school, I'm using someone else's. I'm checking in.

SHE SENT THAT LAST TEXT AFTER TYPING AND DELETING AND TYPING AND deleting. Liberty had never imagined what her mom would do if Liberty were accidentally smuggled, but she didn't expect this.

She didn't expect her to not answer her phone.

Even after four missed calls from the same number she was now texting from.

Liberty was trying not to panic.

She knew there was a logical reason her mom wasn't answering, but every scenario she came up with only made her more anxious.

What if her phone was dead?

What if something really terrible happened with Grandpa and she was busy running around because of that?

Even if all those scenarios were true, someone had reached out by now to tell her what happened to Liberty today and she should be worried—

Hey! Is everything all right?

Came the first text.

Relief oozed through Liberty. The truthful answer was *fuck no,* but her mom finally fucking responded. Things were looking up.

Everything is fine.

Liberty started to text, *We're okay,* when another message popped through first.

Your grandad agreed to go through with emergency surgery. The doctors are going to operate overnight.

Shit. *I knew it,* Liberty thought. Something was really wrong with Grandpa. *Shit.*

Surgery? Is he going to be okay?

Three thinking dots, and then:

Everyone's coming to the hospital. In
case…this might be the last time.

Liberty didn't know how to respond to that.

Of all days for her to be three hours from home accidentally…

When are you coming to get me? Liberty started to type this time, but stopped when another message came through.

I figured you were probably busy
recording the next episode of your show.

Grab some dinner and come straight here
when you're done, okay?

Liberty's heart plummeted.

Her mom thought she'd walked home from school and been holed up

in the basement, as she usually was, working on *Liberty for All.*

Her mom had no idea where she was. Or what happened. She didn't know. She wasn't worried. She didn't…

Liberty looked hard at the borrowed cell phone in her hand. She wanted to throw it like a football, but alas, it wasn't hers. And throwing it wouldn't help.

Finally, Liberty texted back.

OK

SCENE II.

— 7:20 p.m. —

LIBERTY.

Liberty *thought* she was headed in the right direction, but she wasn't sure. The path from the parking lot to the guest services center seemed a little too isolated to be a viable route, didn't it?

It was a footpath surrounded by (and really overrun with) trees and shrubs. She didn't see any buildings up ahead through the tree trunks. And the light was beginning to wane, the sun on the far side of the sky, careening toward the horizon like a slow, slow comet.

Okay, she was lost.

She would just turn around and try again.

Suddenly, a pack of Elizabethan-costumed men appeared through the trees. Behind them was a pound-cake-colored rotunda, so brown on the outside it almost completely blended into the woods.

Liberty's risk radar started to beep, and then the men, seeing her, abruptly stopped, stuck a stockinged leg out and bowed, unfurling an arm over their outstretched legs.

"My lady," they chorused.

Horrified and afraid, Liberty hastened past them without reply. Why did she get the feeling this was about to get so much worse?

Liberty pulled the guest services center doors open, eager to be out of the woods. She then realized that the woods were the only place she might be safe from the carnival of things happening inside this squat little building cake.

"Please," she whispered to any listening benevolent gods. Jesters danced before her. Jugglers juggled. "Please no." Women with intricately braided hair warmed up with a pitch pipe, harmonizing. "No, no, no." Actors rehearsing scenes, rodomontading in ridiculous accents. "No, *no*—"

"You made it," Ashley said as she came into view, a congratulatory smile on her face. Like this was a surprise party made just for Liberty's torture.

"Y-Yeah," she faked a smile.

"Come on," Ashley said. "I found you a change of clothes."

Beside a small fleet of clothing racks, Liberty watched the room. Every bit of disdain she felt for theater bubbled to the surface of her mind, like oil in a water pot.

Anything that involved singing, dancing, pretending to be other people, and/or being stuck in a dark, cavernous space with hundreds of seated people for the purpose of mass enjoyment was Liberty's idea of a bad time.

Ashley must have been in the middle of helping the What You Will people with something, Liberty concluded, as she continued to rifle through the clothing bags.

Liberty briefly considered climbing into a big one while no one was watching. Everyone would leave her alone then, wouldn't they? Upside: Solitude. Downside: She might get accidentally smuggled. For the second time today.

"Hold this," Ashley suggested, swinging a giant dress bag into Liberty's arms.

Oh, great. Now I'm a theater minion, Liberty groaned internally. Not knowing what else to do, Liberty followed Ashley on her errand to a backroom with a handicap symbol on it. Ashley held the door open for Liberty as she maneuvered inside.

The little room almost completely drowned out the noise from the rest of the center.

Liberty finally felt like she could breathe.

"Where should I put this?" She glanced at Ashley, who looked like she was waiting for something to happen.

"Anywhere's fine. Here, let me help you." Together they got the giant dress bag situated on a nearby hook.

"What's in that thing?" Liberty muttered.

Ashley's eyes twinkled, as she flashed Liberty an eager smile. She unzipped it. A portion of a gargantuan blue dress that was quite possibly large enough to pitch like a tent flopped out.

"It's...pretty," Liberty decided. Grotesque, but still sort of lovely. Maybe. A little.

"Isn't it?" Ashley agreed. Then she repeated, "Come on, I'll help you."

"Help me what?"

"Change," she said.

Liberty's eyebrows scrunched together. "Change what?"

"Into this dress."

Liberty about shit a chicken. "There's no way I'm putting that on. I cannot." She didn't know how to make herself any clearer. "*I will not wear that dress.*"

"It's the only extra costume we have," Ashley informed her.

"I can't wear a costume," Liberty insisted.

"Why not?"

"Because I hate them. I hate acting. I hate anything that can be considered socially acceptable lying." Liberty vomited the words out by accident.

She didn't want to spit all over Ashley's kindness, but no.

Ashley dropped her hands to her waist. "It's this or vomit chic for the next three hours."

Liberty was distraught, considering the validity of Ashley's argument. "Um, but...Doesn't Shakespeare write plays about men?" She stalled.

"Yeah. Why?"

"Isn't there, like, a man costume somewhere around here? Something with *pants*?" A.k.a. something she could pare down into, like, bad pajamas, instead of full Juliet.

"Yes, but we gave it to your friend," Ashley admitted.

"He's not my friend."

"Liberty, I'd love to debate this with you, but we've got a show to do in little more than an hour and I still need to run lines, put on my makeup, and do my hair. We only have two spare costumes."

Ashley shrugged, gesturing toward the dress. "We assumed you'd prefer *this* to any of our street clothes—all of which are sweaty and gross on account of our having been on the road for the past three hours."

Her tone was kind, but her meaning was sharp.

Liberty needed to make up her mind and make it up now.

The show must go on, or whatever these people say.

"It's not forever, Liberty. Just for one evening. Maybe it looks like a lot, but Elizabethan dresses are actually quite comfortable."

Liberty barked a laugh.

"See?" A smile lifted Ashley's face. "I knew you had a sense of humor. You're going to need one to get through this."

Thirty minutes later, Liberty was in the thing.

Waist cinched. Boobs smushed, and up way too high.

What if this dress popped her boobs altogether and they never reinflated?

Seeing herself in this getup was like a car crash, Liberty thought. So awful that she couldn't look away.

"I can't breathe."

Ashley patted Liberty's waist, which had begun to go numb beneath this corseted bodice. "That'll wear off."

JUSTICE.

Later, someone knocked on the wood frame outside Justice's stall, making the whole contraption shudder.

"You doing all right in there?" came an ebullient voice.

Justice was mostly dressed. The blue tights were on, making him feel cold and hot at the same time.

This was definitely not a moment when he wanted to chat with anyone. "...huh?" He called, not even sure that whoever it was out there meant him.

"It's Justice, isn't it?" came the voice. "Jack told me you were in here. I'm Ashley Baker!"

Go the fuck away, Ashley.

"Uh, hi!" he tossed the greeting to her.

Who introduces themself while someone is *changing?*

"Do you need any help with the doublet?" she inquired.

"I got it." He assumed she meant the giant puffed jacket. How hard could it be to get on?

Definitely no harder than the *tights.*

(Fourth time was the charm.)

"Okay. Holler if you need anything. I'm right over here," she said, thankfully done badgering him.

Justice had gotten the puff pastry pants on. Now, for the man blouse.

Skateboard Gods of the Universe, give me strength.

— *7:30 p.m.* —

LIBERTY.

Liberty ventured out from the dressing room and hated every second of it. She was wearing the same sort of clothes as everyone else here, but she still felt...not out of her depths. More like on another planet, with no ride home. She found a pair of mirrors in an unoccupied corner and staked a claim.

"You all set?" Ashley asked her.

"I look like a princess, and I hate it."

The full skirt hung to her toes, a heavy blue fabric with threads of gold and brown woven through it, that actually *glistened* when they caught the evening light coming through the casement windows.

A poofy white shirt fit under a matching blue corseted vest. The vest was responsible for the boob-propping, but hopefully not *popping*.

(It had been hard enough to get the boobs she currently had. Replacement boobs were likely out of the question.)

"I look like a lost brown extra in *The Princess Bride,*" she told no one in particular.

Ashley continued talking to her, but Liberty wasn't listening. Her mind slid away to the half-lit classroom, Magdalena's thighs stacked over Adam's. His greedy hands around her waist. Her arms folded around his neck.

If they'd made out any harder, their bodies would have fused together, like conjoined lovers.

Liberty swallowed audibly loud.

Thinking about them kissing made her think about her and Justice in the dark.

Had he really pretended like he was going to kiss her just to make a point? And either way, *why* had touched her so... gently? So kindly? It was so intimate, even in her memory, that her face felt hot. *What the fuck.*

Before Liberty could ruminate further, a woman with a headset dressed in all-black street clothes bustled into the guest services center, came to a stop right next to Liberty, and yelled at the top of her lungs.

"*MUCH ADO*, CURTAIN IN NINETY MINUTES!"

Various members of the What You Will Shakespeare Company, scattered around the room, lifted their heads and shouted back, "Heard!"

"Thanks, Missy," Ashley told her.

Then she returned her gaze to Liberty's.

"We go on in about an hour, so while the show's happening, you'll be on your own at the fair. Keep Jack's cell phone with you so that we can reach you and you can stay in communication with your families. The performance should be done by the time they arrive."

Liberty nodded and then noticed, a few feet away, Justice exiting a nearby dressing stall.

The swampy, underwater intro of *Come as You Are* gushed through her mind. Justice walked up to them, dressed like Romeo in an outfit that matched the scheme and design of her own.

In her mind, with that apathetic frown on his face and that uncaring posture lining his limbs, he looked like a steampunk, Shakespearean hero— an aesthetic she found appealing, despite the fact that Justice made her skin crawl most of the time.

And Liberty was forced to recall that...the truth was he hadn't, always. Seeing him shirtless earlier had been an adventure all its own.

She felt like she'd been on a thirty-second roller coaster; her stomach dropped, her heart raced, she saw her life flash before her eyes, the whole enchilada.

The truth was awful and she hated it so much, but where

Washington went through an ungraceful transition from tweendom to teenagerhood, Justice's transformation could only be described as a glow-up.

If Liberty didn't know him at all, if she'd never met him before today, and she'd seen him for the first time, she would've thought he was...hot, probably.

Not that it mattered. At all.

She jumped as Ashley broke her concentration. "You two look *adorable.* By the way, when your families get here, you should invite them to stay. After the show's done, there's going to be a Midnight Masque, which will be *tons* of fun."

"Tons, really," Liberty muttered, as Ashley disappeared to finish getting ready.

"*Hey,*" Justice said, recapturing her focus.

"Yes, hello," she replied, brushing down the fabric of her skirt, like the unfortunate reality of Justice being hot was stuck on *it* and not her mind.

"You planning to keep the phone for the rest of the year or...?" Liberty's head snapped up.

That's when she realized they were on their own again. Ashley was gone. They were free to do whatever now, she supposed. "What?"

Justice grabbed the phone from Liberty.

She didn't blame him. She was clearly incoherent. Worse, in fact, after the skin of his hand brushed the skin of hers.

"Right. Sorry," she said.

It was weird seeing him now in the light, after spending three hours with him in the dark.

It was almost like nothing that happened inside the box truck was real. It wasn't like she had any proof that anything that happened actually did happen.

If Justice denied it, it was her word against his, and history had taught her that his word mattered more.

Justice proceeded to wipe the phone on his doublet as though she had cooties. She felt the impulse to roll her eyes, but all her eyes wanted to do was appraise him.

His calves looked like royal blue baseball bats, stretching out of puffy knee-length fancy-man shorts. The shorts matched the giant doublet thing.

The blue and brown color combo really complimented him, Liberty thought. Justice noticed her staring and made an unpleasant face. He turned and exited through a different set of doors than the ones they'd entered.

She watched him go.

It was for the best. She was in the middle of a psychological breakdown.

Liberty should have told her mom the truth.

With the rush of nostalgia making her nauseous, the only place Liberty should've been was on her way to a hospital, with or without her sick grandpa. Liberty inhaled the grungy, spiced theater people smell and exhaled the panic.

You're just not used to having him around, her mind rationalized. She and Justice hadn't spent this much time together in three years.

Her body and thoughts were just readjusting.

Liberty feared it was actually the opposite, that after three years, she was still used to having Justice around, and the fact that he was here now only alerted her of the fact that he hadn't been, how much that hurt, and how much she'd missed—*Shut up!* She barked internally.

"He got you *kidnapped,*" she muttered aloud. "Liberty Bell Marshall, pull yourself together."

At least here, with all the theater people, if she talked to herself, no one would think that was odd.

Suddenly, a problem caught her attention.

"Wait, the phone." Liberty began to pace again. "Didn't tell

Mom the truth. Need to tell Mom the truth." Another thought came. "Or..."

She turned to the closest mirror and watched her face.

"Um...hey, Justice. Remember me?" She gave herself a dry, weirdo smile. "We got kidnapped together. I was, um... thinking that since we live on the same street in the same town in the same state that maybe I could catch a ride home with you?"

She glimpsed her oddly intense hopeful face and let a wave of embarrassment crash over her.

"Yeah. That was *crap*."

She shook out her hands. God, can you believe it? Liberty was actually *rehearsing* something.

She tried again: "Look, asshat...since you tripped me and fainted and got us both into this mess, the least you can do is give me a ride home."

She slapped her hands over her face. "Liberty, you are in so much trouble."

SCENE III.

JUSTICE.

Justice found a picnic table on the road to the fairgrounds. He'd dialed Hope, told her the deal, and listened irritably as she'd cackled at him for the past ten minutes.

"Are you—" he started, only to have his words smothered by her guffaws. "*Are you done?*"

He wanted to reach through the phone and pinch his sister's lips closed, the way she used to whenever Justice couldn't keep a secret.

"Sounds like you got wrecked," Hope sighed. He could almost hear her wiping a tear from her eye. More triumphantly, she said, "And you need my help."

Justice sucked in a submissive breath, preparing himself to confirm the (unfortunate) obvious.

"That is...technically correct, yes."

"Can't they get you to a bus station in Providence or something?" She asked, clearly milking this moment for all it was worth.

"No." A trio of dudes playing lutes and lyres wandered past Justice. He gave them a look. "They're scheduled to perform here pretty soon. Plus, I don't even know where in the state we are. Providence could be six hours from here."

"You do know that Rhode Island and your brain are the same size, right?"

"Look." Justice blew a breath out. "Can you come get me or not? If you don't come, I'll be stuck here all night and they're going to force me to go to this Midnight Masque thing. It's like a princess ball or some shit—"

"Why can't you catch a ride home with Liberty?"

"Gimme a sec, Hope. Let me just find something tall to jump off of."

"Tell me the use of me *and* her mom driving three hours each way if we're headed back to the exact same place."

"*Hope.*" He sucked in a breath, feeling the words that would save him come to his lips. "I'm...begging you." He could almost hear her smirking.

"Never fear, baby brother. Dad called and told me about your little predicament about half an hour ago. As soon as I finish getting my nails done, I'll be on my way to get you. I should be there by eleven-ish."

"ELEVEN?" A volcano of annoyance erupted inside him. "You mean I'm going to be stranded in Shakespeare land for *four fucking hours?*" Another thought hit him. "And why the fuck did you make me explain if Dad already—"

"Just wanted to hear you beg," she chirped. Justice held the phone away from him, wishing to God he could punch his sister across space and time. "Try not to get yourself kidnapped again until I get there," she added before the line went dead.

Three literal seconds passed and then... "Hey," a voice said.

Out of nowhere, Liberty was beside him like a jump scare in a horror movie. Justice flinched right off the picnic table, flapping his arms for balance.

He regained his composure and put a few feet of distance between them. There was no telling what she could be hiding under that giant dress.

Maybe another knife to put in his back.

"*What?*" he asked.

Liberty tucked her head into her right shoulder, looking away from him. That was her tell.

That was Liberty Body Language for *there's something I need to say, but I don't want to say it.*

Justice rolled his eyes, exasperation flooding his system. Liberty was like a book he knew too well. He hated that even though they'd been as good as strangers *for years*, he still recognized her. He still felt like he knew her. Like it was just last week that they were gaming in his attic.

"What is it?" He pressed her, knowing she was trying to say something, and wishing she'd get it over with so that he could get away from her.

Her bottom lip fell, but no words followed.

Another memory bowled into him, hard and strong. They were standing together just like this. Eighth grade.

His soccer team had just pulverized South Lake. Sweat clung to their open faces. He and his teammates cheered and jumped and hoisted each other in the air, but Justice pulled away from them when he saw Liberty coming his way.

Liberty made the same face then that she made right now, trying to tell him something, stalling. He remembered tilting his face toward hers—

"Someone kill me."

"Justice?" she said.

"Bye." He turned from her and jogged onto the path leading

toward the fair. He needed to put some time, distance, and people between them. And *fast.*

— *7:40 p.m.* —

LIBERTY.

Well, great. *Wonderful.*

She scared him off. She knew she should have rehearsed her opening a few more times before just...frickin' sneaking up on him. Again.

What now? It's not like she could chase him. Not in this monstrosity.

Not to mention, Justice's legs were built for running. Liberty's legs were built for ripped jeans and exceptionally comfortable pajama pants.

Liberty grabbed her skirt. There was so much fabric that even when lifted up, Liberty still couldn't see her slipper-clad feet. She prayed she wouldn't trip along the path leading toward the fairgrounds. Her face was still sore from tripping on Justice's skateboard.

Once she had walking-in-a-humongous-dress down, she noticed for the first time what awaited her at the end of this road. A decorated wooden arch, which read, in sweeping letters: *Welcome to the Rhode Island Shakespeare Festival!*

Four thin flag posts rose from the top of the sign, banners rippling in the April wind.

"Please, God," Liberty gulped.

She made it through the arch, and then stopped to take in the bedlam unfolding before her.

The entire place was plastered with posters advertising the Midnight Masque. The smells of leather, oil, and copper drew her first toward a large circular stall in her immediate vicinity, with multiple service windows, labeled *The Merchant of Venice.* A crier stood beside it, shouting to the crowds: "Come thee, fairgoers! Trade thy notes for proper coins!"

Spittle flew from the crier's mouth, a small shower of saliva raining into the grass below. Liberty tried to back away and look less disgusted than she felt, which was *hard*.

She backed right into a crowd of people gathered near the scent of greasy fried meats and carbs. Her stomach gurgled apprehensively at the stench.

Behind her was an even larger stall, set up like an outdoor medieval eatery. Above it, an emblazoned sign read *MacBeth's*. A large golden M in Blackmoor font, mimicking the unmistakable McDonald's insignia, rose above the sign like a beacon of anti-veganism.

Patrons of the eatery stuffed their faces with medieval-looking burgers (mutton?) and fries. Everything looked a little sloppy and unsafe to eat, but that only made it a perfect imitation of McDonald's.

Liberty forced herself to take one step, then another. After MacBeth's came a...marriage stall?

White gossamer banners floated from altar posts and ornately decorated chuppahs. Strings of flowers and earthen wreaths overhung the row of altars, and several men dressed like Friar Lawrence stood "marrying" festival goers and passing out little Romeo poisons.

Liberty was unsure whether the marrying was legally binding or not. The ceremonies looked equally too official and too fake for her to be sure.

Another booth was an apothecary's stall.

Shelves stood before the thing, lined with liquids in jewel-toned glass potion bottles. The stall smelled of too many essential oils in one place, rose and hyssop, cedar wood and lavender, all layered over each other and potent enough to make Liberty sneeze.

A jester, advertising the booth, called to the crowds with riddles, holding two potion bottles up. "A poison to dismiss! A potion to summon a lover's kiss!" The dude leered at Liberty and she got out of his way, in a hurry.

This wasn't hell, but it was pretty close.

JUSTICE.

There was a row of painters, seated at canvasses, capturing differently posed festival goers in oil paint.

At least one pair of subjects were steadily kissing.

It was obnoxious, until Justice thought of Magdalena, felt hopeful, and then depressed, and then just mad at Liberty.

Claps, cheers, and medieval jig music reeled him in next.

Nearby was a green pasture, sectioned off by wooden posts. Flowery ropes hung between them, making the air smell nutty and fresh.

A festival vendor was teaching sixteenth century line dances to the festival people inside the rope. A sign posted outside the dancing patch said, *FIVE SHILLINGS A LESSON*.

It was a lot of stepping, clapping, and trading places. If Hope were here, with her *I'm a dance major* bullshit, she would have scoffed, and maybe even have tried to hijack the whole thing and teach Alvin Ailey or something instead.

Justice skirted around the dancing patch and found himself squeezing between bodies in a hollering crowd of patrons. There was another sectioned-off pasture up ahead, though this one was completely different.

It looked like an...amateur wrestling ring? A vendor shouted, "Who among you will best Charles the Wrestler?"

What an original name, Justice thought.

"Call upon the Lord's strength, if thou durst!" The people congregating around the ring cheered as an actor who was meant to be this Charles guy looked threateningly into the crowd. "Three shillings to assume thy fate!" the vendor continued.

Justice kept moving.

He could honestly say this was the weirdest place he'd ever, ever been. And that was saying something.

He'd been to the Halloween midnight showing of *Rocky Horror Picture Show, in drag,* with Washington more than once.

Another section of the fair seemed dedicated to Shakespeare character meet-and-greets, which didn't seem possible because Shakespeare characters—to the best of Justice's limited and don't-care knowledge— didn't have specific looks.

They weren't like Santa Claus, where you could consistently fake it with a fat old white dude and a beard.

Juliet could be a tiny blond girl, or she could be Magdalena, or Dewey, all made up. Or Liberty, if Liberty ever stopped being horrible long enough to pass for an ingenue. (Don't ask him why he knows the word *ingenue*.)

And yet, in true meet-and-greet fashion, actors dressed as William Shakespeare, King John, Richard II, Henry IV, Henry V, Richard III, Henry VIII, and Edward III stood nearby. Justice didn't know any of that from looking at them.

There were signs hanging over each actor's head, and a short line of people ahead of each actor. All Justice knew was that the numbers in their names made the signs above them look like one *really long* algebra problem. "Old guy meet-and-greet. Check," he murmured, turning down the next aisle of stalls he could find.

Ahead of him, a maze loomed. *Why not?*

Justice soon discovered the walls of the maze were each Shakespearean backdrops, where festival people stopped to take pictures. Justice paused in front of the *Julius Caesar* wall where a center space was left open (for whoever wanted to star in the photograph) and surrounded by an illustration of senate members with daggers, poised to strike.

Before he moved on, Justice thought to himself, Liberty would make a *great* Caesar.

LIBERTY.

When Liberty stumbled into the maze, she hoped to find a momentary reprieve from the Shakespearean mayhem beyond its walls only to find that there was plenty of mayhem in here, too.

Festival goers posed for photos, vogueing against different selfie- ready Shakespeare backdrops. She rested her back against the first empty wall she could find.

This corset was seriously limiting her oxygen supply.

Note to self, she thought with exhaustion. *Write history paper on how forcing women to wear ridiculous clothes that keep them from optimal anatomic functioning is a form of historic and systemic oppression.*

The wall behind her had two women in it.

Both looked wicked. An old, tired man sat in the background looking seriously worn down. It only made Liberty think of her grandfather and his tumor.

And her mom, worrying about him in bliss sort of, because she had no idea that she should be worried about Liberty, too. The wall made her feel like crying, so she got away from it and found her way, miraculously, out of the maze.

Outside the maze, Liberty was immediately enveloped by the smells of fresh-cut flowers. Across the way was a flower-crown and braiding station, seemingly manned by fairies from *A Midsummer Night's Dream.*

Patrons at the station got their hair braided into fanciful patterns. The fairies chose flowers from buckets, weaving some into crowns, and others directly into the braids. It was a little too...Barbie meets Coachella for Liberty's taste.

She was fairly certain the English language didn't have a word for how unamused and out of place she felt, wandering down the paths.

JUSTICE.

Justice was two and a half seconds from admitting he was lost when someone bombed him from above with feathers, leaves, and fairy dust.

"What the—!" He sputtered, brushing at himself, and looking up. Strung above him was a zip line.

He followed the thick cord backward with his eyes until he saw a raised platform in the distance, with a sign attached: *PUCK'S FLYING SCHOOL.*

People in fairy gear, seemingly equipped with water balloons full of pixie shit, were then attached to the zip line. Justice watched one of them bomb someone else.

Justice decided this fair must be the place where the government sends political prisoners to be tortured.

LIBERTY.

Someone loves me, Liberty thought as she came across a large group of booths titled *Suicide Stalls.*

Unsure and curious, Liberty tucked behind the entry curtain and looked around. Inside the place were several small semi-private rooms with more illustrated backdrops for picture-taking and tables covered in props.

A few stalls had swords and daggers in them, their backgrounds made to look like grisly battlefields.

Another few stalls were *Romeo and Juliet*-themed. The Juliet stalls were complete with complimentary Romeo poison bottles, a bedroom illustration, a chaise lounge upon which to fake one's own death, two stuffed legs in the corner that were supposed to be dead Romeo lying nearby.

The Romeo stalls had two stuffed legs on a small chaise meant to be sleeping-but-presumed-dead Juliet.

Liberty took it all in.

She heard people reciting Juliet's final words and playacting her dying breaths.

"This is...definitely fucked up," Liberty mumbled to herself. Then, she ducked into a strange-looking stall that was unlike the others.

It had a curtain and a card with instructions on how to recreate the Polonius death scene from *Hamlet*. Liberty read the card aloud to herself.

"If you're Polonius, go behind the curtain and cry out, 'Oh, I am slain!'" She thought about that. "*'Oh, I am slain?'* That's the best Shakespeare could come up with?" she sighed hard. "Will someone please tell me why we are forced to worship this man's work?"

The Clash was a group of British visionaries. Why couldn't they study *them* in English?

JUSTICE.

So far the suicide stalls were Justice's favorite.

He kicked "dead" Juliet's legs aside, alighted on her chaise lounge, and uncorked a bottle of the Romeo poison. It was unmarked, but how bad could it be?

He downed it.

The bitter tang of lemon juice assaulted his throat. His face puckered up. He hacked a cough. A few patrons saw and snickered as they trickled past.

"Just so you know," he called after them, "this poison is fake!"

· · ·

LIBERTY.

Liberty burst out of the suicide stalls, back into the fresh spring air, and stopped.

Directly across the path was an oasis in this desert. The sign read, *WILLIFY YOUR DOG.*

A number of festival goers were gathered around tables, dressing their dogs up in Elizabethan garb.

Liberty staggered toward the place like she'd been lost for months. She sank down on a low stool, admiring several Scottish terriers lapping ice water from polished silver dishes, tails jerking happily behind them like fluffy antennae.

"Time out," she breathed. "Theater people overload."

A poodle strode up to her, wearing a Queen Elizabeth collar and sat, panting happily beside her. Liberty could have cried, she felt so blessed by the dog's presence. For a few brief moments, today wasn't as bad as she thought.

SCENE IV.

— 7:55 p.m. —

LIBERTY.

Liberty and her new friend had been talking for at least fifteen minutes. Liberty didn't know where the poodle's parent was, but she hoped they'd stay away a bit longer.

It was just getting good.

"Ever since we fell out in eighth grade, he's always been bitchy to me..." Liberty unfurled her tale of woe, softly scrubbing the poodle's perfect, fluffy, copper-colored head.

"But he's never actually run away from me in the middle of a conversation before." She exhaled. "That was an understatement by the way. He didn't actually run. He *sprinted* away, like Olympic gold was on the line."

Liberty paused to observe the rhythm of the festival.

Everyone here seemed to be genuinely enjoying themselves. Now that she'd had some puppy rehab time, she was feeling a bit better herself.

She couldn't relate to the excitement others felt, but she

understood it a bit better. Like placing her hands on a door and feeling the heat emanating from the other side.

"I know I should probably be enjoying this festival," she picked up. "Let's face it. Kidnap is the *only* reason I would ever be in a place like this. But honestly, I'm still thinking about Magdalena. How could she not tell me about Adam, you know? I would have understood."

The poodle lifted its head, as though to challenge her.

Liberty was surprised at how hurt and angry she sounded.

One thing was for sure: She'd never expected Magdalena to hurt or anger her.

Not like this.

She didn't like feeling hurt and angry because of Magdalena. Liberty shook her head until her brain thought of something else.

Come straight here, her mom had texted.

Then Liberty thought of her mom, of her whole family gathering at Grandpa's bedside, without her.

Sometimes she felt like a lot of things might be easier without her there, but this wasn't one of them.

In her family, Liberty had a place.

Maybe she didn't have a place in Magdalena's love life or in Justice's friend group, but Liberty was still a daughter. A granddaughter. She was a cousin and a niece and so many other things, and right now, she was not where she was supposed to be. Wait—

Fuck. Liberty shot up from the stool, disturbing her poodle friend. She apologized for interrupting him, but she'd just realized something she didn't think about before.

She was three hours away from Green River, and Liberty's mom thought she was at their *house,* fifteen minutes from the hospital. If Liberty didn't show up to the hospital within the hour, Mom would know something was wrong.

And worse, she'd fear that something terrible happened because Liberty didn't tell her the truth. Mom knowing what happened and being worried is a Sunday picnic compared to Mom not knowing what's happening and being worried sick.

Fuck, fuck, fuck.

— 8:00 p.m. —

JUSTICE.

Justice found his way to a wooden platform decorated like a courtyard below with a balcony above it. A hanging sign pointed to an entryway on the right side of the contraption.

Up, lady, the sign read. *To your balcony! Your lord doth tarry below.*

Honestly, Justice entered the platform thing just to get away from the sight of that god-awful sign.

Inside was dim and cool—like a treehouse in the shade. Justice was thankful for the lower temperature. This doublet, or whatever it was called, was *heavy* and super warm. He was turning into a sweat factory under here.

The little tree-house-ish space had a shelf with copies of Shakespeare's plays stacked on it. There were prop boxes and costumes, too, should any of the festival goers want to do their own renditions of his works.

The left side of the room opened to the miniature platform stage, and the right side of the room was a staircase that led up to the balcony.

Justice took the stairs, jonesing for a moment alone. He still had feathers in his hair from the fairy attack.

At the top of the steps, he found the nearest corner and slid to the floor. Beyond the upstairs landing was a little room that opened out onto the balcony.

Justice took some yoga breaths and glanced toward the balcony and the world above. From down here, it looked as though he'd hidden himself in the skies.

After a while, Justice took out Jack Elby's phone, typed in Washington's number, which he knew by heart (*yes*, even now), and sent his best friend a note.

"*Dude*," he enunciated as he spelled. "He is never going to believe this."

Three seconds after he sent the first message, Jack's phone shrilled between his fingers.

"What the hell, Justice!" Washington exploded the same second he answered it.

"You're not going to believe the afternoon I've had."

Washington was clearly panicked. "Are you okay? What happened? You disappeared at intermission and when I asked Mags, she said she hadn't seen you."

"You talked to Mags? How'd she seem? Upset?" Justice asked compulsively.

Shit, shit, shit.

He'd been worried earlier that Magdalena would mistakenly believe he liked Liberty, and then after being trapped with Liberty he started to worry that Magdalena might think he had feelings for *Washington.*

But the truth was that all Magdalena was going to think now was that he was an asshole who stood her up with no explanation.

"*Focus,* Justice," Washington urged. "What happened?"

"Liberty and I got kidnapped to a Shakespeare Festival." The words sounded even crazier than the reality of it. And the reality of this place was *nuts.*

"KIDNAPPED?!"

"More like, accidentally...taken someplace? Kind of smuggled, I guess."

"Are you all right?" Washington started up again. "Do you need me to call someone, the cops? Your parents?"

"No, it's fine. We're getting picked up. We're in Rhode Island."

Justice stopped him before his friend's worries snowballed any further.

"*What?*"

"Listen, I need you to go into my secret lair and have one of my personal drones airdrop me a survival kit and a fresh pair of jeans."

"But you're okay? Safe, I mean." His voice was starting to calm back down.

"Completely," Justice said. "If you don't count being here with Liberty and a small army of theater people."

Washington went quiet. When he spoke again, he sounded both serious and sort of glum. "Are you...you said Liberty's there with you?"

"The life wrecker herself."

"Are you two...back together?" he asked.

"I'm going to pretend you didn't just ask me that," came Justice's affronted, indignant reply.

Were they really going to go through this *twice* in one day? Hadn't Washington's lunchtime accusations been enough?

Washington gave a great sigh, as though Justice just told him he was cancer-free. His tone was audibly lighter.

"Sorry," he breathed into the microphone, making it sputter. "I know. I just needed to make sure."

"Make sure of what?" Justice said.

"That you weren't a clone," Washington answered quickly.

"If you were testing my clone, 'How do you feel about Liberty Marshall?' would be the right question to ask."

Justice laughed.

"But you're in *Rhode Island?*" Washington reversed course. "As in the place where Taylor Swift's summer house is?"

"Hope's coming to get me. But it's going to take *hours*."

"So much for Kade Park and Magdalena, huh?"

Without warning, Justice remembered him and Liberty in the

dark, talking again, wrestling like kids, remembering each other like they'd never been apart.

Why did *that* come to mind instead of the disappointment he felt about missing his would-be date with Magdalena?

He didn't want to think about it, so Justice ignored Washington's remark and instead added, "What happened with you and Lang?"

Washington laughed the words, "*Absolutely nothing.* I was too busy looking for you." His voice got glum-serious again. "So what are you going to do about Liberty?"

"What do you mean?"

A weird pause. "Nothing. Never mind. Hey, call me when you get home, all right?"

"What are you, my wife?" Justice meant for his reply to sound joking, but he was in an irked mood and, because of it, he missed the mark ever so slightly.

Another *longer* weird pause. "Bye, Justice."

Justice looked at the phone, trying to imagine Washington's face. It felt like something just passed between them and Justice missed it.

After a few minutes of puzzling though, Justice realized what it was. It was standard issue Washington Weirdness re: Liberty.

Washington was weird about Liberty even over the phone.

In this small space, alone with himself for what felt like the first time today, Justice let himself think about that, for real. And when he did, it occurred to him that Washington's weirdness wasn't new.

The weirdness he observed now was actually an evolution of the weirdness he'd observed when the three of them had been friends, since Liberty arrived in their lives to begin with.

And now that he thought about it that way, Justice understood perfectly what this was.

Jealousy.

It had to be.

Even though it was absurd…but then again, jealousy almost always was.

Before Liberty (and after Liberty) he and Washington had been inseparable. But when Liberty *first* showed up?

They became a three instead of a two, and looking back, Justice realized that Washington had never been 100 percent on board with that.

Justice had been, but that's because back then, to him, Liberty was the best thing since a sixty-four pack of crayons.

He and Liberty went together like peanut butter and jelly, and Washington…well, Washington was bread in that scenario because he was on the outside.

Or not always, he wasn't *always* on the outside.

But a lot of Justice's best childhood memories were memories that he shared with Liberty and Liberty alone. And for the first time, Justice thought, *maybe that bothered him.*

It would make sense.

After Angela Devlin's thirteenth birthday party—the one where Justice ended up kissing Washington for reasons that were too embarrassing to explain—Washington used to lord the kiss over Liberty.

He used to joke all the time that Justice had been *his* first kiss and he had been *Justice's* first kiss. And neither Justice nor Liberty had ever had the heart to tell him he was wrong.

How could they without rubbing the truth in his face? The truth was that *Liberty* had been Justice's first kiss.

They were seven at the time. And the kiss happened on a trip to Disney World, a trip Justice, Liberty, and Washington were supposed to take together, that Washington ended up unable to make at the last minute.

Justice doubted that Washington *ever* forgave him and Liberty for going on that trip without him, even though it obviously wasn't their decision. All the tickets and flights and accommodations had been purchased, and they were kids. Their parents weren't going to *not* take them to Disney World just because Washington couldn't make it.

Justice and Liberty HAD A BLAST at Disney, by the way, but they agreed when they got back to tell Washington that the trip had sucked so he wouldn't feel so bad.

They definitely didn't tell him about the kiss.

Or, I guess, "kisses" is more like it, Justice thought.

One on the plane ride down and one in the spinning teacups. But that was beside the point.

Justice had been so preoccupied with his own shit that he'd never stopped to consider what Washington's deal was.

For a moment, Justice considered calling Washington back, apologizing, and...*I don't know, asking him if there's anything he wanted to talk about?*

That sounded dumb, even in Justice's head.

Out of nowhere, memories of his conversation with Liberty in the box truck returned yet again.

Have you ever, past or present, had feelings for Washington?

He still couldn't believe she'd asked him that. Justice. Have feelings for Washington?

That was impossible.

Okay, so...they peed in a bush together when they were five, and they'd spent countless hours together gaming, talking, laughing, staying up all night. Justice was the first person Washington came out to. Justice had been Washington's first kiss.

I guess the evidence is there, he resolved.

But that didn't make it any less wild of an assumption. Justice thought about kissing Washington at that party.

No, not Washington.

Dewey. It'd been years since Justice called him by his first name. Justice still remembered how Dewey smelled as a kid, always like flour and vanilla.

(His mom owned a pastry shop—Edie's Sweets—and was *always* baking *something*. Her red velvet cupcakes? Orgasmic.)

Kissing him was kind of like kissing and kind of like cake.

Justice remembered being surprised by the experience of kissing Dewey. He expected it to be weird or unwelcome or humiliating, but as soon as their lips met, the world around them went dark.

Justice was surprised by how easily kissing came not only to him, but to Washington, too. He'd been surprised by how easy it was to imagine that Liberty was the one he was kissing. Thinking of Liberty was what made that kiss great.

At the time, he'd only been wanting to kiss *her* again for five years. Justice shook the memory from his head.

How would things be different now if he'd kissed Liberty that day at Angela's party, the way he wanted to, instead of Dewey? He'd never, ever know, he supposed.

Just then, Justice was interrupted by the sound of footsteps coming up the stairs.

SCENE V.

— 8:30 p.m. —

LIBERTY.

Even though she didn't know where Justice was and she loathed running, Liberty ran for it, fighting through crowds and checking vendor stalls one at a time.

Where would he be? she asked herself. *Where* might *he be?*

Her mind refused to think, though, while under the assault of less oxygen and heightened physical activity.

She ran out of air by a balcony platform thing.

"*Ugh,*" she rasped. Every minute that passed was another minute her mom and her whole family might be worrying if something happened to her.

All because earlier she was feeling hurt and petty. Why was she such an *idiot?!*

"Nice, Liberty," she muttered to herself as a nearby creak startled her.

A woman stood on the platform, talking to another woman standing on the balcony, figuring out logistics or something.

Liberty wasn't sure.

Strangely, almost magically, Justice appeared around the side of the platform coming through a doorless entryway, fidgeting with someone's smartphone.

He didn't notice her standing there.

He'd aimed the phone at the women, and when one of them looked this way and saw Liberty, she startled.

"Oh, I'm sorry!" she said. "Were you two using the stand? We can come back later."

"What?" Justice lifted his head and flinched, when he found Liberty standing behind him. Then he scowled, as though the sight of her offended him.

"No, it's fine," he told Platform Lady. "Go ahead."

"You sure?" she replied.

"Absolutely," he said emphatically. "Ready when you are!"

On his cue, the women started reciting Shakespeare lines as Justice filmed.

Liberty was so focused on making things right at home that she didn't even register Justice's usual amount of jackass-ery. Urgency compelled her to retrieve Jack's cell phone from Justice's belt without so much as a "please."

She was dialing her mom's cell phone as the thespian women finished up. And as they left, for some odd reason, they thanked Justice *and* Liberty.

It was the story of their lives, honestly. Being thrown together for no reason at all. Liberty got a quick eye roll in as she lifted the phone to her ear.

It rang and rang, but her mom didn't pick up. *Again.*

WHY, she wanted to shout. She anxiously dialed again. The phone rang and rang, but nothing. She toggled into the text message section when something caught her eye, a note from Ashley Baker—

Hi, this message is for Liberty.

We just got a call from your school letting us know that they've had trouble contacting your parents. They were able to leave a message on your mother's voicemail, but her outgoing message said she's dealing with an emergency today, so they're not sure if they'll get through.

Your father's phone seems to have been disconnected.

They were calling to ask if you had any alternate numbers for them or if you could provide the number of someone else who could come get you.

Text our stage manager when you get this message. She'll be labeled in Jack's phone as "Melissa Foley (they/them)."

Your father's phone seems to have been disconnected.

Something came undone inside Liberty.

Why, she wondered, as she suddenly felt close to tears. Again. This isn't about her dad.

Nothing that happened today had anything to do with him, and yet... that was the problem.

When you're in trouble, your parents are supposed to be there for you. And neither of Liberty's parents were. Her dad's phone was disconnected. She couldn't even ask him for help if she wanted to.

And she expected that from him, but still, it hurt.

It hurt to be right about something that wasn't right.

"Having trouble?" Justice snarked.

His voice broke her focus because if it were three years ago, he would've been standing right there, asking her if she was okay. Hell, if it'd been a few hours ago in the dark in that truck, he would've sat right beside her and drawn stupid pictures on her knee to cheer her up.

But he wasn't going to do that.

No, Justice was standing next to her with his exhausted, agitated, why- are-you-always-bothering-me face.

It was honestly a good impression of her dad.

She remembered them fighting in the darkness of that truck. She remembered the way he'd pulled her in, purely to confuse the shit out of her.

She remembered lunch with Magdalena this morning, eons ago, and Magdalena's words, *It's obvious you still love him. What happened with you two again?*

No one could say Liberty hadn't tried.

She'd tried to ask Justice why they ended, but he freaked out on her and wouldn't tell her anything about why the two of them had imploded.

Even now, she was still baffled by it.

She'd been there. She'd been there the past three years as she and Justice hissed and took shots at each other. But why? What truly broke them?

It was the same way she'd wondered, as a child, how Dad could look so happy in photographs with her, but in real life not like her very much at all.

What had she done to make them change their minds about her? What had she done to earn their rejection and abandonment? To merit loneliness?

Justice turned to walk away from her, but she'd had enough of people turning their back on her for one day.

"*Hey!*"

A few minutes ago, none of Justice Garrison's B.S. could have stopped her from calling home, and now, ridiculously, contrarily, she wanted to stop *him*.

She wanted to make a mess. She wanted to burn everything down, annoy him to the very last, rip up whatever final, thinning threads connected them.

Maybe they'd fight again, and just the way that eighth grade fight ended their friendship, this fight would end whatever *this* was—whatever happened between them today, plus their three-year-long antagonistic open season on one another.

Maybe after this, they could settle into tried-and-true apathy. After she'd done her worst and been her ugliest and gotten the same in return from him, she could be sure it was over. Maybe she'd feel a little less wounded if she wounded him back.

Liberty had many talents, but provoking Justice Garrison was the one she was most proud of. She would draw him out with exactly five simple words:

"Give me a ride home."

JUSTICE.

Justice already knew Liberty was nuts, but that wild look in her eyes only added wood to the fire.

"*Not on your life,*" he enunciated, backing away from her.

"Justice—"

"I've already done one road trip with you today," he reminded her. "I'm not trying to make it two. I'd need cyanide to get through three hours of you *and* Hope."

"We live on the same street!" she argued, something weird in her voice. She sounded entitled, almost.

Did she think Justice *owed* her something? After everything that happened today?

After everything she'd done?

Justice felt hot, and it wasn't the doublet insulating him. He turned on Liberty. She was closer than he thought, but he didn't back down and neither did she.

"We could live in the same house!" he retorted. "I still wouldn't give you a ride home."

A smugness came to Liberty's eye. Justice didn't like it.

She dropped her attention to the phone in her hand and started dialing.

She held it up to her face, grinning at him. "Hope?"

The air in Justice's lungs evaporated, eaten up by red-hot rage.

"*Hang up,*" he commanded. Now, Liberty was the one backing away from him. "Hang up right now."

"Yeah, hi, it's me," she continued. Justice stalked toward her. She evaded him as best she could. "I remembered your number."

"Hang up the phone, Liberty!" Justice's tone was three notches away from a shriek.

Damn Hope for making them memorize her phone number in sixth grade. Justice swiped for the phone, and Liberty dodged.

They were headed back toward the balcony platform.

"Nothing's wrong!" Liberty feigned, leaning out of the way as Justice lurched for the phone again. "I was just wondering if I could catch a ride with you?"

"Don't listen to her!" Justice shot.

Justice was only losing right now because he was trying to grab the phone without smacking Liberty upside the head, but maybe she didn't deserve his restraint.

"Okay, thanks! See you soon, bye!" Liberty's words rapid-fired as Justice made a mad lunge for the phone and caused Liberty to trip on the hem of her skirt in the same motion.

The two of them hit the ground, in a heap of surprise and musty costume scent.

For a second, it was like they were elementary school kids again, wrestling on his trampoline, bouncing and laughing, rolling until they fell into the grass.

One second, Justice was furious, *fuming* he was so mad.

The next second, he was losing his edge because he was hunched on top of Liberty, the honey of her eyes and neck and collarbones closer than they'd ever been before.

Well, while he was conscious, anyway.

Even through his ultra-thick doublet, he was aware of Liberty's shape, outlined beneath him. It scattered his resolve like water in a hot oil pan.

It was like the very presence of her boobs had poked a hole in the hull of his anger.

He ignored the way his back suddenly ached, his throat started to close, and his heart began to dribble in his chest.

He shoved off of her, without touching any part of her, without hurting her at all, he hoped. He needed to get away from her again. He didn't want to be reminded that she was someone he used to know, someone he used to—

"I cannot *believe* you," he spat, as she got to her feet. Whether he was talking to himself or her was anyone's guess.

"Get over yourself," she muttered, that crazy gleam in her eye gone. She looked as scattered as he felt. "I need a ride," she said. "It's not like three hours is going to kill you."

"You don't get to decide that!" he snapped at her. Justice felt like he was breaking.

Why did she still have such an effect on him?

He snatched at his curls, frustration swallowing him whole. "I... I'M NOT SUPPOSED TO BE HERE!"

"And I *am?*" she fired back.

"I'm supposed to be on a date right now, Liberty! But you ruined that," he roared.

What did she want from him? What else could she possibly need to destroy?

"*Excuse the hell out of me,* but *no!* I'm not dying to spend another second with you, let alone three hours in a car with you and my sister!"

She scoffed. Not for the first time today.

"A date?" Next, she sneered. "With who? Your ego?"

"WITH MAGDALENA!" He wouldn't have been surprised if Magdalena heard him call her name, all the way from here.

Liberty trilled a laugh. It was fake, just like the rest of her.

"Magdalena's not going out with *you,*" she insisted. "Magdalena would *never* go out with you!"

Justice tried to play off the gut punch in her words. "Well, we'll never know, will we?"

But that's the thing about Liberty. She always surprised Justice. She could always hurt him, just a little more than he ever expected.

So, Liberty dropped another bomb.

"Magdalena has a boyfriend!"

LIBERTY.

The shock on Justice's face was a small, *small* consolation prize for the way he'd treated her the past three years.

If her heart weren't currently dead from recently discovering this information herself, she might have even felt a bit sorry for him.

"What are you talking about?"

"They've kept their relationship a secret this whole time," Liberty charged on, pretending like she knew everything.

Like Mags had told her.

Like these words didn't salt her own wounds.

"He's an amazing guy." The tears, infuriatingly, weren't far off. "He's..." *Let's take a cheap shot, shall we?* "Why would she ever go out with you when she has a guy like Adam Grosch?"

A moment of silence fell between them. And then Justice died laughing.

JUSTICE.

Justice couldn't breathe. He needed ten whole years to properly laugh at how close he'd come to actually believing Liberty's ridiculous, two-faced lie. She had him, until she brought Get Down Goblin boy into this.

"What is the matter with you?" she demanded. Now Justice was laughing at her face.

She looked serious.

She was still trying to pull off this con, even after he'd totally caught her out by *not falling for it.*

His sides *ached* by the time he had enough air to say, "You just tried to pull the biggest prank on me anyone has ever pulled."

Another fit of laughter took him. He let it.

"It's true," Liberty insisted.

He could see angry tears welling in her eyes. Sucks to *suck.*

"Nice try, Lib. You got me. Almost fell for that one."

"I saw them!" she cried. "During the play, they were making out in a classroom."

It was Justice's turn to scoff. "Pfft. *Okay.*"

"Justice." Liberty was even more serious than before. He didn't like that, either. "The reason Magdalena wasn't in Mr. Tanaka's office? The reason I was running backstage before you tripped me with your damn skateboard..." Her shoulders pressed down hard.

"It was because I'd just discovered them. I stepped out of the theater to get some air. I was in the drama hallway, and there they were, in a room, all alone...exercising their *tongues.*"

Justice sighed big, giving his sides a moment to recover.

"Look." He let his tone ease back into serious. "I know you... don't like the idea of me asking her out. I get it. She's your best friend," he paused, unsure he wanted to take this next leap.

"I know you like her, Liberty. You probably want to date her, too. But lying to me like this? Trying to get me to give up on her?" He held up his hands. "It's not going to stop me. She and I would be..."

Justice, for some reason, couldn't finish his sentence.

Usually, the perfect word populated on his tongue whenever

he thought of Magdalena, but he was still scattered.

Liberty still had her claws in him. His annoyance returned.

"Justice..."

When she said his name this time, her voice broke.

It was so unexpected that the sound of it broke something inside him. He was completely unprepared to look up and see her tearful face, crumpled up like paper.

Just...weeping.

He'd only seen her so sad one other time.

When David Bowie died.

Her tears arrested him. They tied his tongue. He couldn't speak. He could only listen. It was out of his control.

She made him feel out of control.

"I love her," she sobbed. "I am...completely in love with her. Do you...honestly think I would lie about this?"

Uh, yeah, Justice thought, but had no ability to say.

"You think I'm happy to tell you that Magdalena's in love with someone else?"

Justice found the strength to speak a few minutes later, but he hated that all the edge to his voice was gone.

His words were soft.

Gentle. Jesus Christ.

"She's not dating Adam Grosch," he murmured, as Liberty dried her tears on her pillowy white sleeve. "She..."

Justice didn't even want to consider it.

"Magdalena couldn't be dating him. Adam's a total dunce."

"He is not a dunce!" Liberty's protest came out a whimper.

She dropped her hands, and Justice glimpsed her heated, flushed face.

Her honey brown skin went almost vermillion when she cried.

For one wild millisecond, he thought about cupping her cheek in his hand. The horror of that thought emboldened him to keep arguing.

Argue like his sanity depended on it.

"He is the textbook definition of dunce," Justice refuted. "He's an idiot. There's no way Magdalena would ever, *ever* go for a guy like him—"

"A guy like *what,* Justice?" she snapped back, voice saturated with emotional intensity. "A guy who's funny and outgoing?"

"He thinks he's God's gift!" Justice scrunched his face together in disbelief. "He thinks he shits gold. He's arrogant."

"That's *you,* Justice." Even when Liberty was a mess, she could cut him. "*You* think everything you do is amazing. Adam isn't like that. You are."

"I am not arrogant!"

"And you're such an asshole," she marched on. "Mags would never go out with you. You're self-centered. And judgmental. And your ego is the size of the sun. You're the type of guy who throws away friends for no reason. Who would want to be with someone like that?"

LIBERTY.

Liberty swore this time, she wasn't even trying. Yes, she'd wanted to provoke him. And she had.

But as soon he'd brought Magdalena into this, all bets were off. She didn't know how they'd gotten here, her insulting him, and him—completely blank with ire.

She could tell by the expression on his face that she'd set him off, even if she didn't know precisely *how* she'd done it. She had no idea what exactly had pushed him over the edge this time.

But the edge was somewhere, and Justice was over it.

It was obvious in the way he said, "What did you just say?"

"That you're an asshole."

"No," he disagreed. "You said I...I throw away friends for no reason." Every muscle in his face was taut.

His bone structure had always reminded her of a tiger. And here he was, about to bite her head off.

"That may be the most *disgusting* thing anyone has ever said to me."

JUSTICE.

After what she did...

Liberty had the *nerve* to call Justice a bad friend?

Let's go over one very definitive, if a bit humiliating, example of Justice being the best friend a person could ever have.

It was March of seventh grade when Liberty spent one afternoon crying in the girls' locker room, because of...well, a vagina emergency.

I look like I rode a horse that was covered in red paint, she'd blubbered. And Justice waited with her while she sobbed. And in the end, he was the one who came up with the plan.

The crazy, unexciting but just might (and *did)* work plan.

Take off your pants, he'd told her, embarrassed by the really awful way *that* sounded. He still remembered the way Liberty's shocked shrill voice bounced off the bathroom walls, saying, "*What?!*"

Take mine, he'd insisted. *I'll run home and grab another pair.*

That's right.

He gave her his fucking *pants.* (*His pants!*)

That is how good a friend he was.

It was the coldest day in March. And Justice gave up his pants, and then ran home—*ran*—in a t-shirt, Iron Man boxers, and a pair of Keds.

It was the coldest run of his life.

And even after *that,* Liberty Bell Marshall had the nerve to call him a bad friend.

"Yeah, I said it." No remorse in her eyes.

"You're such a fucking hypocrite."

"You—"

"I throw away *trash,*" Justice clarified. "I throw away fake people. Not friends."

"Trash," Liberty repeated.

Her tears were dry. Her anger was back.

Good, Justice thought. It was time for a good old-fashioned verbal fight to the finish.

"You're saying I'm trash. That I was *fake?*"

"One hundred percent," he spit back. "Nasty, non-biodegradable, shitty for all environments *plastic.*"

"When was I fake?" she demanded. "When, in the history of our relationship, did I once lie to you?"

"If you thought you could bully him and I wouldn't care, then you were never my friend to begin with." The words came easily. He was just getting warmed up.

But here came Liberty with another curveball.

"Bully him?" Her eyebrows flew up her forehead. "WHO?" Faking it again.

Justice lost it. "DEWEY!"

"WHAT ARE YOU TALKING ABOUT?!" Liberty looked like she wanted to shake him. Justice wanted to shake her back. "Dewey was my friend, just like you, if you can remember that far back! I would never bully him."

Justice scoffed four ways. "YOU CALLED HIM *GAY* IN FRONT OF THE WHOLE SCHOOL!"

"Dewey *is* gay!" she shouted back, as though that was the point.

"THAT IS NOT THE POINT!"

When they were in middle school, calling someone gay was still an insult.

It was a thing you called someone when you wanted to make them feel small and wrong and less human than you, regardless of whether they actually were gay.

And Liberty knew that.

Why was she acting all innocent?!

"George used to bully him all the time and I guess it rubbed off on you, or maybe it was the other way around! Either way, the two of you are a pair of *shitheads*—"

"Leave George out of this! Are you—" she sputtered. "Are you trying to say that I *outed* him or something? In front of everyone?"

Justice groaned loud enough for the state of Rhode Island to hear. He explained it to her, even though she knew.

Even though she was faking.

After Liberty publicly put Dewey down, other guys in their grade started avoiding him. Someone scribbled the F-word on his binder! People started pranking him.

"All because of you and your big mouth!" Justice spat.

"Justice, I swear I didn't know about any of that. And if that really did happen because of the fight we had that day, I'm sorry. But it's not my fault. I wasn't insulting him. I was... I *realized* he was gay, and I..."

She blew her lips out. "I realized it a little too loud. I know that, but it wasn't malicious, Justice. I wasn't bullying him! I swear to you, I—"

Something stopped her from talking.

"Wait..." Her expression froze, and then her lips pressed into a hard line. "All this time..." she murmured. "You've been an asshole to me because you thought I bullied Dewey?"

"You *did*!"

"You mean, Dewey never told you the truth?"

LIBERTY.

Just that one question seemed to break the air between them.

The sun was setting. Festival goers were beginning to clear off the paths, all banking toward a main road. Many of them had already gathered, she suspected, to watch *Much Ado*.

Justice and Liberty were alone.

And something had begun to change.

A muscle in Justice's jaw jumped. "What are you talking about?"

"What did Dewey tell you?" Liberty lowered her eyes mournfully. "About what happened that day."

"He didn't have to tell me anything," Justice said. "I saw it for myself."

"Saw *what*, Justice?" Liberty pressed.

"I..." he faltered, like he was dragging the memory of that catastrophic day out of the vault.

Liberty certainly was.

It was the day they rolled down the hill behind their middle school, Liberty and Dewey screaming at each other on an overcast afternoon.

"I saw you call him gay in front of everyone," Justice recalled. "Like you hated him. You were angry. You were trying to put him down."

Liberty *had* been angry. That much was true. She had hated Dewey, just for a few minutes. But she wasn't trying to put him down. She had never wanted that.

Dewey was her friend, even if he'd been a shit.

"And then what?" She said, making Justice look at her.

"What?"

"After you saw that, what did Dewey tell you?"

"Nothing. He didn't have to—" Justice insisted.

And that's when the past few years detonated in Liberty's mind. Her heart, *her emotions*, were racing.

Liberty froze there, letting out a long shaking breath.

She stood, trying to steady herself, trying to convince herself the ground was beneath her feet and not someplace else. Her world was upside down.

Or rather, her world had *been* upside down the past three years. But now, finally, horribly, unbelievably, painfully, her world was right side up.

Liberty told this entire story wrong.

We need to go back.

THE BEGINNING:

In the beginning, it was Justice and Dewey.

They'd been friends a whole two years before Liberty met them.

Liberty was the one joining a program already in progress.

Liberty entered the room that day in her white shirt and her jean jacket. She met eyes with five-year-old Justice, wearing the same thing.

He perked up when he saw her, Liberty remembered. Justice smiled at her.

Dewey did not.

RE: DISNEY WORLD:

Six-year-old Justice and Liberty on a trip to Disney World, sitting beside each other in their plane seats. Justice's mom leaned over to hand them a Nokia phone.

"Say hi to Dewey," Chelsea instructed them. "And be extra sweet," she'd whispered. "He's really sad he couldn't come along this time."

She'd handed them the phone.

Justice leaned in with his left ear and Liberty leaned in with her right. "Hi, Dewey," they said together.

Dewey blubbered on the other end: "Don't...go...without... me."

. . .

THE REASON LIBERTY WOULD NEVER WEAR WHITE PANTS AGAIN:

In seventh grade, she was twelve.

One afternoon she was severely late for science. After balling up her reddened, formerly white jeans and throwing them away, she darted into her classroom and sunk into her seat. The one between her and Dewey was empty.

"Were you...wearing that earlier?" Dewey asked her.

"Nope," she'd replied.

"You totally missed it. This kid ran by outside, totally streaking."

"Yep."

Dewey was there.

Everywhere.

In almost every memory Liberty had with Justice, Dewey was present. And he was there the day they rolled down the hill. Dewey was the one she fought with, and ironically, fighting with him is what ended her friendship with Justice.

Liberty tried to collect herself.

She didn't want to believe something so simple and horrible and wrong had come between them, but the picture was clear now.

Liberty readied herself to explain the truth.

The whole truth.

JUSTICE.

Liberty was starting to scare him.

He braced himself, but what good would that do? Liberty got through his defenses like a knife through butter.

"Justice, you're wrong about what happened that day," she

told him.

Here comes the next bomb, he thought.

What kind of fallout shelter would he need this time? "When did you find out Dewey was gay?" Liberty sighed.

The memory of Dewey coming out to Justice was far from his mind at that moment.

"I found out in eighth grade," Liberty continued. "On that day. It just so happened that other people were there when I found out. I said it out loud and other people heard me, because I found out while Dewey and I were in the middle of a fight. I was not *bullying* him," she took care to say.

"I was not trying to out him. I just...I made a really loud, angry observation. *That* is what happened."

"No, it's not." Justice didn't know where she was going with this. But he needed to shut her down, before she mixed him up any further than she already had.

"Yes, it is."

"You're making it up." Why couldn't she just leave him be?

"I liked you."

Those three words sent a shockwave through him.

Justice thought his knees might buckle if he tried to make one single move.

"In eighth grade, I *really* liked you. And Dewey found out." She wrung her hands together. "And that day, after we rolled down the hill, on the walk home, I was planning to tell you. But Dewey didn't want me to."

She canted her eyes toward the blood orange residue of the sunset in progress.

"In fact, ever since the moment he found out about how I felt, he tried to talk me out of doing anything about it."

Justice could hardly process one word she was saying. He could barely breathe.

"Dewey wanted me to keep my feelings a secret. The fight you saw was about that," she confessed, nothing but honesty in her eyes. "I kept asking him why he hated the idea of me liking you so much. And that's when I realized he was jealous." Her jaw set, lips wobbling a little.

"I realized *he* liked you. Dewey had a crush on you, too. And that's when I said it. When I called him gay. Out loud. That part of our fight, everyone heard including you."

Justice was gobsmacked. Flummoxed beyond all imagination.

"I..." he stammered. "I don't believe you."

"Fine," Liberty replied.

She handed the phone to Justice, emotion brewing in her honey brown eyes.

"Ask him yourself."

ACT IV.

SCENE I.

— 9:10 p.m. —

LIBERTY.

Liberty was gone, hurrying down the path, following the thinning trickle of patrons toward something.

She couldn't see what. She could hear applause building as she got closer, but tears had filled her eyes again, turning everything shapeless and strange.

The orange in the sky was fading.

So many things were fading that Liberty couldn't even name them all.

Her hatred toward Justice was fading.

Maybe her denial was fading, maybe the walls she'd erected between them were fading too.

Maybe...Liberty didn't know how to do any of this.

Liberty must have taken a wrong turn, she thought, as she reached a field of stages, set up almost like the maze.

Everyone at the festival seemed to be crowded around the biggest of them, at the center.

The stage itself was nothing short of enchanting, lit up with the last of an April sunset smudged and cascading behind it.

Rows of chairs lined the field ahead of it.

Every seat was full. Audience members sat in the grass in front of the chairs, in the aisles, too.

Everyone had a place.

Liberty waded toward the show, infiltrated the seating area, and plopped down in the first open patch of grass she found.

Laughter rippled through the audience as Ashley Baker, performing as Beatrice, said something spunky.

And for some reason, it hit her right then. This show...

Much Ado About Nothing.

That was the subtitle of her life today, or better, it was the subtitle of her entire feud with Justice. They'd been bitter enemies for *years* over... nothing.

Absolutely nothing.

The reason Justice hated her?

It never happened, it didn't exist.

She'd been without Justice for three years over a *misunderstanding.*

As much as she still wanted to hate him, as much as she wanted to hold on to all the absurd, petty things they'd done and said to each other in the past three years, in this moment she was overwhelmed by the tragedy of it.

How much fire had she swallowed?

How much pain had she tortured herself with?

How many times had she just wanted him by her side but said to herself instead, *you don't deserve a friend like him*—all to find out, she was not flawed.

The fault of their destruction was never hers. Or was it?

Magdalena was right, Liberty realized with a twinge.

You don't exactly stand up for you, either.

Liberty didn't fight for herself now, and she certainly hadn't fought for herself then.

Or for him. Or for their relationship.

She never stopped to say, *Let's talk this out. Let's get everything straight.*

No. She assumed. She *assumed.*

She traded her deepest, truest friendship for misery over an *assumption.* She would have followed Justice to the ends of the earth, gone anywhere with him, done anything with him. Done anything *for* him.

Except fight to keep him in her life. Liberty covered her mouth.

The tears made her hiccup.

Eventually, she had to drop her head and watch, with wet, distorted vision, as tears turned her blue dress black, one tiny puddle at a time.

JUSTICE.

Like a zombie, Justice gave Dewey a call.

When the line opened, Dewey's voice was uncertain. "Justice? That's you, isn't it?"

Justice stood, immobilized, holding Jack's cell phone to his ear. He didn't know how to speak or where to start.

Damn it, Liberty.

He felt like his heart had just been through a meat grinder.

"Yeah. I'm here." His voice was unnatural. He fumbled, "Dewey, did you..."

"You haven't called me that in years," Dewey replied.

It killed Justice. *Killed* him.

Dewey was his best friend.

He didn't want to question him. He didn't want to consider that Liberty was telling the truth, but she'd said things he couldn't ignore.

Today, with her, here, he'd *felt* things he couldn't ignore.

"The day we rolled down the hill…" he forced himself through it. "I cut my arm and when I came back, you and Liberty were fighting."

"Yeah." Dewey's voice changed. "What about it?"

Justice could almost hear his friend swallow.

He hated it. This. All of it.

He was so worked up, his eyes stung.

Come on, Justice willed himself.

"What did you two fight about?"

"I don't remember," Dewey said. "I don't know. Probably nothing." Justice hated the way Dewey didn't sound innocent.

Why couldn't he sound *innocent*?

"She called you gay…"

"Yeah," Dewey agreed. "She sucks." And then the tears sprung full force. Because Liberty didn't suck.

Before that day with Dewey, Liberty had done no wrong. All she'd ever done was be there for the two of them.

Justice was shocked by the way hot tears pricked his eyes. He wasn't an angry crier. He hadn't cried hot tears since his parents decided to divorce. These were the tears he cried when he was painfully, undeniably, woefully wrong.

And he was, he realized with an awful twinge. He'd been wrong this entire time. Liberty wasn't mean-spirited. Liberty wouldn't bully the bumblebee that stung her. She wasn't like that.

Why had he believed all this time that she was like that? When it wasn't true, when it had never been true.

"Justice, are you crying?" Dewey almost whispered.

Justice's voice wobbled. He squeezed the phone too tight. "Dewey, I need you to tell me the truth."

"Why do you keep calling me that? 'Washington' was the nickname *you* made up, remember?"

"I'm being serious."

"What the hell is wrong with you?"

"Liberty told me what happened," Justice confessed.

Dewey went silent.

It didn't make anything better.

"She told me that..." Justice gripped the phone so hard his hand shook. "That you tried to talk her out of telling me she liked me back then. Is that true?"

"Justice."

"*Is it true?*" Justice was giving Dewey the benefit of the doubt, even though he had not given Liberty the same consideration.

Justice had called her the worst, when really, Justice was.

"No," Dewey finally said.

"Because you knew I liked her," Justice fought. "*You knew.*" His mind was careening. "You told me that she liked George, that the whole time she was into him. You told me that *she told you that.* But I asked her about it and she said she never liked George. Never."

It was so hard to believe.

Justice felt like his whole life was a lie, but he could see it now.

Impossible as it was to believe, as betrayed and hurt and devastated as Justice felt now that he understood, he couldn't see any other truth but this one.

"You played us against each other," Justice sounded lifeless as he submitted the accusation. "Didn't you?"

It was a scenario Justice had never once considered. But now it seemed the only explanation.

His voice was *shaking.* "I liked Liberty and Liberty liked me, and we both confided in *you.*"

He hated how the math worked out so perfectly, *too* perfectly. He hated the tears rolling down his fucking face.

"And you told her not to tell me how she felt, and you told me she liked someone else. And we—you, you let me think that—"

And then Dewey broke too. "I liked you first."

After that first sentence, the rest of Dewey's confession came easy. Terribly, horrifically easy.

"You were my friend first. And you were...going to leave me behind." He sniffled.

It seemed everybody was going to cry today.

"You two were always going off by yourselves. Leaving me out. Ever since you met her. I just...I didn't want to lose you."

"So you sabotaged our relationship," Justice concluded.

"I didn't, I swear. I wanted...I just wanted to *stall* you two dating so I could figure out how I felt about you."

Dewey's shaky breathing shook the line between them.

"I wasn't trying to manipulate you, I just—I did fight with Liberty about asking you out, that's true, but at the time, I didn't know why. I didn't realize I might have actual feelings for you until she called me out."

"You let me think she bullied you. For three years. You let me hate her. You *watched* me hate her. For no reason. You..."

"What was I supposed to do? By the time I figured my shit out, you were...at the bottom of the ocean. You hated her so much, you bit anyone's head off who mentioned her to you. Even me."

"You should have told me."

"You'd come up with so many other reasons to hate her. I wasn't even sure you cared about that day anymore."

"You should have told me."

Everything Justice said sounded like an accusation. Or maybe Dewey just sounded guilty.

"I didn't know how," Dewey admitted. "I saw how you treated her. How you just threw her away, no question. No discussion. And she didn't even do anything wrong! I knew if I told you, you'd throw me away too and I couldn't...I couldn't risk that. You're my best friend."

Liberty's words returned to Justice's mind.

You throw friends away for no reason.

Justice suddenly and wholly realized the gravity of the past three years.

"I throw friends away for no reason," he spoke them aloud, the words that described him.

"Justice, I'm sorry. Please don't—"

"I gotta go."

SCENE II.

— 9:20 p.m. —

LIBERTY.

Tremors of laughter radiated through the audience.

As Liberty's eyes drifted over the crowd, they snagged on the poodle she'd met earlier. He was sitting with a parent and child.

Like a water balloon to the face, Liberty suddenly remembered she'd never connected with her parents.

It was dark out. It was full-on nighttime.

And they might have no idea if she was alive or dead.

She lurched to her feet, not for the first time today, and started moving.

The backstage area, she thought.

The What You Will people were back there. One of them would have another phone she could borrow.

Backstage was a network of small circus tents.

There was an orange tent that served as an antechamber to the stage. Another tent that had racks of costumes.

Another with a small folding table, covered with water bottles and protein bars and cookies. Led only by her stomach, Liberty drifted to the food table, grabbed a plate, and piled it high with cookies.

She hadn't eaten since lunch.

Nearby, there was someone talking quietly and intently into a walkie- talkie. A stage manager! They knew everything, didn't they? They were professional problem-solvers.

The woman glanced at Liberty and came her way.

"Are you one of the stowaways?" She asked. Liberty nodded.

"Could I borrow your cell phone to call my mom?"

The stage manager slid a phone from her pocket into Liberty's hand, and Liberty dialed like her life depended on it.

It probably did.

Her mom answered on the second ring, 12 out of 10 panicked.

"Hello? Liberty?"

It was so good to hear her voice that Liberty nearly cried all over again.

"Liberty?" Her mother prompted.

"Mom."

"Where are you? I got a message from your school that—"

Liberty found a private spot and sank into the grass. She let her mom's panicked but caring voice soothe her, and then Liberty told her mom about her day.

All of it.

Not just the smuggling part.

She started at the top, from them arriving at school. She worked her way through every single detail for the most part. The only details she left out were the ones about her and Justice, all of their fighting, the wrestling in the truck, the almost kiss? Yikes.

Her mom didn't even know they'd been feuding the past three years. Liberty had tried to convince her that they'd grown apart naturally but were still civil (which, of course, was a very, very white lie).

She didn't even know where to *begin* explaining everything that'd happened with Justice, so she didn't. She just skipped it. The details weren't the most important part.

The most important part was that Liberty was talking to her mom. This was the longest conversation they'd had in weeks, maybe months.

"Liberty, thank you for that thorough account of today's events. I appreciate it and I'm so sorry that all of this happened, but I still don't understand why you didn't tell me all this the minute we made contact earlier this evening," Mom said in her nurse voice.

Her Someone-Fucked-Up-And-That-Someone-Is-You-But-I'm-Trying- to-Be-Nice voice.

Here was another hole in her story.

She was so ashamed of the truth that she briefly considered lying about it.

But she'd had enough lies to last her a damn lifetime.

"Believe it or not," Liberty came out with it, "I didn't want to worry you. You were already worried about Grandpa and when we were texting and I realized you had no idea where I was, I just...I didn't want to make matters worse."

"Liberty, worry about that when you break something. Worry about that when you scratch the car. Do not ever worry about upsetting me when you've been accidentally smuggled to another state, baby."

"It wasn't just that," Liberty heard herself say. "I was worried if I told you...that you wouldn't come to get me."

"Why would you be worried about that? Of course, I—"

"Because I come second," she blurted out.

Her mom was silent on the other end, and Liberty was genuinely so terrified of what her mother's response might be that she kept talking just to stall for time.

"I mean, it just, um...it feels like if you have to choose between

Grandpa and me, you always choose him. If you have to choose between work and me, you choose work. Because sick people need you more than I do. And I get that, but it...it just sucks, Mom. *It sucks.* I hate it."

Liberty blew out a huge breath, fear and relief exiting her body at once.

"You may not know this, but school isn't exactly paradise for me. I have one friend. Everyone else thinks I'm a horrible person. If I'd been kidnapped today for real, no one at PSM would've really cared. And with Dad and everything, it's just...it's hard to go to school and feel like no one cares and it's hard to go home and feel like no one cares."

If today had taught Liberty anything, it was to *speak your truth.*

Speak it early, speak it often, speak it even when it's scary and you're afraid you'll be rejected.

Liberty was scared shitless that she'd be rejected, even after all that'd happened today.

But she also wasn't pretending like she was fine when she wasn't, for once.

It occurred to Liberty...maybe if she was her whole self, all the time, maybe if she stood up for herself, all the time, not just when she was at her wit's end, maybe then she'd feel... free. *Liberated.*

Wouldn't that be something?

When her mom did finally speak, it was obvious she was crying, which only made Liberty cry more.

"I'm sorry," her mom said. She apologized over and over.

"It's okay," Liberty eventually said, and it really was okay.

"You know, I...I didn't used to be like this," her mom said. "A workaholic."

"You? A workaholic? *No,*" Liberty joked, which made her mom laugh, despite herself.

"All you need to know is that you are the best kid anybody could ask for, and you're perfect and wonderful and amazing.

Please don't feel like I don't *care,* Liberty. I love you more than anything in the world."

Liberty exhaled hard. *There* were some words she'd needed to hear. "I love you, Mom."

"I love you, too."

Maybe there was nothing left to say.

Liberty had already told her mom that Hope was coming to pick her and Justice up and that she should stay at the hospital, that Liberty would be there as soon as she could be.

Mom had already told her about the tumor and the surgery and the prognosis, all of it.

It felt like they'd covered everything and then some, but then her mom saw fit to add one last insight.

"All I can tell you, sweetie, is...stay away from prop trucks and when it's your turn, *pick better.*"

Liberty laughed. "Pick better? What do you mean?"

"When it's time for you to fall in love, pick someone better to fall in love with than I did."

Liberty's heart slipped and fell in her chest.

"What am I talking about?" Her mom let out a wry laugh. "I don't need to tell you this. You're wiser than I was at your age, you already know that. What I mean is...if I could go back and change something and still get you, I'd go back and I'd marry someone who was my best friend, you know? Someone like Justice."

"*Mom!*" Liberty whined to cover her own inner chaos.

"Okay, okay. Sentimentality overload. I copy." Mom sounded like she was smiling. "Send me a note *the minute* Hope gets there, and if anything changes, you let me know."

"I will," Liberty promised.

"I love you," her mom said again.

Liberty felt it that time, all the way in her pinky toes.

— 9:35 p.m. —

JUSTICE.

The clouds overhead looked more silver by the minute. The changing light and an optic-white moon lit the sky in shades of blue, black, and shining gray.

It was nighttime now.

And Justice certainly felt like he was in the dark. He laid down on the platform.

Maybe if he stopped moving, his world would stop spinning out of control.

You're an asshole.

Liberty's hurt, decided eyes haunted him.

All this time, he'd been so sure she was in the wrong. And yet —Justice thought about screaming again.

The rows of vendor stalls and activities had quieted now. Small forked flags snapped and shuddered against the breeze high above the tents. Justice held his hands up to the sky, and suddenly imagined Liberty's hands beside his.

Just then, Jack Elby's cell phone pinged.

Justice didn't want to look. He hadn't been looking. But this was the fourth ping in a few minutes...

When he finally did look, a tower of text messages looked back at him:

> Justice
>
> Please don't hate me
>
> I know what I did was messed up, but you and Liberty were my only friends
>
> I could stand to lose her, but I couldn't stand to lose you.

Justice deleted all the messages and then took a few breaths, trying to force his lungs to get back to work as usual.

He dialed and held the phone to his ear.

Dewey answered almost immediately, but Justice spoke first.

"Please don't talk. Just listen." He pushed out a big breath. "I'm sorry, Dewey."

His eyes still stung.

"Fuck, this is the worst day *ever*. Right up there with Toys R' Us going out of business. Uh..." He clenched his teeth, trying to wrest iron into his rickety crying voice. "I'm sorry I made you feel like...you couldn't tell me the truth. I'm sorry that I didn't...pay more attention to you, I guess."

Dewey snuffled, making the microphone snap at Justice's ear. Justice swiped at his eyes with his other hand.

"It wasn't on purpose," he continued. "Liberty and I were just..." Words failed him, but not Dewey.

"*Magic.* You two were magic."

Those words caught Justice off guard, but he tried to keep it together. "I wasn't going to leave you behind. No matter what happened with Liberty. And Dewey, I...I'm really sorry that I, you know...that I couldn't love you."

Dewey choked on a laugh.

"You don't have to apologize for that."

"I know."

A long sobering pause unfolded.

It felt like their friendship just got power-washed. Like they were sparkling clean, somehow.

Brand new.

Not okay. But fresh.

"If I were into dudes, you know it would totally be me and you." Dewey hacked a laugh that time. Justice could feel his friend's delight, and it helped ease the pain of the storm raging inside him.

"Justice?" Dewey asked when his laughter fell away. "Are we going to be okay?"

Since the theme of today was Tell The Truth, Justice came out with it. "I don't know."

☙

LATER, WHEN THE PHONE BUZZED AGAINST HIS CHEST, HE DIDN'T KNOW what to expect.

Was Hope here? Was it another message from Dewey? Was it… Liberty? He held the phone up tentatively.

It was a message for Jack Elby, actually, but in the process of checking, Justice did happen to notice one that wasn't for Jack…

> Hi, this message is for Liberty.
>
> We just got a call from your school letting us know that they've had trouble contacting your parents.

Justice read on, and without warning, a weight bore down on him, pressing in on his chest.

The pressure was so acute he briefly worried it was a medical problem, until his brain went, *You're a dumbass.*

The pressure evened out, making his neck and face feel hot, almost like he was embarrassed.

But it was more than that. Justice felt…*guilty.*

He tried to sit straight up, but failed beneath the weight of the doublet and flopped backward again.

But in his heart, he sat straight up because everything Liberty said was right.

He was an asshole.

Earlier, when he ran away from her, and an hour ago before they fought, she was trying to ask him for a ride home.

Not to ruin his life.

Not to affix an awful end to an awful day, but because she didn't have another way home.

Something's going on with her mom, and her dad...

Justice didn't have many memories of Don Marshall. He was more of a shadow in Liberty's life. He was there at birthday parties, entertaining the adults.

He was standing next to her mom at all their school recitals, but you couldn't tell he was Liberty's dad at all. You couldn't tell because he never looked at her. Even when he was somewhere *because* of her, he never looked at her.

She was never his reason.

No matter how bright Liberty shone, her father was one corner of the world her light couldn't reach.

And today, when she really needed someone's help, asking Justice—the asshole who'd been mean to her for years with no apparent basis in reality—was easier than asking the man who was supposed to have her back the most.

Justice recoiled at the words he'd said, the way he'd *exploded* on her in her time of need.

Even if Liberty hated him and didn't want a ride home (both of which were absolutely legit), she would probably need to call someone and she couldn't even do *that* because Justice had been hogging the phone all this time.

With difficulty, Justice finally rolled off the platform.

His reflexes kicked in, so he didn't eat grass before getting his bearings.

Maybe he couldn't make the past three years right. But he could at least properly apologize for this, couldn't he?

SCENE III.

— 9:45 p.m. —

LIBERTY.

What a fucking day.

After returning yet another borrowed phone, Liberty rejoined the audience watching *Much Ado*. She still felt warm from talking to her mom, finally.

She couldn't explain the immense relief washing over her in gentle waves. She'd spoken her truth and she felt so light, she might just float away. But then her thoughts snagged on the last thing her mom said.

I'd go back and I'd marry someone who was my best friend, you know? Someone like Justice.

Yeesh.

How was it that parents were so versatile? Liberty wondered.

They could embarrass you from near or far.

Why did she have to bring up Justice like that, when they were in the middle of reconciling?

Justice...

And then everything stopped. Her whole world and everything in it stopped for about thirty seconds because something occurred to her.

She could never see Justice again.

The last time Liberty saw him, in addition to the massive spat they'd had, she'd...

Oh, God, she'd... She'd told him...

*I liked you. In eighth grade, I **really** liked you.*

Horror suffused through Liberty like a virus.

Had she really admitted *to her archenemy* that she had a crush on him in eighth grade?

This was the Motherload, the horror to horrify all other horrors. Liberty would have to change schools, change streets, maybe even move to a new state.

There was no way she could face him after saying something so completely moronic and embarrassing.

Justice Garrison would never let her live it down.

In a million years, he'd never *ever* let her live it down. It was awful and it was true, which made it worse.

He...he was her greatest weakness, and she'd basically told him that to his face.

There was no telling what kind of torment he'd have up his sleeve, come Monday at school.

No sooner had she realized she could never face him again did Liberty remember that she'd voluntarily signed up to spend three hours in a car with him and his sister on the drive home.

No, no, no, no.

What would she do now?

She'd already talked to Hope, who said Liberty was more than welcome to ride along. She'd already told her mom, who was in agreement.

Justice hated the idea.

Good. Maybe, she could call her mom and say, *Hey, Justice is repulsed by the idea of me driving back with him, so can you actually come get me after all?*

Yeah, right.

"Liberty, *why*," she whispered to herself.

There was no way out.

When she'd needed a ride, Hope and Justice were the perfect solution. But now that she'd gone and embarrassed herself so thoroughly, there was no way she could go through with it.

But she would have to, wouldn't she? Getting home soon was too important.

Liberty needed to be at home as soon as possible.

Grandpa was undergoing surgery tonight, and the truth was Liberty kind of knew how that felt.

For her, today was like surgery.

An involuntary one—a botched hack job where all the nastiness inside her was amputated, except there was no anesthesia to numb her and no stitches to keep her from bleeding out.

Now she knew she and Justice had separated for no reason. Their three-year feud was based on a lie.

And what would come now?

Her motivation to hate Justice was gone.

And the pedestal she'd put Magdalena on crumbled the minute she saw Adam's tongue.

Maybe I should give up on love and friendship until college... She'd given it her best shot and look what happened.

Liberty was just going to have to pretend like today never happened.

Yeah, that's what she would do.

She would just...well, she would act.

She would perform the role of Non-Embarrassing-Normal-Teenage-Girl for the next four hours, and once she was home, she'd petition her mother to let her go to boarding school until she graduated.

Because even though today had been such a wild ride, it didn't change anything.

Even though Liberty was heartbroken and mad at Magdalena about Adam, at school, on Monday, she'd act completely normal around her.

What else could she do?

Magdalena didn't know that Liberty knew anything, so of course, Liberty would act natural. They'd go through their normal routines, sit everywhere they usually sat.

And when Liberty saw Justice and Washington together in the hall, or in the cafeteria, or at RC meetings, nothing would be different.

Justice wouldn't look at her and she wouldn't look at him.

Liberty was not the kind of fool who thought one crazy day could change three years of cold, hard, hateful muscle memory.

Everything that happened today proved how tragic the last three years were, but that was it.

All that was left was to go home and move on.

Even though she was mortified by it and wished she hadn't told Justice she used to like him, she was also a little proud of herself.

In the name of speaking her truth, she'd done something for her eighth grade self that her eighth grade self never got the opportunity to do.

There was some good closure in that.

Or at least, that's what she would tell herself on the painstaking drive back to Green River while she tried not to cry from her anxiety over it in the backseat.

What a fucking day.

JUSTICE.

Justice still had that power-washed feeling as he navigated

through the all but empty fairgrounds toward the sounds of an audience cheering and laughing.

Everyone must be watching the show, he concluded.

It was weird. He was walking, just like he normally walked every single day, but his heart was pounding.

He was walking, but his heart was running.

It was like his heart wanted to get to Liberty faster than his feet would take him.

What was *that* about?

Their relationship the past three years, to put it nicely, had been *hostile.* If there was like a...Presidential Medal of Fuckery, it would go to Justice.

Hands down.

He'd been mean. Beyond mean. But...

*I liked you. In eighth grade, I **really** liked you.*

Thinking about those words made him feel like he had a chocolate fountain in his chest. Those words gave him a hot, melty, sweet, overflowing feeling inside, and it was really, really gross.

She liked me back then, he allowed himself to believe. Liberty Bell Marshall liked Justice *in middle school.*

That said something, because his middle school self was not exactly what one would call...a catch.

His middle school self (his scrappy, scrawny, never-considered- contact-lenses self) swelled at the thought.

Who was he kidding?

His middle school self was *swooning* inside of him.

Before Magdalena, before he misunderstood the fight and wrecked everything, there was Justice, with the biggest crush in the world.

A crush that felt like he was carrying an elephant on his shoulders every day.

A crush that had him up at midnight in early July, running

down a quiet street, just so he could be at Liberty's window, the first to tell her happy birthday.

That crush was...wild.

And really humiliating sometimes. (He already told you about the pants.)

But it was April then when the crush started, just like it was April now. It was sixth grade. Liberty walked into their homeroom wearing a Spock T-shirt.

The same one he was wearing, and it was like a repeat of second grade. It was like Aunt Shan's ghost touched his shoulder *a second time*, Justice swore to God.

It had scared him how much he liked Liberty.

I was honestly terrified, he remembered. Justice had never been so terrified of anything in his life.

In eighth grade, Justice was trying to start a relationship with Liberty while also watching his parents' relationship fall apart.

He'd been so afraid that falling in love with someone and taking a chance might end in the same misery his parents had plunged them all into...

Justice was so afraid of finding out that what he and Liberty had might not be real...that he destroyed their relationship before he ever got the chance to find out.

Like he was so scared of him and Liberty dying in a car crash that he destroyed their car before they drove it anywhere. His actions sounded really dumb when he put it like that, in his head.

Justice followed the cheering sounds until they were right in front of him, the lane opening like an artery into an organ. The field of stages expanded before him.

As he approached the audience, he slowed down. Everyone at the whole festival must be here.

He glanced up at the stage, and that Ashely girl was there. Benjamin Franklin was up there with her. It was the same show from this afternoon.

The name suddenly stuck out in Justice's mind, *Much Ado About Nothing*.

Is that the story of us?

He scanned faces in the semi-darkness, looking for a mane of curly nut-brown hair. And then he saw her, seated near the back, off on her own.

Justice gravitated to her, heart really kicking now.

What's the big deal? It's just Liberty.

He'd seen her a thousand times. Why was his heart reacting like this?

"Liberty." He said her name out loud and immediately understood that something was different now.

He didn't know if it was him. Or if it was her.

Or if it was both of them, or some sorcery or something. But everything felt different.

Really different.

Liberty startled, eyes popping up to find Justice there, breathing hard, standing over her, squeezing the cell phone in his hand. Tiny tears beaded in her eyes.

Because the menagerie of audience members were focused on the show, it felt like they were alone.

Again.

"Can I..." his mouth started. The crowd quieted just enough for Justice to get the rest of the sentence out. "Can I give you a ride home?"

Applause drowned her voice, as she said back, "Yes."

His cheeks felt like tea bags in boiling water, hot and diffusing emotion. *She said yes,* his brain kept repeating.

One simple answer to one simple question shouldn't feel like *this*. He knew that.

He knew that, and yet his heart stuttered the way his mouth used to when he was four.

Seeing Liberty now was just like the movies. Like he was

moving through a time lapse with a Childish Gambino song pulsing hazily in the background.

Liberty wasn't looking at him. But Justice was looking at her, like he hadn't seen her in three years.

Her hair was more voluminous now, as though her head was too small for her mind, and she'd begun storing her ideas in the curly annex attached.

Her honey skin. Her full, parted lips that he'd tried to sketch many times and had never done justice.

Liberty adjusted herself in the grass.

Justice realized that she was trying to get up from the ground but having trouble because she was wearing a sixteenth century monstrosity.

Without giving it one single thought, he held his hands out to her. She saw them and froze, slowly lifting her head.

Their eyes met again, and it was intimate somehow.

Snug. Like a key in a lock.

Though who was unlocking whom was a question with no answer. Yet.

Her cool hands came to alight in his and he pulled her to her feet, and he probably held her hands a few seconds too long and she probably noticed.

And that's why Justice turned away from her super fast, like an overactive robot, and marched away from the crowd and the stage, hoping to God she was following him, even while he was being crazy.

Why am I thinking so much?.

And why were his lungs acting all new, like they'd only converted air into CO_2 a few times before and not for 17 years?

When they were away from it all, housed by the crisp darkness of an April evening, Liberty broke the charged silence between them to ask, "Shouldn't we go get our things?"

"What?" Justice had forgotten about their things, even about his skateboard, which sort of started this all.

"Isn't...Hope here?" Liberty's head fell to the side a little.

Maybe Justice thought her head was going to fall off. Maybe that's why his hand suddenly wanted to hold her cheek. Again.

Yeah. That's it.

"She's actually—" He blabbed and tried to get it together. "She's not here yet."

"Oh."

"Yeah."

"Then..." Her lips pressed together and then released. Justice suddenly felt like could watch a .gif of *that* for hours. "Why did you come find me?"

Focus, he urged himself.

He tried to find the words. *Right. Yes. I wanted to...extend...an apology for my behavior earlier when I...acted like a douche-canoe.*

A...douche-canoe?

"I just wanted to... About earlier, about *everything*, I—"

"Justice, stop," Liberty held up a hand in protest.

"What?" He blurted.

"Look, I know today has been...*bananas.* And we've, uh, we've said a lot of things. But nothing's different, okay? What I mean is that...*nothing's changed,*" she explained.

She let out a breathy laugh.

"You and I both know that come Monday, we're going to go right back to hating each other, so you don't have to pretend like today has been anything other than what it is, all right? An anomaly. One that will never happen again."

Justice was *completely* lost. Zero idea what she meant. "What are you saying?"

"I'm saying I don't expect you to be nice to me all of sudden or treat me any different just because we fell down the rabbit hole today."

Justice barely heard a word she said.

He was too busy thinking *her eyes are bigger*, their honey color trapping the light of the torches, which illuminated the path around them.

Her lips were *so* pretty. The most perfect lips he'd ever seen. Her lips were what inspired him to categorize lip shapes to begin with.

Justice knew that he was supposed to like other things about girls. *I fucking do, don't get me wrong.* But Liberty's lips were limited edition perfection.

Her bare collarbones made his heart skip.

He was so nervous all of sudden that he didn't dare officially notice the way her corset thing was squeezing her tight everywhere.

The way he suddenly wanted to...

Christ, he felt *ill.*

He felt just...lousy with attraction, with *affection.*

I liked you.

Those three words had apparently been the key to a vault of repressed feelings, and now that the vault was open, Justice was dealing with a deluge of thoughts and feelings he'd never expected to revisit *ever* again.

How could he make it stop?

He was just standing there, like an idiot, staring at her but not saying anything and she was trying not to look at him but didn't seem to be doing a very good job.

Say something.

"Uh." But that's when Justice realized he had questions. He had questions for Liberty about...a lot of things.

Or maybe he just—Justice didn't know what he wanted to say. All he knew was that he suddenly felt like everything he understood about their eighth grade year was wrong and he would really love some additional perspective.

"Can we talk about eighth grade?" he finally asked.

He watched Liberty's eyes go wide and her whole body freeze up. "No."

"What?" Justice sounded like a confused broken record.

"We don't need to talk about eighth grade," she asserted. "What's passed is past. We don't need to talk about eighth grade ever again—"

"But I want to." Justice surprised himself *and* Liberty with that remark. "I want to talk about how...we..."

The words "I can't do this" fell from Liberty's lips in a mush, and then Liberty Marshall proceeded to do something Justice had never once seen her do.

Liberty turned away from him and ran. She turned and *ran*.

Except that, Liberty doesn't run.

She was brave. She was confrontational.

She was like a giant rock.

It took Justice a good minute to actually *believe* that she was running away from him before his legs kicked into soccer mode and went after her.

It was full dark now, as they hightailed it through the fairground grass. The dark colors they wore turned black and gray in the cool darkness, but Justice could still tell.

They were matching. Justice and Liberty.

We match, he thought.

Thoughts came faster when Justice ran. He understood in those few seconds that they'd always matched.

With a start, Justice realized he might actually believe they still belonged together, even now.

I have to talk to her.

He pushed his legs faster.

Abruptly, his costume caught on a tent pole he didn't see before it was too late. His feet tangled beneath him, and he went down sprawling. He lost sight of her.

When Justice got to his feet, Liberty was gone. But the certainty inside of him wouldn't wilt.

Do it differently, Justice, he commanded himself. *This time can be different. It will be.*

LIBERTY.

This is insane! Liberty screamed internally. *I've never run away from another human being in my life.*

She'd seen people do it in movies.

But usually, she'd pull out her sixth grade taekwondo moves way faster than she'd run.

Maybe the difference right now was that she wasn't in real danger, not that anyone could tell that from the way her heart was slapping around in her chest like a panicky fish out of water.

Liberty didn't even know what was wrong.

She obviously didn't want to talk about eighth grade. She'd been through enough today without Justice mocking her childhood crush or worse, retroactively rejecting her.

But did the fear of those outcomes really warrant *this?*

Liberty, hiding in the *Romeo and Juliet* stand from earlier?

Her back was pressed up against the wall right next to the side door. It was dark enough in there that it should've scared her.

Unfinished wood and gruesome shadows.

She should have been afraid of being in this pitch-black creaky thing, not of Justice's quick footfalls as he ran this way. And yet.

"Liberty!" He shouted her name, his voice too loud in the quiet of these darkened empty lanes. "*Liberty!*"

She glanced toward the sound of it and realized that she could *see* him, with his back to her as his head swiveled left and right.

There was an opening between the room (if you could even call it that) Liberty now stood in and the open-air platform, which Justice stood just beyond.

Which meant that if Justice turned around, he'd be able to see Liberty, which freaked her out so much that as soon as her eyes locked onto the darkened staircase to her right, she hurried up the steps, forgetting altogether about being quiet.

She was immediately given away by the wooden steps beneath her feet which *squealed* as she climbed, loud enough to be a car alarm. She froze.

Justice was mid-word when the squeal broke the quiet.

His voice cut off in the middle of saying Liberty's name, though she wasn't sure if that was because it was hard for her to hear anything over the fucking squeal or if it was because *he* heard it, discovered exactly where she was, and was now entering the platform shack.

Liberty leaned against the wall for support, breathing hard. This was the worst game of hide and seek she'd ever played. She'd never wanted to be invisible so badly in her life. She just wanted to get away.

Why couldn't she get away from him?

He'd left her, so why did she feel like she couldn't escape him? Same street, same school, same club, same clothes, same crush, same freak accidental kidnapping, same horrible medieval costumes.

Why was the universe always throwing them together?

WE'RE NOT SUPPOSED TO BE TOGETHER! She wanted to scream into the cosmos.

Liberty was ashamed that she ever thought they were supposed to be together—

"Liberty, I know you're in there," Justice called, making her muscles lock up tight. "I know you're there, so even though you hate me...would you just listen?"

She covered her mouth with her hand again, like words would fly out of her if she didn't.

She just stood there, frozen.

Caught.

Her stomach twisted, like someone gave her a good pinch on the *inside.* Why did the thought of being caught by Justice make her feel like there was a circus in her chest?

"I talked to Dewey," Justice said next, shocking Liberty. "And he told me the truth."

More shock for Liberty.

Her breath hitched. She held it in.

"What I'm trying to say is that...I believe you. About what happened." Huh? Justice *believed* her?

"Liberty, I...I need to say something to your face." Somehow, she heard him exhale. "Could you come out here?" Justice asked. "Please."

It took Liberty too long to realize he was actually *asking* her. He legit wanted her to come outside.

See him.

She was still pretty freaked out, but she managed to convince her legs to carry her up the remaining three stairs and walk her cautiously onto the balcony above him. It was higher up than she thought it was. It felt like a real balcony.

Stars twinkled beyond the treetops.

Her skin tickled, but she didn't know if that was due to the evening breeze or Justice's face, tilted up toward hers from one story down.

Justice was standing on the Romeo platform, looking...well, like Romeo.

Like a guy...in love.

But that wasn't real. Or possible. It wasn't *plausible.*

So Liberty tried not to notice.

This moment was too saturated, too full of words they'd said and not said, insults they'd thought and hurled at each other. It felt like something was breaking apart.

Like a Band-Aid needed to be ripped off, and Justice wanted to do it fast and Liberty wanted to do it slow.

But Liberty had no idea what the Band-Aid *was* in that metaphor. Liberty didn't know what was being covered up, and she also didn't know what had healed.

Was it her? Was it him?

Liberty certainly didn't want to think about the idea of *us*. But that idea seemed written in his upturned eyes.

Liberty was still holding her breath.

This wasn't the Justice she knew and resented.

What the fuck is happening? Liberty touched her fingers gently to the wooden railing. She held onto it, to keep herself from flying away, and then...

"Liberty, I'm sorry."

She never imagined she'd ever be here in this moment, him apologizing, earnestly, honestly.

His face blurred in her vision as a teardrop fell to the railing separating her from the open air.

"I misjudged you," he told her, as her shoulders lifted and shook. "I didn't even...What I did wasn't fair. I—I really fucked up, Liberty. I know. I know it. Fucked up and beyond. And I'm really sorry."

"Fuck your apology!" Liberty was surprised by the amount of happiness, vulnerability, and real rage she could feel all at once. "I don't care what you think of me. And I don't need you to like me, Justice, so just—"

"Good! Because I don't like you!" Familiar irritation brightened his eyes.

Liberty supplied a mad laugh, in response. "Wonderful! Because I don't give a shit!"

"EXCELLENT!" He roared. "*SO WHY DIDN'T YOU EVER TELL ME?*"

What the hell was he talking about *now*?

"Tell you *what?*"

The confidence in Justice's voice dwindled down.

"About...you know."

"I thought you knew," Liberty replied. "I thought Dewey told you. I assumed that you took Dewey's side in the fight."

Justice shook his head, like she was wrong. Like she'd misunderstood him.

"I'm not talking about the fight."

His voice was soft and smooth, like cashmere. The circus inside her livened up at the sound.

"What?" She managed.

"Why didn't you ever tell me that you liked me?"

Why the hell was he asking her *that?*

If this was some sort of setup that ended with Justice making fun of her for having had a crush on him, she was going to beat him to death with that doublet he was wearing.

"I told you. I was going to, but then Dewey and I—" She said the words too hard and started over. "Look. Does it even matter?"

Liberty feared the circus inside her was starting to show.

He could probably see the carnival lights glowing at the back of her throat.

"It matters," he asserted, voice heavy.

The look on his face was layered so intensely with an emotion Liberty didn't want to face that she had to look away.

"Why?" It was not the question Liberty should've asked.

Then, almost out of nowhere, he yelled, "BECAUSE I GAVE YOU MY PANTS!"

(Liberty hoped someone would literally kill her if she ever tried to wear white pants again.)

"Because we used to write comic strips together," he barreled on, making her heart bounce. "Because you were my first kiss!"

"We were seven."

"Because I even told you that time...that I loved you."

"You were drunk. On *one sip* of champagne at New Years after Hope beat you at cards," Liberty pointed out. "*So what?*"

Justice didn't say anything.

His frustrated gaze was cast toward a darkened stall with a *Leathergoods* sign in front of it.

Why hadn't she told Justice she liked him back then? A Jeopardy question from pubescent hell.

The words stung as they passed her lips. "You had more memories with Dewey. And back then, I'd recently figured out that I liked girls too. I thought it was possible and highly likely that you maybe...loved Dewey. However you might have felt about me."

"You did not seriously think that," Justice concluded. "There's no way you honestly thought that."

Liberty got defensive. Immediately.

"Justice, you were *his* first kiss for crying out loud."

"Yeah, but I only kissed him because *you weren't there!*"

"I *was* there!"

Justice dragged a hand down his face like he was... He actually looked embarrassed.

What exactly was he about to say?

"Angela's party. We're there and Henry Feldon tells me that we're about to play truth or dare. And I...I asked him to...I asked him to dare me to kiss my best friend."

Liberty wasn't following.

"We start playing, you're there, Dewey's there, and it's almost Henry's turn. And then Angela needs you for something, I don't know. You disappear and you don't come back. Then it's Henry's turn and he dares me, like we agreed, but...*you weren't there.*"

Justice drops his hands to his waist and briefly hangs his head. "So I...I had to kiss Dewey. But I wanted it to be you. I imagined it was you, every second."

Liberty wanted to accuse him of lying right now. She wanted to say he'd made this entire tale up.

But no one would voluntarily invent a story that made them look pathetic.

Which meant...Justice had to be telling the truth.

"Liberty," he pressed on. "I was crazy about you and you know it."

Something turned to goo inside her when he said those words. *Ignore it,* she commanded herself.

"I *hoped,*" she clarified. "But I had no idea."

"How could you not have known?"

"Because someone who was crazy about me couldn't have thrown me away like that."

"Well, I was a fucking idiot. We've established that," Justice said. "Did I mention I'm sorry? Because I am, Liberty. Please believe that, even if you never forgive me."

Liberty watched him take a big breath.

"Here's the thing. My aunt Shan...she told me something when I was little. Just before she died. She said to find someone I belonged with, that I'd be able to recognize them easily...because they'd be wearing the same thing as me."

His eyes darted away before returning to hers.

"I know it sounds crazy, but that was *you,* Liberty."

An emotion in his voice had begun to overpower Liberty's anger, her hurt, her *hate.*

"That was you in second grade. That was you in seventh grade. That's you right now, here, today. We...*we match.* So before you never speak to me again..."

He dropped his head, and then lifted it back up.

"Can you let me pretend for a second that none of this ever happened?"

"What?" Liberty replied, at a loss.

"Can we...play a round of Let's Make Everything Up?"

Here we fucking go.

This is something Liberty hated about Justice—his penchant for random, weird-ass solutions to problems.

He didn't solve problems with viable solutions. Not even with temporary solutions, like Band-Aids.

Justice solved problems with his imagination.

With fun and games and ridiculousness that rarely had anything to do with the problem itself.

"Justice—" She started to deny him, but he was gone.

A nearby creak startled her, and that's when she saw him hauling himself onto the balcony beside her, making the entire stand shake.

Damn this Romeo and Juliet Instagram trap.

Justice was halfway up the balcony's rope ladder before Liberty could say, "What are you *doing*?"

His hand appeared on the railing, followed by his head rising about it. He hoisted himself over the balcony's ledge.

The balcony itself was far too small for both of them *and* all of their relationship drama. Liberty didn't even want to give a thought to weight capacity.

Why couldn't she have picked a better hiding place?

"I know you hate acting," he said first, making her groan. "But we used to do it all the time when we were eight."

Oh my god, Liberty covered her face with her hands. This was all wrong.

Yes, it was tragic that their friendship ended the way it had, especially considering that apparently they'd both had crushes on each other, but—

"Give me *one* good reason," she demanded.

"Because this is the closest to a time machine we'll ever have. If I had one, I'd go back and make everything right," Justice went on. "If we do this now, if you do this with me, at least I can pretend that I did."

He was looking hard at her, turning on the full power of his pancake-syrup eyes.

Not the eyes, Liberty begged. *Not the IHOP eyes.*

Liberty attempted to collect herself by massaging her temples. Justice was trying to apologize to her, and part of his solution was playing a children's game?

It would be like the UN trying to de-escalate international tensions with Candyland. And still Liberty was closer to saying yes than any rational, sane person should have been.

"The world is this one," Justice said softly, just *assuming* she was in.

What a dick.

"We are ourselves. Our thirteen-year-old selves."

He got that kid-gleam in his eye. Making up the world was always his favorite part of this game.

"This archway," he motioned toward the opening from the balcony into the upstairs antechamber area of the R&J stand. "It's a time portal. When we step through it—"

"We're thirteen again?" Liberty dragged a hand down her face. She didn't want to agree to this.

She didn't *think* she wanted to agree to this, but after everything that'd happened, she could feel it.

A desire. A fruitless, pointless, innocent, nostalgic strand of hope that wished they *could* have a do-over.

That they could go back to the perfection of their friendship and keep it alive.

A small, tiny, pitiful part of her yearned for that. Despite the scars that bound them.

Before Justice disappeared through the doorway, he asked, "Are you ready?"

Liberty let the chilly April evening air prick at her skin for a few more seconds, and then she stepped in after Justice, following him into the past.

SCENE IV.

— 10:00 p.m. —

JUSTICE.

If you think Justice had a plan, you're wrong. Justice had no plan. Zero plans.

He was just a guy, pretending to be the thirteen-year-old version of himself.

The one who was skinny enough to fit through a crack in the door. The one who discovered porn with Dewey one afternoon, about four minutes before Liberty burst in and scared them to death.

He and Liberty were just pretending. It wasn't real.

So why did it feel so real? The awkwardness, blooming through his body, was immediate. Like he never grew out of it, like it'd always been there, under the sheet of time.

Justice felt like it really was three years ago when Liberty stepped through the door. Her eyes weren't on him, but when they finally did find his face a few minutes later, they were warm.

Familiar.

They were the eyes Justice remembered drawing and redrawing in his sketchbook.

"Are you okay?" Liberty suddenly asked.

"What?" He bleated.

"About your parents..." she mumbled.

Right, his brain caught up with her.

It wasn't easy, letting himself slip back into the turmoil of those days. But if Liberty was game, there was no way Justice was going to back down and back out from his own stupid, spur-of-the-moment idea.

"Fine," he lied. " Everything sucks, actually," he tried again.

He remembered something from the divorce, something he wasn't sure if he'd ever told Liberty.

"My parents are discussing where we're going to live."

"Who?"

"Me and Hope."

Liberty went still after he said that.

"Dad wants to move into the city, and they actually talked last night about separating us. One of us lives with him, one of us stays with her."

Justice was surprised by the real emotion that sprouted out of his chest. The anger he'd felt, that his parents would even *consider* separating him and his sister.

The fear that he might be chosen to live with Dad, and the fact that that would mean no more Dewey. No more Liberty.

Justice glanced back at her.

He couldn't see her expression in the dark, as she moved toward one wall and pressed her back against it.

"That's terrible," she said.

"Tell me about it." Justice drifted toward her, until they were standing side by side.

She nodded, then gave a sigh. "Right up there with Angela Devlin's birthday party."

Justice cracked an irrepressible smile.

"That was honestly the *worst*."

"The good news is that nothing is going to suck worse than that," she added. "So technically you're prepared. For whatever your parents decide."

"I wouldn't say that." Justice held his breath. "Boston may have better skate parks—"

"And comic book stores."

"Yeah, but it doesn't have you."

Goddamn, Justice. Turn the fuck down.

Justice's actual thirteen-year-old self would've fallen out of a chair if he'd said that in real life.

"Or Dewey," he recovered.

"*Right*." Justice recognized Liberty's signature brand of sarcasm anywhere. "And if you don't have Dewey, who will you watch porn with?"

Justice hung his head. He could feel, like, real actual thirteen-year-old blush on his cheeks.

This was a horrible idea, Justice realized. He *had* to suggest a game of Let's Make Everything Up.

"Once. That was *once*," he iterated. "And it wasn't even my idea." She laughed, and the sound vivified him.

When was the last time Liberty Marshall had laughed *because* of him?

"Whatever," she snickered.

With her easy posture and her hair so long, she wasn't the girl Justice remembered, until she smiled in the dark, and suddenly, she was.

"Liberty Marshall, I like you." The words were out, hanging between them like a rope bridge.

Seventeen-Year-Old Justice knew how Thirteen-Year-Old Liberty felt, but Thirteen-Year-Old Justice didn't know.

Not yet. Not really. Not like this.

Liberty's eyes fell to their feet, which made Justice feel nuts inside. Absolutely wild.

"This is insane," she said, which sent his heart crashing against his ribs. A car driven into a brick wall. "We're not thirteen anymore." Her voice was adamant.

She looked up at him.

"No, we're not," Justice heard himself say, just before he bent his head toward Liberty's, and pushed his mouth to hers.

He pulled back just as soon as he'd leaned in, though, because WHAT THE FUCK WAS HE DOING?!

Until a few hours ago, he'd hated Liberty Marshall.

As far as he knew, Liberty Marshall still currently hated him—*anyone* would hate him after everything he'd done—and after today, Liberty was probably going to avoid him until the end of time. Justice knew that, and yet, he'd just... *kissed her?*

Not even a real kiss. A bird kiss.

WHAT WAS WRONG WITH HIM?!

Liberty didn't move, and Justice, for some reason, leaned in and gave her another peck.

Heart *flying,* he pressed his lips to hers again and this time dared himself to leave them there longer than 0.1 seconds.

Something happened to him when her lips opened against his. His mouth opened, too, and then it was a real kiss.

Relief washed him; his self-respect was back in place. He pulled away slower this time.

"Justice," she said his name as he leaned in again.

"Hmm?" He was a little distracted by the way their noses fit perfectly together.

"Why..." Another kiss. Another. "Why are you kissing me?" she finally murmured.

"I want to." The answer to her question left his mouth without pre-approval.

Justice leaned in again, but Liberty stopped him with her hands. He looked at her in the darkness.

They weren't pretending anymore. He wasn't thirteen-year-old him. She didn't want a thirteen-year-old answer, either. Why did pretending feel so easy when this, right now, felt so hard?

Her eyes were magnetic. Those bare collar bones were tripping him up again.

Justice shook his head.

"Honestly? I haven't figured that part out yet," he admitted, taking a step closer to her. "But would you do me the honor? Liberty Marshall, will you kiss me back?"

Not bad, Garrison.

Justice waited for her to say no, crazy anticipation flooding his veins. She stood there contemplating his request so long that he started to forget what he asked her, then she abruptly met his eyes and said, "I must be crazy."

Justice watched her falling eyelids, her parting lips, as she pulled him in. How had he gotten this far in his life without kissing these lips?

Without kissing *her?*

Their breaths heated their faces.

Her forehead rocked into his as their lips mixed together. He touched her waist and she jumped a little, like she forgot she had a waist.

"*Liberty,*" he found himself saying, lips against hers.

His fingers traced the slope of her neck. He didn't know why her bare skin against his fingers started a riot in his chest, but there he was.

Him. Justice Garrison, kissing her, Liberty Marshall. And liking it. *More* than liking it.

He could already tell that this was a moment he'd come back to in his mind, more than should be allowed.

This kiss was so different from the kisses he'd had before. He couldn't even *remember* the kisses he'd had before. Not when this one was so outstanding, so *liberating*.

"Okay, you're freaking me out," Justice admitted later.

They were sitting in the corner of the upstairs room, his back against one wall, Liberty's against the adjacent one, with her legs draped across his.

"What?" She mumbled.

They'd been sitting in silence for five whole minutes. Justice could still feel her kisses against his face, but she hadn't said anything since she pulled away and came to sit down over here and he'd followed.

"You're really quiet," he explained.

"I'm thinking."

Hmmm. Hope and dread sprung up inside Justice like a fountain. "About what?"

She supplied him an unamused look in the darkness.

"Okay," he amended, gently tapping the fabric mountain of her skirt. "Good things or bad things?"

"The world isn't black and white, Justice," she sighed. "I'm thinking about...true things."

That didn't sound good at all.

"Like...?" He prompted.

"Like I'm in love with Magdalena."

His heart flopped over like a fish.

Duh. Of course, she'd mentioned that earlier, but he hadn't been really listening because they were fighting.

And even if he had been listening...the way Liberty kissed was so intense he would have forgotten.

As it currently stood, if not for Hope, Justice wasn't entirely sure he could be prevailed upon to remember which house was his.

"That's too bad," Justice replied. "I hear Magdalena is dating Adam Grosch."

Liberty burst out laughing, and Justice felt like he'd just made a winning goal. Making her laugh felt that victorious. He smiled, enjoying the moment.

He thought back to their conversation about Mags—which now felt like forever ago—back in the box truck, when Justice had tried and probably failed to articulate what drew him to Mags in the first place.

Thinking about it now…

"You know, I think I fell for her because she reminded me of you." The weight of his words hit him *hard.* He treaded water with, "And because she's super hot."

Liberty just looked at him, face blank, gaze pointed, which made the hair on the back of his neck perk up.

"What?" She asked him.

"Mags is hot," he shrugged.

SHOULD YOU REALLY BE TALKING ABOUT YOUR EX-CRUSH WITH LIBERTY?

Wait. Was that true? Was Magdalena really his *ex-crush?*

As in, was Justice…over her? Already? Since when? Since ten minutes ago?

"She reminds you of *me*?" Liberty reflected back his words.

"The first few times I saw her, I think the reason I even noticed her was because she was with you. Even though I hated you, I knew you wouldn't be friends with just anyone. They had to be special."

Justice's heart started to trot.

"And then she showed up at Model UN, and I started to notice things about her I knew you probably loved." He understood the words more as they fell from his lips. "And then, I guess...I started to love them too."

"Justice, is this a joke?" Liberty's tone made Justice's blood run cold. He leaned forward in the dark.

"What?"

"Am I like...are you doing all of this because Magdalena doesn't want you?"

"*What?*" Justice felt like he was choking on nothing.

Literally, what was Liberty talking about? "Did you hear anything I just said?"

Liberty didn't reply. She only moved her legs off of his and got to her feet. She'd done it before Justice thought to stop her. Something was wrong. Very wrong. And Justice knew that it was probably his fault. Again.

Liberty was quiet as she marched toward the stairs. Justice scrambled to his feet and followed her.

"Liberty?" No response. "*Liberty,* what's—" They were out the side door and into the grass. The moonlight turned the whole fair silver. "Talk to me!" He finally shouted.

"NO!" She roared.

Okay, anger's back.

"You haven't talked to *me* in three years! And now what? You're telling me you're sorry for giving me hell, that you were crazy about me—"

"*I was!*"

"I'm not falling for your shit all over again! It doesn't work like this!" Basically they were reenacting the final scene of *When Harry Met Sally*...only they were seventeen, brown, wearing tights, and Justice had no idea how their movie was going to end.

"You're impulsive, Justice! You change your mind every few seconds! A few hours ago, I ruined your life because I stopped you from going on a date with Magdalena, and now you're...you're romancing me!"

She forced a breath out. "You can't be an asshole to me for three years, change your mind one day, and then expect me to—" She shook her head hard.

"What?"

"WANT YOU BACK!"

"*Why not?*" He demanded.

She'd stopped walking again. The look on Liberty's face scared him, because she looked scared *of him.*

He felt like he was trying to fight through a cement wall of her justified fears and trepidations all to get to the girl on the inside, the one whose laughter could fill him up like a helium balloon.

"I wrecked everything in one day; why can't I put everything back together the same way?"

Liberty cut her eyes at him.

"Because one day can't erase three years of shit, Justice." She stomped toward the path. "Because you hated me and I hated you. Because I love someone else and so do you!"

"Not as much as I love you!"

sdvygbhuinqdsjabhdijnqfvnr *WHAT THE FUCK?*

When did this become about *love?*

Justice, barring one drunken encounter, had never told anyone he loved them before. Justice was so shocked by his own actions that a big part of him wished Liberty would keep walking and leave him alone to take a psychological assessment or something, but she stopped.

She turned.

"You what?" she said.

"And I never hated you," he added.

She made a face, because they both knew he was lying.

"Okay, so I did hate you. But that doesn't mean that I didn't also like you at the same time!"

Liberty resumed walking away from him.

"And if you hate me so much, then why did you kiss me back?" He lobbed the question at her back.

Her steps faltered again.

Got her.

A few quick steps, and Justice was standing next to her.

"I must be an *idiot,*" she concluded softly.

"Then we match," Justice said. "We're two of a kind."

His heart was in his hand as he reached for hers, braiding their fingers together so that their knuckles kissed.

"Don't break up the team."

"I didn't break up anything, *you did.* You...you never even said you wanted to be a team."

"Well, I'm saying it now."

He was? Was he? Was this actually happening?

Liberty sniffed, as a tear fell.

"You don't mean it. You can Romeo me all you want, but that doesn't change the fact that *you ditched me,*" she whimpered, breaking his heart.

His own actions, reflected back to him in her words, cut more than anything he'd ever ascribed as her fault.

"And I let you go. And then I let me go too, and I...I can't..." She reached for the right word with her eyes. "I can't *care* about you again, Justice. It's not safe. You're...you're a wrecking ball."

Justice couldn't breathe.

He had something in common with a Miley Cyrus song. This truly was the lowest point of his life.

Justice was such a dumbass and he knew that now, and boy, ignorance really was bliss.

Liberty dropped her eyes and it felt like *no.*

Of course, it did.

This entire conversation was a *no.* She didn't want this. Even if they did match, their relationship was so tattered and ripped up that Liberty would rather throw it away than...

Oh, God.

Justice finally understood what Dewey meant about the fear of rejection.

This...this was fucking awful.

Justice could feel his heart beginning to rip down the middle, one awful, painful popped stitch at a time.

Now he was the one who felt like running. Jack's phone suddenly trilled. Justice answered. What else could he do?

When he hung up, Liberty had crossed her arms.

"Hope's here?" Liberty was guessing, but it sounded more like she was *wishing*.

If it was time to go home, then she could get away from Justice sooner, he realized.

Wow, this moment hurt.

Justice didn't know a moment could hurt this much.

"No, actually." Justice exhaled. "Robo-call."

He tried to find the words, any words, that might turn this ship around, but none arrived.

"Liberty..."

"Let's just get out of here."

Without another word, she turned back toward the field of stages, walked away, and didn't wait for Justice to follow.

SCENE V.

— 10:45 p.m. —

LIBERTY.

Well, I'm saying it now. Liberty shivered.

Even though they weren't talking anymore, all Liberty could hear was Justice's voice in her head.

His words and his reckless, romantic, absurd ideas.

I wrecked everything in one day; why can't I put everything back together the same way?

Liberty scoffed under her breath.

Who the fuck did he think he was?

Hey, Liberty, I know I carpet-bombed your country yesterday, but today, do you want to sign a peace treaty and marry our nations into a world superpower?

How could anyone be so arrogant?

So...so... It was just too much.

Justice could rope her into a lot of things, but not this. She didn't even know what *this* was.

Was he honestly asking her, after all of their shit, to go out with him *now* or something?

She didn't care that they'd been on this whole adventure and gotten things sorted out. Her highest hopes coming out of this situation included, hey, maybe they wouldn't detest each other so hard anymore or maybe they'd acknowledge each other in the hall once in a while.

But dating?

Liking each other?

None of that was possible now.

Why would it be? They were different people. They both loved someone else. They couldn't just forget about everything and start again.

Relationships weren't Netflix. You couldn't just pause a relationship for three years, then just hit play again when you felt like it and pick up the relationship where you left off.

She was still reeling from the fight in his voice. That scared and unnerved her more than anything.

Justice might have wild, creative, outlandish ideas, but the reason those ideas worked for him was because he was persuasive. If Justice legitimately tried to convince Liberty, honestly, after everything they'd been through, that they should *be together* now, he might just do it.

He was that persuasive, and Liberty was unfortunately that... persuadable. It was like her immune system was weak and it was all too easy for Justice to infect her.

More than anything, Liberty's mind kept coming back to the question, *Did Justice really want that?*

Did Justice Garrison genuinely want them to be together?

It was extremely difficult to believe that was possible, but...*We match. We're two of a kind.*

Liberty hated how she didn't feel sure. About any of this. Of him, of herself.

Liberty hated how her name sounded catchy when Justice said it. Like something she wanted to hear again and again.

It didn't make any sense.

They woke up that day archenemies.

Liberty had ended their conversation because it was crazy that they were even talking about any of this.

The idea of them dating now, after all this time, was a mediocre idea at best. But the idea of them dating now, hot off the heels of this weird, impossible magic day?

That just felt like asking for trouble.

It felt like putting on a pair of white pants.

She felt preposterous, thinking *he* could actually want her.

The idea was so unbelievable that Liberty didn't even get around to wondering whether it was something *she* wanted.

She glanced sidelong at him.

He'd caught up with her, and they were walking back to the field of stages in silence.

Hope would be here soon, she guessed.

Liberty certainly hadn't expected she'd feel so down right about now, as their adventure here was ending.

Even though she hadn't taken a proper breath in *hours,* she'd gotten kind of attached to her corset. It'd held her while she cried, so they were kind of close now.

Liberty guessed one could say she and Justice were kind of close now, too.

She suddenly remembered his tongue against hers, and she had to look away before he caught her staring at him.

Liberty could not BELIEVE they'd kissed.

Something her eighth grade self used to daydream about had finally come true. It was a strangely effective kind of closure, she thought. And that was good.

Closure was what they needed.

They needed to put the past and today's events behind them and get back to their regular lives.

She knew and believed that to be right, so why did she feel so glum inside?

They were still together and would be for the next three hours at least, but why did Liberty feel lonely already?

And if you hate me so much, why'd you kiss me back?

They turned right at the parchment stall and followed the lane to the end. Soon the field of stages came into view, and the very back of the audience was visible at the end of the path. Liberty snuck another glance at Justice, who looked so crestfallen it made her own heart pang.

She tried to beat her empathy back with a stick, with little success. Liberty swallowed hard and kept her eyes forward.

As they reentered the performance space, *Much Ado* seemed to be wrapping up. The stage was crowded with actors. Ashley, as Beatrice, swiped for a letter in someone else's hand, making the audience and other characters titter.

Justice and Liberty made their way toward the backstage area.

"Peace!" Ashley shouted to the crowd. "I will stop your mouth!" She pulled her scene-mate's face to hers. How anyone could pretend so passionately was beyond Liberty.

The crowd went nuts for it.

Everyone screamed and applauded.

Someone in Liberty's way threw their arms in the air so triumphantly that she had to step aside quick, which sent her stumbling over her dress, straight into Justice, who steadied her. But then, she made the mistake of looking into his eyes.

They were a maple syrup mudslide, and she was just slipping, and slipping, and slipping into them.

She didn't have a chance to recompose herself before he said, somehow audible even with all the commotion around them.

"Liberty...be with me."

On stage, someone struck up a band.

The audience began to clap along to some medieval rendition of a Top 40 hit. Everyone, actors and audience members alike, began to dance.

Justice and Liberty were the only ones standing still, like the earth was them and it had stopped spinning.

Will you do me the honor?

Liberty was frozen to the spot.

Her heart was trying to climb out of her chest and fly to him. She couldn't believe it. She didn't want to believe it.

It was supposed to matter to her that he'd been a jerk these past few years. She was supposed to be too angry for this. She was supposed to be so into Magdalena that no one else mattered. *He* was supposed to be so into Magdalena that no one else mattered. They were both supposed to love her.

Not as much as I love you, he shouted in her mind, making her whole body feel carbonated.

It came down to one simple question: Did Liberty Marshall dare to believe those words? Did she dare to believe that Justice could be trusted, that he really felt the way he said he did, that he wasn't just getting caught up in the moment, that this wasn't a cruel trick?

Could she bring herself to believe in him, after he'd done her so wrong? The truth was that...she wanted to.

(When Justice got to college, Liberty thought he should major in Heart Stealing, because he was definitely good at that.)

But what Liberty *wanted* to do and what she was *able* to do, what she *should* do...

They weren't always the same, were they?

"And that's curtain!" Liberty heard the stage manager call from nearby. Recognizing that voice released Liberty from the trance she was in, staring at Justice like she'd never seen a boy before in her life.

Without words, Liberty made a beeline for the backstage area, Justice close behind her. The music was steadily getting louder, and audience members still dancing and cheering had begun the process of moving the chairs out of the way.

When they made it back to the orange tents, Ashley Baker and Jack Elby were there too, clearly satisfied and exuberant after taking their final bows.

They actually looked excited to see Justice and Liberty.

"All set?" Ashley asked them. Liberty was in such a weird head space that she just looked at her, saying nothing.

It was Justice who replied.

"Almost." He checked Jack's phone. "Our ride should be here within the hour."

"Oh, good!" Ashley cheered. "That means you'll have time to enjoy the masque!"

The volume of the music and the revelry unfolding behind them had reached the level that required Justice to shout in order to be heard by someone standing right in front of him.

"The *what*?"

"The Midnight Masque!" Jack shouted back. "It starts now and goes until one!"

"What should we do with the costumes?" Liberty babbled mindlessly.

"Take them to school on Monday." Jack adjusted his giant Shakespearean man belt. "Your drama teacher agreed to dry clean them and send them back to us."

"And when you're ready to go, your things should be where you left them. Back in the dressing rooms!" Ashley added.

"Which reminds me!" Jack said before ducking into a nearby tent. He returned, Justice's skateboard in hand.

Justice lit up when he saw it, like it was his firstborn son.

All Liberty could think about was the way Ashley said *back in the dressing rooms.*

To her, it sounded more like *back in the real world. This is it,* Liberty thought to herself. *Our show's over.*

— 11:00 p.m. —

So, basically, there was only one way to get back to the guest services center, and these renaissance festival people decided to throw a giant medieval dance party on top of it.

They could *see* the guest services building from here through the trees at the edge of the fairground, nearly blending completely into the night, but actually getting to it?

Hope would probably be there by the time they'd walked either all the way around the dance party or fought their way through the middle of it.

Liberty had to admit it was beautiful, though.

Everyone at the festival, smiling, laughing, and cheerfully dancing quadrilles, which, as far as Liberty could tell, were joyous, synchronized group dances.

She watched the stepping and the turning and the clapping with envy.

What would it be like to be in a place like this because you wanted to be? she wondered.

Suddenly, a hand grabbed hers. It was Justice's.

She was surprised to find how different his hands were. They were bigger than hers now.

When had he grown these paws?

They were walking around the perimeter of the Midnight Masque. They were far enough from where the band sat that they could hear each other at normal volume.

"You never answered my question," he told her.

"You never asked me a question," she replied.

"Liberty, I'm being serious."

"Are you?" She drew back to look at him. "Why should I believe that?"

"Because it's the truth." His eyes drilled into hers, and she felt so crazy inside that she actually laughed, a weird, fake, wrong kind of laugh.

"The same way it was *true* that I bullied Dewey?"

"Liberty—" She watched his lips move.

They were saying something she couldn't make out because she was backing away from him. She backed away until lines of dancers came between them and the soundtrack of the Midnight Masque filled her ears to the brim.

She left him on the sidelines, and this time, he didn't follow. That was probably for the best.

ACT V.

SCENE I.

— 11:05 p.m. —

JUSTICE.

Well, as the old saying went...*that's the ballgame.*

It was over.

And Justice had lost. Big.

No one could say he hadn't given it his all, though. He absolutely had. And that was worth something, right?

Not as much as I love you.

He couldn't keep from cringing.

Sure, he might want to dig a hole and bury himself in it for the next ten years, but loss did that to people.

And Justice was a sore loser. Always had been. The sting of defeat rankled him for *years*.

And if past experience was any indication of how long he'd be processing *this loss*—the loss of the only girl he'd ever loved—then he might as well go ahead and buy a decade's supply of ice packs, heating pads, bandages, and soccer balls.

Because was going to be taking this pain out on the field well into his twenties.

Mostly, Justice just couldn't believe it.

He and Liberty once had something so amazing, so wonderful, something that happens once in a lifetime if you're lucky, and he'd thrown it away.

He couldn't take it, knowing that his actions broke his own heart. He'd broken his own heart and he couldn't fix it.

The damage was too old, too deep, too permanent.

That special thing they had that he'd thrown away had gone to the garbage dump and been trash-compacted and melted down into nothingness.

It didn't exist anymore, and that was his fault.

He'd never felt so utterly and completely lost before. He'd never hated himself, either, but there was a first time for everything.

Justice stood there alone, watching the Midnight Masque unfold like a creepy loser, dressed appropriately for the occasion. *What now?* he wondered aimlessly.

His options were stand there like the sad act he was and wait for himself to die, slowly and excruciatingly from self-loathing, or he could return Jack's phone, go to the guest services center by himself, and then wait for Hope in the parking lot. She'd be there soon.

Liberty would eventually show up, and when he saw her, he'd...well, he supposed he wouldn't say or do anything in particular.

She'd made her feelings perfectly clear.

What they had in the past was not to be, not then, and not now. There was no way to understand why she felt that way, other than to accept that she wasn't in love with him.

Because if she was in love with him, she would've said yes when he told her to be with him.

But that thought snagged in his mind as wrong. His thinking was off. His *math* was off, wasn't it?

He thought about Liberty's words.

You never asked me a question.

She was right, he realized with a lurch. The proof was in his own thoughts.

When I told her to be with me...

He hadn't asked her to be with him. He told her to do it.

That one simple distinction suddenly stood out to Justice in brilliant, blinding contrast because it was also the summary of what was wrong with him.

It was the reason why he was in this mess, the reason why everything was so fucked up—Justice didn't ask questions. He almost always made assumptions instead.

If he'd just been like, *Liberty, what happened?* that day when he walked up on her fight with Dewey, she would have told him the truth and their friendship would probably still be going strong right now.

If he'd asked Dewey, *Hey, what were you two fighting about?* he would have discovered Dewey's deceit so much sooner, and maybe if he had...maybe their friendship would be okay right now.

Right now, all Justice knew for sure was that his friendship with Washington was on hiatus, until he could sort his feelings out. Trust took years to build but seconds to break, and today that trust had been demolished.

Decimated in every sense of the word.

But if Justice had asked one simple question, being lied to by his best friend for three years might not have happened.

Or if he'd said, *Hey, Liberty, I like you so much I think I'm going to die. Will you please go out with me?*

If he'd just been bold and asked her out back then, instead of anxiously trying to figure out what she wanted *first,* now he knew she probably would've said yes, and they could've been together.

Hell, if he'd…if he'd just asked Liberty today if she was okay, after she tripped on his board, she never would've stormed onto the truck after him. He might've still fainted, but they wouldn't have been smuggled.

Justice could see it now in stunning clarity.

His failure to ask questions was the linchpin in some of his life's worst mistakes. And it was obvious to him now why that was. *When you ask a question, you give someone the chance to give you bad news,* he thought to himself.

You give someone the chance to reject you, to disagree, to disapprove, and that possibility scared him. Justice didn't ask questions because he didn't want to get hurt. But he'd never asked questions, and look how hurt he was.

If a play isn't working, as Coach Hennessy always said, *try a new one.*

Maybe…

If, fifteen minutes ago, he'd been bold enough to *ask* Liberty to be with him, maybe she would have said yes.

What a dangerous thought.

That thought made half of him yearn and ache to run into the masque after her. But he'd chased her down twice in one night. Was his motivation to go after her this time going to be *third time's the charm?*

Liberty was sick of him. Justice understood that.

He was sick of himself. It wasn't often that Justice felt truly mortified by his own actions, but today was the day.

He was so…*ashamed* of everything he'd done wrong that he couldn't bring himself to do anything else at all.

Liberty had made it clear that she was unreceptive to A) his feelings and B) his crazy idea that they should be together.

There was no point in embarrassing himself further. Justice would go on alone.

He started walking.

The Midnight Masque was huge. It would take him a while to walk all the way around the festivities and return to the Guest Services center, but oh, well.

It's not like he had anywhere urgent to be.

He watched the dance mindlessly, taking in the swirl of skirts as women turned, the handclaps of the men, as they performed their part of this particular number.

All the movement and the liveliness, the colors, *the expressions* on participants' faces—it made his hands ache for pen and paper.

He wanted to sketch the scene before him.

What a perfect subject—and that thought shook something loose inside his mind, an old memory he hadn't thought about in years.

A sixth grade trip to the zoo.

Justice and Liberty got separated from their class. Justice had his sketch pad with him, and as soon as he got caught up in all the park's movement and merriment, he eagerly sat down to start sketching.

But Liberty didn't see him sit down, and when she lost sight of him in the crowd, she had a panic attack.

A full-scale panic attack. Thankfully, he found her.

If he'd been even two minutes later, she might have collapsed. But that was the day Justice learned that Liberty and large crowds didn't mix.

The thought startled him. He looked up again at the *sea* of fairgoers enjoying the masque.

Liberty was in there somewhere.

Was she okay?

SCENE II.

— 11:10 p.m. —

LIBERTY.

Getting away from Justice was easy at first.

Once there was a line of dancers between them, they lost sight of each other, and that was all the distance Liberty needed to clear her head and calm herself down.

Liberty had been slowly zigzagging her way through the Midnight Masque, trying to avoid dancers and get to the other side. Doing it this way seemed like it must be quicker than walking along the outskirts, but Liberty was beginning to fear she was wrong about that.

She took another deep breath, as a fanciful chorus unfolded, signaling the beginning of a new dance.

Liberty took the opportunity to shimmy between two couples and make it to the next open patch of grass, but as soon as she got there, someone grabbed her from behind.

Two giant hands perched at her waist and before she had a

chance to figure out who'd grabbed her, she—and about a hundred other women—were lifted into the air in sync.

The women laughed and trilled at being picked up, but Liberty instead felt panic.

She hadn't meant to, but she realized, horribly, that she'd been mistaken for someone participating in the dance.

As soon as the person put her down, Liberty tried to run.

She hated being touched by strangers. She hated dancing like this. But the faster she stepped, the more in tune with the dance she appeared.

Another stranger, smiling and jovial, materialized in her way, grabbed both her hands and pulled her more forcefully than she'd expected into a circle.

They rotated three times, but it felt like ten because Liberty's panic level was rising by the millisecond.

When Liberty got too anxious or panicked, it felt like her throat closed up, rendering her temporarily incapable of speech.

She felt her lips moving as she tried to tell the person to let go of her, but she couldn't feel any sound leave her mouth, and the music was so loud that anything she said would have been drowned out anyway.

The stranger released her and moved on, only for a new stranger to appear.

Liberty couldn't breathe.

The new stranger grabbed her hands and began spinning them. By the end of their final rotation, it was apparently time for all the women to be lifted into the air again, and without warning, she was hoisted up toward the stars, feeling positively ill.

I hate this, she cried internally. *I hate this, I hate this, I hate this. Why is this happening?*

Liberty wanted to get away, *needed to,* before her muscles started to lock up, before she got so scared and dizzy and breathless that she passed out.

With all the people at this masque, she'd probably be trampled and dead before anyone noticed anything amiss.

The moment she was on the ground, Liberty began to sprint—despite her distaste for and severe lack of talent for running. She bumped into people but she didn't stop.

She forced her way through throngs of people dancing the quadrille or watching the quadrille.

But she didn't know where she was going.

In all the commotion, in being pulled into the dance, she'd become completely turned around. Her only point of reference was the stage, but everywhere she looked, she only saw people.

There were so many people moving, packed together all around her, that the stage was invisible from where she was.

Where was she?

As Liberty struggled for breath, the hopelessness of her situation began to dawn on her. Her eyes became bleary with tears, even though it felt that there wasn't a drop of water left in her whole body.

Her hands were shaking as she gripped her dress, running with every ounce of energy she had left. Her head had begun to pulsate with the strain.

Memories, doubts, insecurities began to chip at her mind all at once, all while she forced herself to put one foot in front of the other.

Hadn't she been admiring the festivities awhile ago?

Hadn't she thought these people looked so lovely, dancing together and smiling and having a wonderful time?

Why wasn't Liberty among them? She suddenly wondered. Why wasn't she joyous? Why couldn't she enjoy this the same as the rest of them?

How was it that in the end, even after she'd made up with her mom, even after she and Justice had reconciled and the mystery of their destruction had been solved at long last, Liberty was still alone?

Liberty was still drowning in her own fear and anxiety.

She was still running away.

Shouldn't she feel better right now? Shouldn't she be relieved?

Maybe good didn't always vanquish evil, but shouldn't today's events have balanced the scales just a little bit?

But then Liberty started to see herself in her own mind, like she was dissociating, like she was watching herself in her memories from above it all.

Maybe Liberty was a runner after all.

Because running away from her problems was a theme with her, wasn't it?

When Dad interrupted her performance on her thirteenth birthday, she ran. When Justice walked up on her fight with Dewey, instead of telling him what was going on, she took one look at the rejection on his face and she ran.

When she saw Magdalena and Adam together, she ran.

She and Justice wouldn't even *be here* if she'd just stood her ground. If she'd found the strength somewhere to confront Magdalena about her secret instead of running for the hills...

When Justice wanted to talk about eighth grade, she ran away from him. And now she knew that whatever she'd feared he might do or say was wrong.

All he was trying to say was that he was sorry, that he messed up. And she was so afraid of his retribution that she'd run away without even giving him a chance.

As soon as he'd mentioned that Magdalena reminded him of her, the second it occurred to her that she might be a consolation prize, Liberty was gone.

As soon as it felt like Liberty was about to be hurt, she took off.

But running away didn't protect her. It only guaranteed she'd be alone every time she *did* get hurt.

Whether Justice's feelings were real or not, today Liberty had not only rejected, but *cruelly* rejected, the only boy she'd ever loved for being an idiot and an asshole to her.

She'd stood up for herself, but that's not what the rejection was about. Rejecting him and protecting herself weren't the same thing. If they were she'd feel better right now, she'd feel safe. But she didn't. She felt out of control.

The world seemed to move slower as Liberty's mind continued to race, speeding up by the second.

Liberty realized the truth in those time-warped seconds.

Justice Garrison, actually, was the only person she'd ever want to be accidentally kidnapped with.

If she had to do today all over again and she could pick who got trapped with her, Liberty literally wouldn't pick another person.

There was no one else on the *planet* that she would have preferred to go through this with.

Not Magdalena. Not George. Justice was right.

They were two of a kind. They fit together in a way that didn't exist with anyone else in her life, and Justice realized that today.

That's what the past few hours had been about. That's what he'd been trying to tell her.

What the two of them had was too precious not to fight for. Liberty wanted to think both of them knew that now.

On top of all her panic and anxiety, Liberty started to feel shame creep in, like mud in the water.

She had been so terrified that Justice might make fun of her for liking him in middle school, only to turn around when he confessed all of his feelings to her and throw those feelings back in his face.

She brought up all his mistakes. She'd made him feel bad for being an idiot. As if being a dumbass was his fault, and not...a part of the human condition.

As if she'd never been an idiot.

As if she'd never had complex feelings she'd been terrified to share with someone.

She knew that experience intimately, and yet she'd had zero compassion for someone going through the same predicament.

And not just anyone.

Someone she used to love.

Oh, God.

Someone she maybe still loved.

The panic swelled and Liberty went with it.

SCENE III.

— 11:20 p.m. —

JUSTICE.

The people at this fucking party seemed to be *multiplying*.

After diving into the crowds of people dancing, he'd been searching (probably for no good reason) for almost fifteen minutes. Justice was beginning to think Liberty was already at the guest services center.

She'd probably already made it out safely and that's why he couldn't find her anywhere, but Justice couldn't get himself to give up until he felt certain he'd done a thorough search of the field.

This would be a lot easier if there weren't so many people. He turned in circles.

Luckily, he was tall, so he could see over heads and between faces and other limbs, but he saw nothing but smiling, jubilant dancers as far as the eye could see.

Maybe the reason Justice couldn't find Liberty was because she wasn't in distress.

Maybe she was happily dancing the night away along with everyone else here. Maybe she didn't—

Justice stumbled to the right, as someone barreled past him. He looked and was shocked to see Liberty running for her life. Bumping into him had barely fazed her, and she would've kept going, he was sure, if he hadn't caught her by the hand.

When she turned back, he saw her face, red like she'd been holding her breath, damp from tears and sweat, eyes wide and frantic, staring blankly at him.

At first, her face was full of fear, but as she seemed to register that it was him, the fear deflated bit by bit.

He had to shout again. "Are you okay?"

And then with more strength than Justice knew Liberty had, she grabbed at him. She grabbed his arm and pulled.

If she'd yanked him any harder, he might've fallen onto her. Justice thought she was pulling him to her, but when she thrust her arms around his neck and squeezed him, hanging on for dear life, he realized that maybe she was pulling herself to *him*.

She was scared.

Scared shitless, he guessed, by the way her body trembled.

Justice held her tight, relief pumping hard and fast through his veins. He was so grateful that he'd made it in time.

There were no words for it.

He couldn't go back and change the past. He couldn't change their present either. He couldn't change how she felt about him, no more than he could change how he felt about her. The one and only thing Justice could do was keep Liberty from going through all of this alone.

And he had.

Justice led them out of the masque as quickly as he possibly could with Liberty still attached to him.

The best way for her to manage her fear of crowds was to close her eyes, which she couldn't do unless someone was there to guide her, and that was Justice's job.

In a matter of minutes they stood in the semi-darkness, several paces from the edge of the party, nearest to the guest services center.

He could see the darkened vendor stalls, the quiet zip line, and the empty marriage altars, their gossamer banners rippling in the breeze.

"You can open your eyes," Justice told her.

His voice sounded different now that they were away from the crowd and the music.

Liberty did open her eyes, and he helped her sit on a nearby rock. And then he backed away from her, saying, "You ready for this?"

Justice Garrison then proceeded to dance like it hurt.

He danced like he was trying to retroactively embarrass his future children. He danced like he had no concept of what dancing was. He pulled out all the stops.

His fake ballet moves, his parody of the wack old-school dance moves his parents used to do. He even did all the choreography from MC Hammer's *U Can't Touch This* music video, which he honestly deserved a medal for because that choreography was just full-on nineties high-energy aerobics.

He was sweaty and gross and *tired* by the time he was done, but he was also successful.

Liberty was laughing harder than he'd ever seen her laugh.

Oddly, seeing her smiling again and knowing that he was the reason—even after how badly he'd fucked everything up—was enough.

Today had definitely kicked his ass, but maybe it hadn't been as bad a day as he thought.

How bad could it really be if he'd made Liberty Bell Marshall laugh so much?

SCENE IV.

— 11:35 p.m. —

LIBERTY.

Liberty's whole torso hurt from laughing so hard within the confines of her corset.

She could barely breathe, but what she lacked in oxygen she made up for with pure joy.

There were few things so universally enjoyable as Justice dancing very badly. Liberty didn't believe there was a human being on Earth that could watch him dance so terribly and not be wholeheartedly amused.

It certainly had always worked on her.

When Justice finished his routine, he laid down in the grass by her feet, where he was still reclined, panting from all the exercise.

She was so beside herself with humor and relief that she didn't know what to do. So she just stared at him, lying there breathing with his eyes closed.

He...

Justice, he'd...

She didn't even know how to articulate what Justice's actions meant to her.

It was too weird and wrong and cliche to say he'd rescued her when she was in trouble. That's not how it worked. Panic attacks weren't equal to being locked in the highest room in the tallest tower.

Being prone to anxiety and panic wasn't glamorous. It was messy and scary and dangerous.

Honestly, it was a part of herself that Liberty would feel more ashamed of if she hadn't met Justice all those years ago.

But meeting him made it okay.

Because they both had a psychological kryptonite. For Justice, it was blood, vomit, and fainting spells. For Liberty, it was crowds, stress, and self-esteem.

And when they were young they'd made a pact to always help each other, if ever they were struggling with their kryptonite.

And Justice had *more than* made good on that eight-year-old promise. But that wasn't what got to Liberty.

What got to Liberty was that he had no reason to do it. Justice had no incentive to help her.

They'd been sniping at each other all day. He'd poured his heart out to her, and she'd as good as kicked him in the balls.

But Liberty knew it the moment she saw him back there in the masque. That unalloyed concern on his face?

He wasn't there to dance or have fun. He wasn't even there to find her or tell her something.

He'd been there to make sure she was okay.

"How did you know I was in trouble?" She mused aloud.

"Let's call it a hunch," he huffed.

"How long did it take you to perfect those moves?"

"Many years of dedicated study." They both laughed.

"Why'd you do it?" She finally asked. "Why'd you come back for me after I…"

Justice opened his eyes into hers. "Can't an old friend help out an old friend?"

They stared at each other for a long, long moment, and then Justice struggled to sit up. But once he had, he gave her a look Liberty had never seen on his face before.

What was that? Humility, maybe?

"Liberty, I know you don't want to do this and that's fine," he exhaled hard. "But I just, uh...I need you to know that this isn't a joke to me. *You're* not a joke to me."

Liberty realized that Justice was picking up where they left off, back by the R&J stand. Justice was picking up with all kinds of stuff today.

"This isn't about Mags and Adam," he continued. "You're not a consolation prize, Liberty. If anything, Mags was a consolation prize for you."

Liberty didn't want to be impressed by him, but she was feeling wooed. Who wouldn't be?

"I liked you when we were seven, and I like you right now. I know I ruined everything. I feel so awful, so *shitty,* about what I did that I want to run away to the moon. The only reason I'm not actively banging my head against a wall right this second is because you're more important."

Her heart lifted up so high in her chest when he said that, she thought it might pop out of her mouth.

"Even just zero point zero zero zero zero zero zero zero zero zero one percent of you is more important. Basically I'm doing this for like, one fifth of your pinky toe."

Liberty snorted before she could stop herself.

"I get it if you don't want to date me. Who would want to date an idiot?" He scrubbed the back of his neck. "But could we...at least, be friends again? It'll be...*tough,* probably. Because of, you know, back there with the..."

Liberty's cheeks heated, remembering his lips against hers.

Justice cleared his throat. "But it would also be enough. Liberty, *I would do anything* to get my best friend back."

He was radiant, honestly.

Liberty didn't know how the whole world wasn't glowing. Liberty was. She definitely, definitely was.

She couldn't even speak.

"Anything, seriously," he reiterated. "I would willingly relive Angela Devlin's twelfth birthday party for you."

"No, you wouldn't."

"I would do her One-Direction-Harry-Potter-Crossover-themed ice skating fiasco again. For you."

"You'd kiss Dewey all over again and everything?"

Justice shook his head again.

"No, I'd...I'd make sure I kissed you."

Liberty wanted to tackle him, but that felt like a lot for right now, so instead she observed, "All of this happened... because of a skateboard."

"Not just any skateboard," Justice said, reaching for his board instinctively. "This is my lucky skateboard. I got Nyjah Huston to sign it."

Everything Liberty knew about skateboarding she knew because of Justice. She still didn't know very much, but she did know that the day Nyjah Huston signed Justice's board, Justice probably cried like a baby.

The thought made her smile.

"I'm kind of glad I tripped on it," she breathed. Those words made Justice's face go blank.

He was staring at her like every thought in his head had evaporated at once, like his mind had gone fishing, and all that was left was his body, sitting there beside her.

His gaze was so rich, so concentrated, she didn't know how she'd ever look away.

And then Jack's cell phone rang, making both of them jump.

Justice took one look at the phone, and Liberty knew.

Hope was here, which meant it was time for Justice and Liberty to leave this magical place and return home.

Liberty rose from the rock where she was perched. She waited for Justice to join her and realized this time *he* needed help getting up.

When she offered him both her hands, he took them. But once he was on his feet, he only let one of her hands go.

And Liberty was just fine with that.

Their final goodbyes to the What You Will Shakespeare Company were awkward.

(Sorry we accidentally kidnapped you! Thanks for not being human traffickers!)

But they survived.

They started back toward the guest services building, and because the masque was in full swing, no one seemed to be going in the same direction.

The building itself looked dark and sad as they approached it. It looked like a lonely chocolate cake, standing in the darkness.

If you're wondering, Justice didn't let go of her hand.

Even when he gave Jack his cell phone back and shook his hand. Once they entered the darkened building and the lights started to flip on automatically, Liberty was convinced that he might even follow her straight into the changing room where she'd left her things.

But they went their separate ways at the dressing rooms to retrieve their this-morning clothes.

The ones with blood and puke on them.

Thinking about that should've grossed her out, but all it really did was remind her that they'd spent three hours together confined in a dark, enclosed space and everything had still turned out okay.

It was nothing short of miraculous.

They hadn't spoken a word to each other since Hope called. But the silence wasn't strained or awkward, it was comfortable and worn-in, like a good pair of jeans.

When Liberty stepped back out into the central area, holding her disgusting clothes in a paper bag that Ashley for some reason had on hand, she gravitated toward the mirrors.

She soon caught Justice's reflection behind hers, just standing there like an axe murderer in a horror movie.

"Your serial killer impression is really coming along," she informed him.

Justice didn't reply, and it was almost like he was waiting for what Liberty knew she had to say next which was, "Okay. So the thing is that...I've missed you. So fucking much."

Everything inside her ached to run, but she planted her feet.

Justice closed the distance between them in seconds, dropping his stuff in the process. He came her way and leaned in until their foreheads brushed.

Liberty was reminded of the bruise there, still slightly sore, but she felt something else: a butterfly garden between her ribs. Cherry soda bubbling in her veins.

This was Liberty Marshall, feeling...happy.

"Me, too," Justice said, as Liberty pressed her open mouth to his. His arms circled her waist. In his giant doublet, this was a bear hug and a kiss in the same moment.

Kissing Justice was...yeah.

"I don't want to be friends," she gave in, the first second he let her breathe. His hands at her sides tightened.

"Oh, thank God." His lips pulled at hers eagerly.

When he kissed her cheek and temple and forehead, she added, "I don't want to date either."

"Dating sucks," he agreed, plying his lips to hers.

"So..." Liberty pulled back, leaving her hands on his shoulders.

"I'm your guy."

Liberty was completely burning up. Maybe it was the combination of thick threads and no AC in here.

Or maybe Justice was an open fire.

"Is that okay?" he asked, when she didn't say a word.

"One hundred percent," she mumbled, burying her face in his heavily clothed chest.

It shouldn't have made her laugh, but she couldn't help it when he squeezed her to him and said, "This time, you're going to have to get rid of *me*."

SCENE V.

— 11:45 p.m. —

JUSTICE.

They heard Hope before they saw her.

She was idling in a large parking lot labeled *Patrons,* blasting Third Eye Blind in Mom's black Jeep Wrangler.

All the windows were down, and she had one of her bare feet stretched out the driver's side, toes balancing on the sideview mirror. (*My sister, everyone. She's beauty and she's grace. Please, no applause.*)

When they walked up together, wearing matching Elizabethan costumes, carrying a skateboard and Big Y paper bags, first Hope froze, thick coffee tumbler in hand, and then she spit really hard.

Whatever she was drinking flew out of her mouth and onto the pavement.

Hope laughed so forcefully it sounded like she was choking. She cackled, falling back against the headrest and honking the horn.

She'd never been quite *this* embarrassing, but nothing was going to kill Justice's mood. He struck three poses, playing up the tights and the giant doublet sleeves.

Hope died.

Hope died and died and died, then she pulled out her cell phone and recorded him walking up to her door so she could Snapchat the glory of this moment to all her friends.

She could turn this into a meme. Justice might go viral, but nothing was going to kill his mood.

"Hi," he said, leaning in the window frame with his giant puffy Shakespearean-sleeved arms.

Hope's voice was hoarse.

Tears streamed from the corners of her eyes.

"What the fuck, Justice," she replied, a last chuckle trapped in her throat.

"You done?" Justice asked.

"Not for ten years."

"There's someone I want you to meet." Justice turned around and found Liberty standing awkwardly.

She so obviously had been laughing at him, too, but was now trying to hide it for God knows what reason. She strode up to his side, keeping her distance, which Justice somehow found adorable.

He grabbed her hand so she'd stand a little closer.

"Hope Garrison, I would like to introduce you to my girlfriend, Liberty Marshall."

For a split second, Justice was afraid that Hope was going to do another spit-take, this time on his face.

But instead she went still again, all humor dripping off her features. She looked between their faces.

And then Hope SCREAMED.

She *screamed* at them in excitement. She started stomping her feet and honking the horn again.

All of New England could hear her.

She drummed on the steering wheel, retracted her leg from the window, opened the door forcing them to back up, and then she hugged them both individually really tight, still somehow screaming.

Her lung capacity, *Christ.*

Then, she shoved Justice.

"It took you long enough!" She growled. She went back to hugging Liberty again.

"Mom is going to freak out. *Dad* is going to freak out," she said, turning the two of them in a circle.

"In a good way?" Liberty piped up shyly.

"In an amazing way," Hope assured her. "They've only been waiting for this since the beginning of time."

Because she knew Justice hated it, Hope clamped both her hands on his cheeks and pulled hard enough to make the cut on his chin hurt.

"ahp!" Justice said, unable to fully form the word.

"Congratulations, asshole," she said. "You've finally graduated." Justice smacked her arms away. "Break her heart and we're putting you up for adoption."

Justice straightened his doublet, stealing a glance at Liberty who looked stupidly happy.

"Let's get the hell out of here," Hope said.

She opened the back door of the jeep with a flourish.

"Juliet," she said sweetly. Liberty climbed in. To Justice, she said, "Twerp, after you."

Hope hopped back in the driver's seat, still laughing and whooping. She turned the engine over, grabbed at her phone, muttering something about "the perfect song for this," and hooked everything up.

Before she hit play, Hope cranked the stereo volume up to max. Justice had half a second to cram his hands over Liberty's ears before *All 4 Love* by Color Me Badd, one of the cheesiest, catchiest *worst* songs ever made, blasted them to hell.

Hope had a deep love for bad boybands. And making Justice cringe. Anything by Color Me Badd killed both birds with one tap of her thumb.

Liberty laughed.

Hope pulled them out of the lot, screaming along to the lyrics. Even...*the rap bridge.*

Oh, the horror.

Usually, Justice would've attempted to fling himself from the car, but tonight, nothing could move him from that spot, sitting next to Liberty Marshall, the dream girl of all dream girls. She was his best friend, his best arch nemesis, and now also his girlfriend.

And the best one a guy could ask for at that. She pulled his hands down from her ears.

Color Me Badd thankfully died down into the whimsical, rainy, cobblestone sounds of The Smiths.

Hope's exaggerated singing was contagious. Liberty joined in on the first verse. She always did understand Hope's taste in music. A morbid chorus swayed through the speakers as Justice leaned over to kiss her.

It wasn't easy, fighting a doublet and a seat belt all to get to her lips, but you know what? Justice didn't care if anything was easy ever again, as long as he got *this.*

Sitting by her side.

Hope must've noticed them. (That or they were about to die.)

But she started screaming and honking the horn again.

Liberty pulled away laughing, "We're going to get stopped by the cops, aren't we?"

"Most definitely."

"I should call my mom." She provided him with a perfect smile. "I should tell her we might be late."

"Yeah."

"And also maybe...maybe I should tell her that I have a boyfriend."

"Yeah." His cheeks ached, he smiled so hard. He kissed her again."Maybe you should."

GREEN RIVER ROMANCES
SERIES INFORMATION

Justice & Liberty
Maria Magdalena
George Washington
Adam & Eve
Jack & Gyl
Rebel Hope

ABOUT THE AUTHOR

Regan M. Humphrey is a nonbinary writer, psychologist, educator, filmmaker, and multi-hyphenate creative. She specializes in sci-fi, fantasy, and contemporary young adult fiction, writing for the young and young-at-heart.

ACKNOWLEDGMENTS

There are so many people I want to thank. I wish to thank the organizers of DVpit, and all the agents and commenters online who showed me that this book was not only important, but important for the moment we're in right now.

I'd like to give special love and thanks to everybody at the Atlanta Shakespeare Tavern Playhouse, where I received all of my formative theater training. Special thanks to Andy, Katie-Grace, Matt, Kelly, Tiffany, Laura, Tony, and all the incredible kitchen staff, Mike, Garrett, et al. My love of Shakespeare started with you all, and I'm so grateful for the way delving into the bard's work has influenced my creative practice.

I would also like to the thank the MFA program at Antioch University Los Angeles for all the growth and development I gained while studying there. This book would not be what it is without the teaching, encouragement, and support of the Antiochian community. Great thanks to Victoria Chang, Lisa Locascio-Nighthawk, Francesca Lia Block, Aditi Khorana, Aminah Mae Safi, and all my Meadowlarks! (Shan, Aldo, and Debbie, especially, my fellow YA warriors.)

Special shoutout to Zach Benton for introducing me to Jan Terry. And the biggest, hardiest gratitude and love goes to my mom, the first person to discover that I was a writer. I absolutely could not have gotten this far without your love and unwavering, unconditional support.